The Buckeye

The Buckeye

Ronald Troy Allen

2017

The Buckeye
Copyright © 2017 by Ronald Troy Allen

Printed in the United States of America

First Printing, 2017

ISBN-13: 978-1545369715

First Edition

Cover Design by Mariah Sinclair, www.mariahsinclair.com

Dedication

To my Great Uncle Wilber Thomas Reinoehl

Killed in Action May 19, 1944

B-24 Navigator U. S. 8th Army Air Force, 392nd Heavy Bombardment Group

Wendling Field, Norfolk, England.

Chapter 1

The setting sun, cast its brilliant rays on a low bank of clouds producing soft pastel shades of orange and pink creating a beautiful tapestry in the evening sky — a fitting backdrop to the fall events. Realizing the cool air and the shorter days signified the changing of seasons, squirrels hurried their work of gathering and burying nuts. A blue jay's cry echoed through the woods, an audible warning of the coming hardships of winter. It was autumn, a transitional time when nature says goodbye to the warm days of summer before the cold days of winter rush in. The true color of leaves, concealed for an entire year behind a blanket of green, were revealed in a panoply of colors. The changes in the physical environment impart introspection to those who slow down to let it take hold in their minds and draw out the lighter subtleties in human personalities: an appreciated time of rest and relaxation after the busier months of summer.

A slender, middle-aged man with sandy brown hair and light blue eyes named Tucker McQueen sat in his worn rocking chair and stared out a large picture window. Wrinkles could be seen on his face from his oft-used expressions. The cool temperatures allowed Tucker to open the house and invite in the smells and sounds of the forest. It was his favorite spot to relax. He balanced a mug of hot black coffee on his right leg. Periodically, a small wisp of steam wafted off its surface. Tucker rocked slowly and took in the beauty of the season. The gentle, cool breeze pushed the leaves across the back yard. He watched them roll along until his gaze fixated on a solitary red-leaved tree. The breeze was invisible except for the movement of the leaves and the branches that swayed in a rhythmic manner. A leaf slowly wafted back and forth as the effect of gravity pulled it gently down to its final resting place in the grass. Purpose and blessing washed over him as he remembered what this solitary tree represented. Staring at the tree, he remembered the day he had planted it. Thirty years prior, Tucker's life had been changed drastically by a man that he would come to know but would never meet. "What a journey," he said to himself. His memories came flooding in as quickly as a dry creek bed floods during a heavy storm.

It was a work-related accident that stole his father from him. He was in his junior year in high school. Without his father's steady hand to guide him, Tucker was adrift and unsure as to what he wanted to do with his life. His high school performance had been mediocre. The only subject that was of interest to him in school was journalism. Although he was talented, it did not attract the attention of teachers who would have encouraged him to consider college had they realized he had a lack of motivation, not ability. After graduating from high school and with no plan about what to do next, he settled for a monotonous factory job. It was a life full of repetition and boredom. At first, the money offset his disdain of the job, but he reached a point where even that did not outweigh his loathing of the menial task that he was required to perform. It did not use even a miniscule amount of his God-given talents. Tucker had always been a thinker, which was at times a great asset and at other times a terrible burden. It had occurred to him that it might be nice to be like others, who just accepted life without further reflection, but he could not turn off his thoughts. Eventually, the drudgery of the factory work and his interest in writing motivated him to apply for a job at a local newspaper named *The Daily Reporter*. The office was located in his hometown of Mitchum, Ohio, one of hundreds of towns that had seen its zenith at the end of the 1800s. With a hardware store, a restaurant that had been owned by three generations of the same family, and a town square, Mitchum was indistinguishable from thousands of other mid-western towns. The town was on the downhill side of its lifespan, but those who loved it would never admit it.

It was on a humid day in June that Tucker found himself dressed in his new suit enroute to the newspaper office building. He found street side parking only a block from the building. Glancing in the rear view mirror, he checked his appearance before exiting the truck. "Well here goes nothing," he said to himself as he approached the front door. Entering, he looked around. People were continually coming and going as they all worked as a team to meet deadlines. Ceiling fans slowly churned the stale cigarette air. They failed to make a noticeable difference. The noise of clicking typewriters and several individual hushed discussions were constant. Spotting a secretary typing at a desk, he approached and waited until she had stopped.

"My name is Tucker McQueen, and I would like to apply for the position." He held out the newspaper, which carried the advertisement. He desperately tried to hide his nerves, but the loose-bound newspaper telegraphed a clear message of how he felt. She looked up from her typewriter and stared at him for an awkward amount of time before she spoke.

"Wait here, and I will see if Mr. Timmons is busy," she said as she pushed back her chair. She walked over and lightly knocked on a door that had the words "Editor-in-Chief" etched in the glass. Tucker could hear voices but could not make out what was being said. A few minutes later she walked back and, without even offering a courteous glance, resumed her typing. "Mr. Timmons will see you now," she said over the click clack of her typewriter.

Kenneth Timmons would become a man Tucker would grow to respect professionally but personally despise. He was enormous with large hands and fingers that looked much too thick to find their work with pencil and paper. His physical features could mislead a person to believe that he found his employment through tough physical labor, but once he spoke, it was evident that his intellect was more intimidating than his size.

"Sit down, Mr. Tucker," he said in an authoritative manner.

Tucker slid into a chair that was positioned directly in front of the desk. It sat noticeably lower, which put Mr. Timmons in a towering position. Tucker sat up straight, but it wasn't enough to bring him up to eye level with his potential boss.

"Bridgett said that you're interested in the position we have open."

"Yes sir."

"Why don't you tell me a little about yourself?" Mr. Timmons said.

After Tucker explained the last year of his life and why he was interested in the position, Mr. Timmons then proceeded to ask him a wide range of questions to determine if he matched well with his needs.

"What year did you graduate from high school?"

"About two years ago in 1966," Tucker said.

"What kind of experience do you have that qualifies you for the position?" Mr. Timmons asked.

Tucker's mind went to work immediately in an attempt to save himself from looking like a wannabe instead of a qualified candidate. "I worked on the high school newspaper and completed a summer job with *The Gazette* over in Hanover."

"Humph, did you work with Tom Keller?"

"Yeah. I mean, yes sir, I was assigned directly to Mr. Keller."

"Keller's a good one to get experience from. He has a good nose on him and can sniff out a story if there is one."

Tucker would soon learn that this was high praise, and the only thing that Mr. Timmons handed out less than compliments was raises. He asked several more difficult questions meant to knock Tucker off balance. The last portion of the interview was a writing assignment in which Tucker was supplied with a set of facts and told he had thirty minutes to compose a story with title. He had it back on Mr. Timmons desk in under twenty minutes. Mr. Timmons read the story.

"A little rough, but with some hard work on your part, you may survive. All of our new reporters are on a six-month probationary period, and the salary is non-negotiable. If you want it, Mr. McQueen, the job is yours," he said in his trademark gruff manner.

"Yes, I want it," Tucker said barely able to contain his surprise and excitement.

"One last thing. Do all of us a favor and do not go strutting around here acting as if you are something special. The senior reporters have no patience for it. You are going to have to earn their respect, not expect it. Be here Monday morning at 8:00 A.M.," Mr. Timmons said as he stood to indicate the interview was over.

"I'll see you on Monday morning, Mr. Timmons," Tucker said as he rose to exit the office. Mr. Timmons already had his head buried in work and simply raised his hand and waved him off in a demeaning manner.

Tucker spent the afternoon searching for an apartment in the downtown area. After asking around at the local shops, he was pleased to discover a small studio apartment on the town square. It was an open concept with tall windows, worn dark wooden floors, and metal tin ceiling tiles with a large star stamped into each of them. At one time the apartment had been the second floor of an old five and dime store. It was exactly what Tucker wanted: affordable, close to his job, functional and charming. The good news came as no surprise to his mother, but it was still difficult for her. She masked her emotions with a smile as he told her everything that had transpired. The remainder of the weekend was spent moving and settling into his new apartment.

When Tucker walked through the door on Monday morning, Mr. Timmons introduced him to Carl Jacobs, one of the senior staff writers. Mr. Jacobs was painfully thin with white hair and a pointed nose that served as a perch for his glasses. His weatherworn face was a testament to his years of experience. "This is Tucker McQueen, the new reporter I spoke to you about. When he is properly trained, cut him loose," said Mr. Timmons.

Carl understood his assignment of turning the raw material in Tucker into a competent reporter. He stopped momentarily from his work and muttered in a squeaky voice that seemed to be befitting of his smallish frame, "Given time, I'm sure you'll get the hang of it." He seemed to be neither a warm nor cold individual, but was more like a machine that, if properly oiled and maintained, could be counted on to perform. "You can sit there," he said, pointing an arthritic finger to a scratched wooden desk that was shoved in the corner with no visible window in sight.

Tucker didn't have any delusions of setting the journalistic world on fire but hoped to hang on to his new position by experiencing at least a modicum of success. It didn't take long for him to identify that the problem was not in doing what was asked of him; it was in receiving assignments that were actually newsworthy. There wasn't much excitement generated by the local area, and thus, little possibility of his separating himself from the pack. His articles were the filler that was relegated to the last pages in the newspaper.

After working for a few months, he discovered that some of the other reporters were college graduates. With an intensified feeling of inferiority, he overcompensated by working even longer hours and hoped that the extra effort wouldn't be overlooked. Nevertheless, his articles were sentenced to the back page, and he continued to mull through one trivial assignment after another. When he first took the position, he felt his life was heading in a positive direction. However, after more than a year of giving his all, it occurred to him that his career ladder might be leaned against the wrong tree. It was his memories of factory life and his thirst for professional success that motivated him to continue his struggle.

In August, Tucker was given what appeared to be another routine assignment. Just like many others, he found it on his desk late in the day. The message was short and to the point, just like Carl's writing style: "Arrive at old military airport over in Farmington at 8:00 A.M. for flight on a WWII aircraft." If he said it once, he must have said it a hundred times. "Tuck, a good reporter knows not to bore readers with too many details. If they wanted to read a book, they would buy one. There are two reasons for brevity Tucker: newspapers are short on space, and readers are short on attention."

Carl was, in fact, working to shape and refine Tucker's writing skills. He saw talent in him and believed if properly cultivated, Tucker could have a successful career in journalism. Although Carl was harsh at times, Tucker listened and applied his advice. The airport assignment would work well as Tucker had received permission to take the afternoon off. His plan was to drive home afterward and help his mother around her house over the weekend.

The following morning, Tucker made the thirty minute drive to the airport. Stepping out of his truck, he walked on a long sidewalk toward the old brick terminal building. It was rectangular and had a small square second level that had served as an air traffic control tower many years ago. Presently, it was an observation deck and lounge area for transient pilots. The city didn't have a need for such a large airport or the aircraft operations required to justify an air traffic control tower. Most of the aircraft that used the airport were small single engine types or occasionally, a light twin-engine aircraft that stopped for fuel enroute to a far busier place. It hadn't been built for a commercial need but to meet the demands of World War II. The construction was completed when money wasn't a primary concern and without consideration of what would be done with it after the war. It was built when the country was fighting for its core principals and survival. When victory was achieved, the need for the airport was no more, and the federal government deeded it to the city. It had always been more of a liability than an asset as it was a real financial burden to maintain. Tucker continued along the sidewalk to the main entrance of the terminal building and pulled on the handle of the old metal framed glass door. The interior of the building was tidy.

Walking down a hallway, he saw an old man with black, heavy rimmed glasses who was sweeping the main lobby area. Noticing Tucker, he stopped pushing his broom and smiled.

"Good morning. Like some hot coffee? It's fresh as a spring rain," he said.

Tucker didn't have to think twice about the offer. "Sounds great." He followed the old man over to the coffee pot where he watched as he filled a white ceramic mug.

"Cream or sugar?"

"Oh, no thanks, black is fine."

He handed Tucker the coffee and then poured a cup for himself. "Somebody flying in to pick you up?" the old man asked.

"Sort of. I'm taking a flight on a World War II aircraft that should be here within the hour. I am a reporter with *The Daily Reporter*."

The old man's countenance seemed to shine even more with news of the aircraft.

"How 'bout a donut to go with that coffee?" he said. Taking one for himself, he then handed the box to Tucker. "Heard they were going to arrive sometime this week, but with maintenance problems, it was undecided when; least that was the last I heard," he said. "Goodness, where are my manners? Name's Robert Miller," he said, extending his hand, "You can call me Bob."

Tucker sat the coffee and donut aside and shook his hand. "Pleased to meet you. I am Tucker McQueen."

"Let's find a place to watch for them and bring the donuts. I imagine a young man like you always has room for another one," Bob said as he picked up his coffee and walked over to the front of the terminal that afforded them a good view of the runways. They both set their coffee on top of a display case that was full of pilot supplies.

"It's a privilege to have that old Liberator stop here; I imagine it will draw a sizable crowd to this sleepy old terminal. We all owe a debt to the men who fought and died in those bombers," Bob said in between sips of coffee.

Early on, Tucker had been taught by Carl to ask questions and then listen with no expectation. It had been drilled into him, "Tucker, the story is found in what they say and not what you expect them to say. Don't force the story; let it unravel on its own." Tucker had found this to be true. It worked well in finding a story where it first appeared that none existed.

"Is that what kind of bomber it is, a Liberator?" Tucker asked, reaching for a second donut.

"Well, that was the official name given to it. She had other less affectionate ones like the Flying Boxcar, the Pregnant Cow, or the Flying Prostitute."

"Flying Prostitute?"

"Oh, well, that was because the new thin style wing on it looked odd to the fellas, and they said it looked like it had no visible means of support." Tucker chuckled when he understood the reasoning behind the nickname. "Actually, it is a B-24 Liberator, and one of the last ones flying. Most of them succumbed to the aluminum guillotine; that is to say, they were scrapped after the war. Chopped up and made into coffee pots, cooking pans, and other aluminum products." Pondering the information, Tucker began to construct a story in his mind. He could hear Carl's voice in his head once again. "A good reporter learns everything he can about a story and then sifts through the information, separating the wheat from the chaff."

"How about this airport? I saw a brass plaque on the wall when I walked in that said it was built in 1942. Did it play much of a role during the war?" Tucker asked. Bob had just taken a bite from his donut. Since his mouth was full, he did the only polite thing and shook his head up and down. Tucker then noticed his looking around at the old plaster walls, ceilings, and fixtures that could clearly be dated to the early forties.

"Years ago this place was alive with activity. It was built to help train flying cadets for the armed forces and for many other wartime purposes. I had hoped to join the Army Air Force and become a pilot, but my eyesight wasn't good enough. My war was spent on the ground in the infantry. See that long fence over there?" he said, pointing out the large front windows. Tucker looked across the airfield and could see a long rusty cattle fence. "Kids used to gather there and watch aircraft come and go. I used to stop and stand with them. It was amazing what they knew about the military aircraft. They would talk about the leading fighter pilot aces much like kids today about famous baseball players. Even though I was unable to fly in the war, I did take flying lessons and became a pilot after the war was over."

"Fascinating," Tucker said as he quickly jotted down notes. Tucker ate the rest of his donut and washed it down with his remaining coffee. "Thanks for the coffee and donuts. I think I'll make my way outside; it is shaping up to be a beautiful day," he said as he walked his empty coffee mug over to the sink. Picking up his pad of paper and pencil, Tucker headed for the main double doors that led out onto the apron.

"Wish I could join you, but I have some chores to finish before I can come out," Bob said as he picked up his broom.

"Is there somewhere to sit outside?" Tucker asked.

"Sure, out the door, turn left and about half way down the front of the terminal building, there are some benches."

Tucker made his way along the sidewalk that ran along the terminal building. A man was sitting on the only available bench. He wore powder-blue slacks, a dress shirt decorated with paisleys, and a cream-colored panama hat. When Tucker drew closer, he could see a young boy stretched out on the bench beside him with his head resting on the old man's lap. An old, heavily worn, brown leather flight jacket was covering the boy for warmth. The man was slowly caressing the boy's brown hair as he peacefully slept. When the man saw Tucker, he started to wake the boy to make room on the bench.

"Oh please, let him sleep."

"Are you sure you wouldn't like to sit down?"

"No, I am fine," Tucker said as he leaned back against the old brick terminal building. He didn't have to ask; he knew the old man was waiting for the bomber to arrive.

"Beautiful morning. Have you been waiting long to fly in the bomber?" Tucker asked.

The man turned his frail body to face Tucker. "Most of my life," he said. He started coughing, drew a handkerchief from his pocket, and covered his mouth. Finally regaining control, he spoke, "Flown before, son?"

"A couple of times, in a four-seat, low-wing aircraft Cessna airplane," Tucker said, in an attempt to sound like he knew something about aircraft.

"Hmm, I wasn't aware that Cessna ever made any four-seat, low-wing aircraft," the old man said.

"I could be mistaken—it's been a while back," Tucker said.

"Looks like you have one that's not used to the early morning hours," Tucker said, as he gestured toward the young boy. The man smiled and turned his gaze down toward the boy.

"This is my grandson, Samuel. He has an interest in airplanes and loves to hear of my experiences in the war. I made a promise to him that we would ride this old bomber if it ever came through these parts. You should have seen the smile on his face when my daughter told him it was stopping here this year. He has been counting down the days. His smile makes it worth every penny of the cost."

"I'll bet he is proud to be your grandson."

"Let's hope I can live up to what he believes about me," the old man said, as he clearly felt the heavy burden of a hero. The old man looked toward the heavens as if he were speaking to God. "I tell Samuel the ugly truth about the war. That historic cities that took decades to build are demolished in a matter of hours, families are shattered, and most of all, the good guys don't always come home. Pain is the common denominator for all participants." The old man's gaze once again turned toward his grandson. "I hope he has a life full of peace." Tucker looked off in the distance and tried to absorb the wisdom in what the man had told him and thought of ways to weave the encounter into his story.

Samuel stirred. "Old Pa, is it here yet?"

"Not yet son, but it should be anytime." The grandfather's words brought the boy up into a sitting position, but with his eyes still not wanting to accept the job of staying open, he leaned over against his grandfather and shut them.

"What did you do during the war?" Tucker asked.

"I loaded bombs," he said. "I made many friends and lost many too. It was rough watching your buddies fly off into that meat grinder. They all were volunteers and could request another duty at any time with no loss of respect. The odds were against them completing their tour of duty, which was thirty missions. They knew it, but they kept on going out mission after mission. Such a tough breed."

Tucker began to ask another question, but the old man held up his hand. "Do you hear something?" he asked. The man cocked his head in the same way he had many years before straining to hear the melody of finely tuned Pratt and Whitney engines carrying his overdue friends back to his airbase. His ears weren't disappointed this time, "Only one airplane sounds like that: a B-24 Liberator," he said. "Amazing that a sound can bring memories to the surface that I thought I had solidly anchored to the bottom," he said the words explaining his sad expression. The old man reached into his hip pocket, pulled his handkerchief out, and slowly pressed it against each eye. The movement of his grandfather caused the boy to open his eyes.

"What's wrong, Old Pa?" Samuel asked.

The old man smiled through his tears and patted the boy's knee. "Nothing son, nothing at all," he replied, "just the sound of an old friend that I haven't heard from in a long, long time." The boy knew what his grandfather was speaking of as he too could hear the sound. He sat straight up with his eyes now open.

"It's here, it's here," he shouted, clearly excited. As the bomber drew nearer, the sound of its engines could be heard echoing off of the buildings and surrounding woods announcing to the crowd of admirers inside the terminal building that the guest of honor had arrived. Tucker strained to catch a glimpse of the bomber through the early morning fog. Heading towards them, it first appeared as a shadowy form over the far end of the runway. It was clear the pilot was letting the old Liberator make a grand entrance. Pulling great amounts of power from her four radial engines, she was thundering down the main runway. The slipstreams created by the massive propellers were creating a dramatic effect by whipping the fog into long swirling columns of dense white vapor. Vibrations from the bomber were pounding rhythmically against Tucker's chest, and a sense of adventure and excitement stirred deep within him. He could feel the hair on his arms and the back of his neck bristle as the mechanical monster drew closer. When it reached the midpoint of the runway, the crowd erupted in cheers and applause. Tucker's attention was diverted to the old man's movements. With some effort, he rose, placed his feet side by side, and swept his hand up his body, to salute the aircraft as it winged its way past them. The young boy looked up in admiration. His hand slowly reached up and slid into the old man's other wrinkled hand as they watched the awesome display of power and strength. The bomber passed the far end of the runway, pulled sharply up into a steep left-hand turn, and began a downwind leg preparing for the landing sequence. After the landing rollout, the bomber proudly made its way toward the crowd lumbering along like an old soldier full of confidence and stories. As it turned onto the apron, the blinding sun raced along the highly polished aluminum side. Tucker was forced to avert his gaze. As it drew nearer, he could make out the name it had been given, *The Buckeye*. The name arched over a hillbilly cartoon character who was sitting down, leaning against a large tree. The brakes were applied on the bomber, and it slowly came to a stop. Once the engines had been shut down, the stars and stripes were unfurled and hung out of the pilot's side window. The early morning breeze snapped the colors to life and stretched them out displaying their beauty. The admirers watched as the crew slowly emerged from the bomber and performed their duties as efficiently as bees tending their hive. A couple of crewmembers erected fencing around the bomber with an entry point for those who wished to take a tour.

The old man needed no invitation. He walked directly to a crewman who was collecting donations and handed him a twenty, waived off the change, and proceeded slowly around the bomber. His grandson was at his side already busily asking questions and pointing at the bomber. The old man's hands stretched out to touch the bomber as he walked along its side. Moving slowly down one side, the two disappeared through the rear main entrance hatch.

Tucker stood there watching as the crowd grew like a thundercloud on a hot humid summer day. A man walked over and stood near him. He was wearing an old army issued hat with the brim bent upward. It looked to be original as it was faded and heavily worn. Tucker, still searching for the bits and pieces needed to write his story, seized the opportunity. "Were you in the war?"

"Yep."

"Did you fly on a B-24?"

"Nope. I was a grease monkey assigned to the Eighth Air Force in England." Before Tucker could ask another question, the man explained that he was a crew chief in charge of the maintenance of a B-24 named *Anna Belle*. "The worst part was not the long cold evenings spent repairing the blown engines and bullet holes. It was the gut wrenching wait for the bombers to return from a mission. Those fellas on the bomber were my best friends. I remember sweating out some stress-filled moments and praying all of the bombers would come back. They rarely did. When they did get back, any aircraft with wounded aboard would shoot a red flare to alert the medical crews. Once it had landed, the ambulances would race toward it to try to save some poor crewmember who was in bad shape. They flew out looking their best and came back looking like they had been in a back alley knife fight. Boy, what a relief when I would spot *Anna Belle*. It was rare when there wasn't some type of damage that needed repaired."

Tucker ventured a question that he feared might be too personal. "Did your bomber ever fail to return?"

"No, I was fortunate. There were a few times that I thought the Germans had got the best of *Anna* Belle, but she always came home. One of the worst ones was back in December of '43 when scanning the skies we waited an extra hour. With each passing minute, I became more convinced that I had lost ten friends and a bomber that I knew better than my wife. When all hope seemed lost, I heard a low rumbling off in the distance. I stopped and listened intently," he said, holding his hand to his ear reenacting the moment. "Call me a liar, but I knew from the sound of the engines that it was my *Anna Belle*." His grin grew and worked to push his bushy eyebrows up on his forehead. Working his hands, he explained. "The pilot brought her in fast and set her down long on the runway. He jumped on the brakes, and the left tire blew out, but he managed to getter stopped. You never saw ten men so happy to be back on the ground. Their story of how they fought through fighters and flak to make it back to base was nothing short of miraculous, yet commonplace among the crews. I think often about the ones that didn't make it. Just like you, they were just getting started in life. He looked off in the distance at nothing in particular. They had dreams of building families and living peacefully into old…" his voice cracked. The man shuffled his feet as he looked at the ground struggling to gain control. Clearing his throat, he began again, "Anyway, I brought this just in case the fried eggs and bacon that I had for breakfast decide they want to show themselves again," he said. He held up a dark paper bread sack. "I get kind of green around the gills when I fly. Like a dead fish that's been on a stringer too long. You can always tell if they're safe to eat by checking their gills for color. Dead too long and their gills lose their bright red color. You know what I mean?"

"Yeah, I know what you mean," Tucker said remembering when his father had taught him the same method. The thought of a bloated, smelly fish on a stringer caused him concern. He hadn't felt queasy about the flight, but the comments combined with the thought of seeing the bacon and eggs reemerge began working on him. Tucker excused himself and worked through the growing crowd of people to seek out a member of the crew who could tell him more about the bomber.

Coming upon one of the crew, Tucker held out his hand. "Hello, I am Tucker McQueen."

"Name is Justin Meeks. What can I do for you?"

"Well, I work for *The Daily Reporter* and am writing a story for next week's newspaper. I saw you in the cockpit. Are you the pilot?" Tucker asked.

"Yes, I am," he said.

"Would you be able to tell me a little about the purpose of your visit and the history of the bomber?" Tucker asked.

"Sure. We have been touring around the U.S to keep the memory alive of all the men who fought and died for our country. This is a B-24 Liberator built back in 1943 at the Ford factory in Willow Run, Michigan. From what I have been told, its crew flew it across the ocean to an airbase in England. After completing an unbelievable amount of missions, she was flown back to the states to go on a war bond tour.

"What was a war bond tour?" Tucker asked.

"It was a means for the United States to finance the war. In simplest terms, it was a way for a private citizen to loan money to the government, and then when the bond matured, they were paid back principal and interest. When the war ended, she managed to escape the scrap yard and was sold as surplus to the Zenith Oil Company. They turned her into a first rate executive transport. I wish they had kept her until we purchased her because their maintenance was excellent. We were fortunate in that the oil company had stored the original gun turrets in one of their warehouses—minus the guns, of course. After ten years of hauling big shots around, she was sold to a fire fighting company in California. She took a real thrashing, flying low and slow through horrible conditions. I am sure you can imagine that when we purchased her, she was in need of some major repairs; stomping out forest fires is not for flimsily built aircraft. The thermals created by the fires create some hellish updrafts. A weaker aircraft would have come apart years ago, but the Liberator was built to withstand flak and fighters. We acquired what was left of a once proud warrior from a not-for-profit group who had sworn to come up with the money to restore her. Turned out, their financial backing never grew to the size of their dream. I suppose they figured since they couldn't do it, somebody should, and so they sold her to us. Her rough handling as a fire bomber had taken a heavy toll, but after throwing buckets of money at the project, along with countless volunteer man-hours, she was put back into her original flying condition. In the end, there was much discussion by all as to what nose art she should wear. Interestingly enough, the decision was made for us. At the end of the restoration, we removed layers of paint and, to our surprise, found some of her original Army Air Force serial numbers and remnants of the original nose art. That was a real surprise, but it was not as amazing as what followed. During restoration, we would have days where the public was invited in to view our work. We would rope off the bomber so they couldn't touch it or climb in it. One afternoon when I was working on the bomber, an old man, withered by the years, slipped under the ropes and walked over to the nose of the bomber. He took a pencil from his pocket and started tracing the nose art. He wasn't hurting anything, so I just watched him. After about ten minutes, one of our volunteers saw him and was going to stop him since we had a strict policy of no one working on the bomber except approved personal. I waved him off as something amazing was happening. Over the next hour, everyone just stood and stared. It became evident that he wasn't just tracing the obvious outline of the nose art, but he was adding details that were too faded to be seen. We just stood back in fascination as he continued to outline the faded artwork down to the smallest detail. Once he finished the outline, I grabbed various colors of paint and set them open by him. His hand delicately painted what his mind's eye was seeing. A small crowd gathered to watch him work. His relatives, who were standing close by, were stunned. I spoke with his son, who verified that his father had fought in World War II. I am not sure what the old man's name was, but he did initial his artwork. See right there are his initials, B.L.M. His son told me it was rare for his father to speak about the war, and sadly a few years earlier, he was diagnosed with Alzheimer disease." Tucker looked at the nose art in the light of the story and tried to envision this feeble old man painting from a long ago memory. "Well, you're looking at the finished product. He spent two hours straight completing it. Every time his family asked him to take a break, he would wave them off and mumbled something, about 'it was the least he could do for the crew.' He was clearly reliving some past memories. When he finished, he stood at attention and saluted. Some thought he had just traced the faded outline that was already there, but as I said, I saw him add detail to the artwork that had been completely worn away. I suppose we will never know for sure, but I believe that sometime, in 1944, he painted the original nose art. How else could he have done what I saw him do?"

Tucker was furiously jotting down notes. Justin finished by saying, "Take a good look at her. To appreciate how rare she is, consider that there were over 18,000 Liberators built, and she is the only one with combat experience left flying."

"Thanks for the information," Tucker said, as he shook Justin's hand. "I appreciate your taking the time to speak to me."

"My pleasure," Justin replied.

Tucker began to explore more of the bomber. Wondering about the history of such a magnificent warrior, he reached out and touched the smooth aluminum side. Continuing, he worked his way around to the business end of some fifty-caliber machine guns that were protruding from the tail turret. He noted three small Nazi swastikas painted beside the turret and guessed they indicated the number of aircraft that were shot down by the gunner. Walking along the side of the bomber, he noticed two old men standing under a wing in conversation. They were both laughing and reliving some of their experiences. Eventually, their smiles faded, and he saw one of them place his hand on the other's shoulder. Finished with his walk-around inspection, Tucker sat down and leaned back against the nose wheel. The pieces of the story were loosely assembled in his mind. It would contain a historical overview with some of the individual interviews and finish with the sacrifices made by the men that had fought and died in the air war. There were many good pieces, but he needed a common thread to draw them all together. Leaning against the side of the bomber, he closed his eyes and daydreamed about what it would have been like to leave his home, travel to a distant land, and put his life in jeopardy to fly over an enemy that was intent on killing him. Men who endured such tragedies would be amused at his petty worries. His mind swirled deeper and deeper into thought until he became oblivious to all that was going on around him. He was drawn out of his trance by an annoying clicking sound.

"Hey, Tucker, smile for the camera. Opening his eyes, he was blinded by the flash of a camera bulb. "You're not sleeping on the job are you? Let's go, I have another assignment I need to shoot after this one." Pete Evans, his assigned photographer, had arrived.

"I uh, wasn't sleeping."

"Sure you weren't. Just resting yours eyes, right?" Pete loved to tease others, but he wasn't too keen on being teased. He was a middle-aged man who had taken his avocation and turned it into his vocation. Rumor was that job offers had been made, but he had settled for the comfort zone that lures so many people into accepting less than their best; there was no doubt he was talented. Tucker was glad to have him along as he knew he did quality work, and his pictures would spice up the article. Wearing khaki pants and a functional shirt that was outfitted with big pockets to hold extra film or whatever else found their way into them, he looked the part of a photographer.

"Old man Timmons wouldn't like seeing you resting your eyes like that on company time," Pete said. Tucker knew he wasn't about to snitch on him as it was no secret as to how Pete felt about Timmons. Pete tolerated Timmons because he enjoyed his job; Timmons kept Pete because of his talent. Tucker had witnessed them going at it in Mr. Timmons's office, and they could never seem to agree to disagree. Pete had told Tucker that Mr. Timmons had a weakness for the bottle, which had cost him a marriage and his career at a large newspaper.

"Tuck, what time is this old battle wagon going to defy the laws of gravity?" Pete asked as he loaded a roll of film.

"The pilot told me as soon as they finish up with some minor repairs," Tucker said. Pete's grin departed his face, and he took on a more worrisome look.

"Repairs, what kind?"

"If I remember correctly, it's something with the propeller governor on one of the engines. He said it's like shifting gears in a car: low gear for hills and high gear for high-speed travel. More or less, that propeller is stuck in low gear, which is inefficient in cruise flight. I suppose with the age and flight time on the bomber, there must be systems breaking down all the time," Tucker said.

Pete worked his way around the bomber, and as he snapped off pictures, a crewmember asked everyone to clear the area around the bomber. Tucker watched as Justin entered the aircraft through the bomb bay doors and then reappeared in the cockpit window. When the crowd was back at a safe distance, the mechanic made a wide arcing swing with his hand. The radial engine spit and sputtered and, finally, with a little coaxing on the throttle, caught with blue smoke emitting from the exhaust stacks, and the propeller instantly became a blur. The mechanic continued to use signals to communicate with Justin. Opening his hand with his palm up, he raised it toward the sky. Justin brought the engine up to a deafening roar and began cycling the propeller through its various pitch angles. With a thumb up, Justin conveyed that all was well. The mechanic took his hand with thumb extended and made a sweeping motion across his throat. Instantly there was a reduction in the noise as Justin pulled the throttle back. He then moved the mixture to idle cut-off, and the engine shut down stopping the propeller. The mechanic pushed a roll-around ladder to the engine and climbed it, flashlight in hand, and did a visual inspection. Once he was satisfied, he descended and told one of the volunteers that the aircraft was fit to fly.

Tucker's attention was drawn to a woman that was working towards the middle of the crowd. She wore an army green jumpsuit and a leather flight jacket. When he moved closer, he noticed a patch sewn on it. It was a cartoon character of a young woman wearing goggles, a leather flying helmet, and a white silk scarf. The old woman, who was deeply wrinkled from too many days in the sun, bellowed out, "There is a brief preflight meeting in five minutes for anybody who is going on the morning flight."

"That would be us, Tuck," Pete said, heading toward the small group of diehard aviation enthusiasts who had gathered on the shady side of the bomber. Once she called names and checked them off her list, she began the briefing.

"My name is Betty. There are a few things you need to know before the flight," she said, with authority in her voice. "Our takeoff position will be between the bomb bay doors and the cockpit. I will show you once we board the bomber. If you have a weak stomach, I got some barf bags," she said, holding them aloft. "Make sure and use them. If you don't, and puke in the bomber, you have to clean it up. Whatever you do, don't puke out the waist gunner windows cause it will dry hard on the sides of the bomber, and it's a bitch to scrub off. One last thing, once the wheels depart the runway, you can unbuckle and walk throughout the bomber, but a word of caution: be careful around the bomb bay doors. If you step off of the catwalk onto them, you could trip the safety sensor, and they will let you go like a bomb that's wiggled loose from the rack." Nervous laughs rippled across the group.

Tucker felt pretty good but wondered about the old man who was fumbling with the bread sack. He saw Tucker look over at him and winked in reply.

"Just in case," he said, holding up the bag. Tucker responded with a weak smile and a slight raise of his eyebrows.

Betty directed the group into the bomber through the bomb bay doors. "Watch your heads. All I have is a 1944 rusty needle in the medic bag and nothing to dull the pain," she said, with a big grin on her face. Once everyone was safely seated and buckled in, Betty put on a headset and spoke to the pilot. Tucker could see her lips moving as she silently counted heads. "All of the passengers are buckled in," she said. Sitting down, she latched her safety belt. "When you hear the bail out bell sound, you can roam the aircraft. In preparation for the landing, the co-pilot will sound it again, and you will need to head back to seat and strap in," she said. As they sat and waited for *The Buckeye* to come to life, Tucker studied the patch on Betty's jacket.

"Hey Betty, I am curious about that patch on your jacket," Tucker said. She looked down at it and smiled.

"I was in the Women's Army Auxiliary Corp," she replied. "Spent the war ferrying aircraft from factories to airports. It was an exciting time for me and the other girls serving our country. We flew hot fighters, heavy bombers, and cargo aircraft."

"I'll bet you have a lot of interesting stories," Tucker said prying for more details.

Proud to share her experiences as a pilot, she was glowing like a new father announcing the birth of a baby. "Well there are a few stories worth sharing. One that comes to mind was in 1943 when I was flying in a four-airplane formation from a factory up north headed to an airport in Georgia. I had ice buildup on my wings. 'Bout cashed in," she said. Before

Tucker could ask a follow-up question, he heard the familiar whirring sound of the inertia starter followed by the coughing of an engine as it was started. One by one, the pilot managed to coax the big Pratt and Whitney's to life. A unique smell of exhaust fumes wafted into the bomber's interior. Tucker could feel his back vibrating against the bulkhead that he was leaning against as the pilot added enough power to get the bomber rolling. Looking around at the expressions on the passengers' faces, he noted nothing but excitement. He could feel himself being caught up in the experience, and a smile broke across his face. After a short taxi, the bomber lined up on the main runway and came to a stop. Moments later, with a deafening roar, it rolled forward on its takeoff run. Once again the old bomber proved the Wright brothers' theories on flight and broke ground. When less than one hundred feet off the ground, the bell sounded and everyone unbuckled. The passengers quickly began exploring the bomber. Like loose metal shavings being drawn toward a magnet, the passengers were drawn to the open waist windows. Even the thunderous noise from the engines couldn't drown out the loud excited discussions taking place. Once the area cleared, Tucker worked his way to the waist gunner window and watched the shadowy silhouette of the bomber as it raced across the treetops. The other passengers explored other stations in the bomber; some heading towards the flight deck, while others were intrigued by the ball turret that was located in the belly of the bomber. One man was letting his imagination go as he sat in the tail turret working the hand and feet controls envisioning fighter attacks. Tucker thought of the bond the crew must have felt as their very lives were held in each others' hands. He stuck his head out of the waist gunner's window to get a better view of the engines and was instantly deafened by the oncoming air, which nearly ripped his sunglasses off his face. Pulling back into the bomber, he straightened them and then worked his way to the ball turret. It was round with a steel framework and had many glass panels to afford the gunner a good view of enemy aircraft. Studying the open hatch door that allowed the gunner to access the turret, Tucker could see how cramped the position was. Clearly, only a small crewmember could squeeze into the tight space. The gunner straddled a set of handles that he used to turn the turret, as well as fire the twin browning fifty-caliber machine guns. It was designed to fight off any attacks that came from below the aircraft.

"Hey, Tucker," he turned and was blinded by a white flash of Pete's camera. Worried that he might try to engage him in conversation and keep him from exploring more of the aircraft, he started toward the front of the bomber. Heeding Betty's advice, Tucker took each step with extreme caution as he worked his way along the catwalk that spanned through the bomb bay. He finally worked his way up to the navigator's station in the front of the aircraft. The table where the navigator sat was about half the size of a small coffee table. Tucker sat at the seat and imagined the stress endured by the navigator when required to block out everything and focus on plotting a course home for a damaged bomber and wounded crew. After exploring the area, he stood up to investigate other areas. Just as he started toward the tail turret, the airplane hit a rising thermal and pitched up. The sudden pitching of the aircraft caught him off balance, and he felt himself falling. His hand shot out for a bulkhead to stop his fall, but he was unable to grab ahold. On the way down, his head hit the corner of the table; he felt like a prizefighter had dealt the finishing blow. His knees buckled, and he slowly melted into a reclined position. Slowly he started to regain consciousness. As he first opened his eyes, he remained confused and struggled to make sense of anything. As he lay there processing the visual information that flooded his brain, his hearing rushed in with the many sounds of the noisy flight. It all came back to him, and he realized that he was lying on the floor staring up at the bottom of the navigator's table. His attention was drawn to one of the corners where he could see a small portion of white pages being blown by the swirling wind vortices that were whipping through the bomber. Reaching up with his hand, he touched the corner. Scooting directly under the table, he felt around the bottom of the table for some way to free it. He pushed his index finger into the gap where the white paper could be seen and noticed that the gap became slightly larger. As he pushed on the metal bottom, the book fell upon his chest. Picking it up, he noticed a small amount of olive drab overspray on it from the restoration paint job. Tucker blew on the cover of the book and in the dim light made out a name but was unable to read it. Slowly, he rose to a sitting position, leaned back against the bulkhead, and put the book in his jacket pocket. His attention shifted to the throbbing pain he felt from his injury. He reached up, pushed back his hat, and felt where his head had struck the table. His hair was wet and matted. A trickle of warm, sticky blood oozed down over his eyebrow. Pete saw Tucker sitting down by the navigator station and approached him.

"What happened kid? You look washed out," he said, with a genuine look of concern. Pete reached out and offered Tucker a hand. Tucker grabbed hold, and Pete pulled him to a standing position.

"Some turbulence caught me off balance, and I fell and hit my head on that table," Tucker said.

"Here, take this," Pete said handing him a handkerchief. Tucker dabbed at his forehead and looked to see the sharp contrast of red blood staining the white cloth.

"Thanks, Pete."

"You feel okay?"

"My legs feel a little shaky, but I think it will pass."

"Here, clean your cut with these." Pete handed him some alcohol pads that he carried to clean his camera lenses. Tucker dabbed at the wound and grimaced as he loosened some clotting blood and the alcohol seeped down inside the cut. Opening his wallet, Tucker took out a bandage and handed it to Pete.

"Let me give you an estimate on the damage," Pete said as he slowly pushed Tucker's hair up out of the way to get a good look and apply the bandage. "You may want to stay with someone tonight so they can check on you," he said, while staring at the cut. I always heard that it's good to have someone wake you through the night when you take a blow to the head," Pete said.

Their conversation was cut short by the sound of the bail out bell ringing. "Guess that's our cue to go buckle in for landing," Tucker said as he moved toward their seats.

The bomber gently sat down on the runway with the main wheels touching first and the nose gently settling after the bomber had slowed considerably. Taxiing up to the apron, the pilot worked through the shutdown procedures. Still seated, Tucker felt a gentle nudge from Pete.

"You taking the rest of the day off?" he asked while gathering up his gear.

"Actually, I was already scheduled to be off half a day. I am planning on going home to see Mom," Tucker said as he stood.

"You may want a doctor to look at your cut. It may need a few stiches," Pete said.

"Ah, I don't think it's that serious. I think I'll just have Mom clean and dress it when I get to her house." He was hoping to play down the situation since he did not want to become the brunt of the next few weeks' worth of office jokes. Exiting the bomber he headed to the parking lot.

Chapter 2

Tucker climbed into his Ford pickup truck, started the engine, and drove out of the parking lot. The hum of its motor and the soft ride provided by the coil springs in the bench seat always took Tucker to a peaceful place. The interior smelled of warm leather with a faint hint of motor oil. Driving it brought back many good memories. His father had bought it many years ago. When he received his license, his dad took him immediately to the hardware store and had a key cut. Without saying a word, he handed it to him. Some men are born athletes; others are perceptive businessmen; he was a natural father. There would have been more children, but it wasn't meant to be.

Many aspects of Tucker's life had changed in the past few years. Lately, his life had been lacking the slow, peaceful pace that he had enjoyed while living with his parents. He was happy to retreat to the serenity of his childhood home. Tucker drove down the gravel driveway that meandered back through a

canopy of tall poplar, sassafras, and maple trees. Shutting off
the engine, he heard the quiet hum of the motor fade and sat
listening to an assortment of songbirds. Closing his eyes, he felt
peace wash over him. He breathed in deeply, taking in the
earthy, woodland smells and savored the moment. Looking out
across the property, he knew there was a season for everything,
and this too would certainly end. Exiting the truck, he headed
to where he was certain his mother would be — her garden.
The vegetables that it produced were enjoyed by many, but she
allowed herself to be stingy with her flowers. She admitted that
she had an emotional connection to them, and they were where
she found her great joy. Tucker recalled her telling him that if
he ever questioned the existence of God, he should plant a seed
and watch it grow. Gardening was a spiritual experience for her,
and she often voiced that she could not understand people who
saw the obvious fingerprints of the Creator and then turn and
deny His existence. When he drew close to the garden, he could
see movement in the pole beans and knew she was down in the
trenches fighting weeds, a never yielding enemy. Years ago a
friend had suggested to his mother that she spray herbicide, but
she was a bit of a purist and was unwilling to use poison in her
garden; instead, she used grass clippings as mulch to smother
the weeds. It wasn't foolproof and some pushed through the
matting and had to be pulled by hand. She claimed anyone
could duplicate her garden and that the miracle was in the seed
and soil, not her hands, but anyone who paid attention saw
through her modesty. As he walked the length of the garden,
Tucker enjoyed the sea of colors that her flowers produced.

"Hi, Mom," he said, somewhat startling her. She stood up and smiled. Walking towards him, she opened her arms and greeted him with a hug.

Noticing the bandage, she asked, "What happened?"

"Oh nothing. I will tell you about it later."

"Are you hungry? I made some vegetable soup," she said as she brushed the dirt off her knees. Tucker bragged about her cooking to anyone that would listen, and one of his favorites was her soup. Her method of making vegetable soup meant it always tasted slightly different each time. The variance in taste was a result of her being frugal and her humble beginnings. In order to not waste the smallest of vegetable leftovers, she poured them into an empty one-gallon plastic ice cream container and stored them in the freezer. Most of the time, the soup consisted of corn, green beans, peas, onions and beef roast; it took about a month for it to fill. Typically, she made it on a Saturday. Preparation began at noon with her pulling the hodgepodge out of the freezer in the morning to begin thawing. In the early afternoon, she added whatever ingredients were missing and set it on the stove to begin cooking. By the time Tucker and his dad wandered in for supper, the soup was bubbling up and dispersing its mouthwatering aroma throughout the house. His father said he was unsure as which was more attractive to him, her beauty or her ability to take his meager salary and feed him like a king. She drew great satisfaction in taking care of them.

"Shall I grab your tools?" Tucker asked.

"Yes, thank you."

Tucker grabbed the hoe that was leaning against the old rusty fence. It seemed everything had a memory attached to it. He had helped his father erect the fence in an attempt to stave off any critters who might turn his mother's hard work into their free meal. It stopped most thieves, except the raccoons; they were ingenious in getting through or around any barrier. More than once, Tucker had heard his dad scold some masked bandit that had managed to get into the garden but failed to figure a way out.

Walking toward the house, his mother spoke. "You know, I've been thinking about selling this place and moving closer to the city. It's been a little over two years since your father passed away, and sometimes the memories overwhelm me. I don't mean to trouble you with my burdens, but I feel so alone especially in the evenings. So many memories whisper to me.

Tucker could feel the weight of emotions pouring from her as she spoke of what it meant to live without his father. He felt the same emotions, but he hated the thought of her selling the house as it was a powerful connection to his past. Knowing that she was looking for his support in this difficult decision, he spoke. "Well, you would be closer to me and Aunt Vicki if you moved in town."

"Your father and I worked hard on this place," she said pausing and surveying the property. "So many memories, so many good times. We built a wonderful life here. I feel lost without him," she said softly. Tucker could hear quivering in her voice.

"I understand," Tucker said. "Well we have the next couple of days to discuss it. Let's go up to the house and get some of your soup," he said. She nodded her head in agreement.

It had been a few weeks since Tucker had been home, and when he entered the house, a torrent of memories rushed him. His mom placed the old aluminum coffee pot on the stove as Tucker reached into the cabinet and grabbed a couple of bowls and some old soupspoons. She pulled a silver ladle out of a drawer, filled the bowls, and then set them on the table. Tucker proceeded to stir the soup and blow on it. As he stirred the soup, the familiar colors of the vegetables rolled to the surface. He added a touch of pepper and took his first bite, slightly burning his tongue. His mother set out an assortment of crackers, sweet pickles, and extra sharp cheddar cheese. Once they finished, she walked over to the stove and moved the percolating coffee pot off the burner.

"Why don't we sit in the living room? I will pour our coffee and bring it in," she said as she opened the cabinet. She selected a dainty china coffee cup for herself and a stout ceramic one for him.

Tucker walked into the living room and started building a fire as the house had cooled considerably with the setting of the sun. Grabbing the antique iron tongs from the rack, he added some small firewood to the kindling, which had caught nicely. After a few minutes, the fire had grown, and he added a sassafras log. He watched as the flames licked up the sides of the log and caught on the dry wood. The fire spit and crackled as it came to life and began to remove the chill out of the cool, fall air. A mellow glow lit the room. Once finished with the fire, he walked over and sat down on one of the two couches that were separated by a coffee table. The couches faced each other and were arranged perpendicular to the fireplace making an ideal place for conversation. His mother sat down across from him.

"So tell me, what is new with your job?" she asked.

"Well let's see. My assignment today was to take a publicity flight aboard a WW II bomber. The pilot said it is the only surviving B-24 Liberator that flew in the war and is still flying. It was stationed at an Army Air Force base somewhere in England."

"That sounds interesting."

"At first I wasn't that excited, but it turned out to be more than I had expected," Tucker said. "That is how I ended up with this band aid on my head. The aircraft hit some turbulence, and I was caught off balance and fell. On the way down, I hit my head and was knocked out."

"Are you all right? Did you see a doctor?" she asked with concern in her voice.

"No, it wasn't, or at least I don't think it's serious," he said reaching up and touching the bandage. "Perhaps you can look at it in a little while? For a while, I lay on the floor unconscious. When I came to, I found a small leather book. Actually just the edge of it was visible. It was hidden behind a false bottom that had been built in the small navigator's table."

He was uncertain why he had not thought of the book earlier. It could have been the thoughts of spending a weekend at the home place or the fear of Pete taking the story back to the office, but regardless it had slipped his mind. Tucker rose and walked into the kitchen to grab his jacket that he had hung up by the back door. Returning to the living room, he reached into the pocket and pulled out the darkened leather book. He set his jacket beside him and studied the leather book more closely. Overall, it was in good condition; although, it did have a coating of grime on it.

"It appears to be a personal journal," Tucker said as he took a closer look at the leather strap that was sewn to the binder. The strap wrapped around the back of the book and ended at a thin square brass box lock that was in the middle of the front cover. The lock was to stop an individual from stumbling on to the book and reading its contents, but certainly wasn't meant to secure it from a determined reader as cutting the strap would easily defeat it. "Looks like the lock is all that stands between us and an answer to my question," Tucker said while studying it. His mother rose and walked back into the kitchen and returned with a damp washcloth. Tucker handed her the book, and she gently wiped it off.

Holding the book under the lamp that sat beside her, she turned it until the light shone just right, and she could make out faded gold lettering. "Lt. William Alan Pritchet," she said aloud and then handed it back to him. He brushed more dirt and grime off the old weathered book and looked at the brass lock.

"I have some old keys. Do you want to try them?" his mother asked.

"Sounds like a good place to start," Tucker said. "Could you also grab a knife so if we need to cut the band?" He could hear her rummaging through some drawers in an old writing bureau that sat in the front hallway. She returned shortly. "Try the keys and keep this," she said, first handing him the keys and then the pocketknife. Tucker looked at the old knife and opened the largest blade. It had been thinned by many years of sharpening that had resulted in a slight curvature in the sharp cutting edge.

"Thanks, let's try the keys first," he said. Tucker methodically tried each key. Most were too big for the tiny lock. "May have to cut it."

"Try to use the small blade to pick the lock," his mother offered. He opened the smaller blade, but it was too wide to fit into the small opening.

"Perhaps something smaller that I could fashion into a key?" he said. His mother went back to the drawer and returned with a small paper clip. Tucker bent the end to work it into the lock. With a little twisting from him and some encouraging words from his mom, he finally heard a click as it popped open. Tucker looked up and smiled at her. It felt as if they had just uncovered the entrance to an ancient Egyptian tomb and were standing at the entrance about to discover what had been hidden for many years. Savoring the moment, Tucker took a sip of his hot coffee. His mom was now sitting up on the edge of her seat and watching his every movement, so typical of her curious nature. She had confessed to him that as a young girl she would search the house at Christmas time until she found her presents. Once they were located, she would get them out and play with them without her parents' knowing. She had even gone as far as to tell her sister what color suitcase she wanted when she came across them tucked deep in a closet. Waiting was not an easy task for her, and he could tell she wanted to grab the book from his hands and end the suspense. Tucker opened it. A picture fluttered down and landed between the couches near his mother. She reached over and delicately picked it up. As she gazed at the picture, Tucker saw her smile.

"I have felt that look before," she said as she stared at the picture.

She handed him the old black and white photograph of a young couple sitting side by side smiling with their cheeks pressed together. The young man had on his military dress uniform with ribbons and a pair of wings. He looked to be about twenty years old with short dark hair that was parted to the side. The young woman was wearing a gold cross necklace and had a ribbon in her hair. They were a handsome couple, full of life and energy. Tucker opened the journal and began to read aloud.

Chapter 3

The date is August 2, 1944, and I am headed to war. I have been a card-carrying member of the United States Army Air Force since July 21, 1943. They have invested countless hours of training in me, yet it remains to be seen if it was a sound investment. I have yet to pass the test that the enemy has prepared for me. Uncertainty seems to occupy all aspects of my life. The world is being threatened by evil forces that have plagued man since the beginning of time. My generation has been called on to fight them. It is the same old story that has played out before, just different circumstances and characters. As long as there has been freedom, bad men have tried to forcefully take what all are gifted by their creator. My warhorse is a B-24 heavy bomber known as the Liberator. My crew has trained extensively in this bomber for the past few months, and we know her so well she feels like the 11th member of our crew. We know all of her likes, dislikes, and quirks. She is spoken of affectionately, as we know our survival is dependent upon her ability to dish out and absorb punishment. We dote over her to make sure she is in the best fighting condition possible. I am confident she will not let us down. To say I am not scared would be a lie, for I am deathly scared of how I will perform when in combat. The possibility of my own death concerns me, but letting down my crew is even more disturbing.

Our pilot opened our orders only moments ago and announced we are being sent to England via the northern ferry route. We will fly to Presque Island then a stop at Goose Bay, Labrador. After our stop in Canada, we will have to make a long flight to Reykjavik, Iceland and then finally Prestwick, Scotland and after thousands of miles, finally report to the 392nd Heavy Bombardment Group, 578th Squadron at Wendling, England. It is as dark outside the bomber as the interior of a cave. As we speed along at 215 miles per hour, I sit at my small navigator desk with a lamp that illuminates the page enough that I can pen my thoughts. Everything is built with space and weight in mind, and my area is very cramped.

Just a few weeks ago, I enjoyed my last visit home. It took over a day of travel to get there. I arrived at a late hour, but my family was waiting for me at the train depot. I have a younger sister named Julia, who is 15, and a younger brother named Charlie, who just turned eight. Our house is in a small, quiet town in Indiana, which has a general store, train depot, post office, and two churches. When we arrived at our home, Mother, Father, and I sat up for a few hours and talked. The next morning I awoke to the sound of my mother shutting the heavy door on the wood cook stove as she prepared breakfast. I drifted back to sleep until I was awakened again by the clank of Mother setting her big black cast iron skillet on the stove to fry bacon. It made a glorious popping and crackling sound and filled the air with a wonderful aroma that seeped into my bedroom. The smoky bacon aroma, coupled with the coffee, won out over my desire to sleep, and I slid my feet out from under the heavy warm quilts where they were rudely greeted by the cold hard wood floors. Walking to my closet, I put on a heavy flannel shirt and selected a pair of blue jean bib overalls. Stepping over to the window to check the weather, I saw Dad heading down the path to the barn with Charlie holding his hand. I could hear the cows bawling in the barn for their morning hay and grain. Passing through the kitchen, I headed for the backdoor.

"Good morning Mother, smells good." She was cracking eggs as I passed by.

"Morning, Laddy. Are you hungry?"

She knew the answer to the question, so I just smiled at her and pulled on my rubber barn boots. Walking the path, I noticed that the walnut trees that I had planted a few years ago had grown to well over my head. In a few years, we would be harvesting black walnuts that Mother would certainly put to good use. Stepping into the barn, I saw Charlie helping spread the hay around in the bins while Father was filling the grain troughs. Charlie saw me.

"Hey, William, over here."

Charlie has always been my shadow, and I could tell he was excited to have me home. Father looked over at me.

"Good morning, William. I was going to let you sleep in this morning."

"Guess my internal alarm had other plans for me. What's left to be done?" I asked.

"Just need to slop the pigs, and then we'll head up to the house for some breakfast," he said. I grabbed one of the buckets and went to the bin to fill it with grain. My father usually raises four pigs each year. On a bitterly cold weekend in February, most of the extended family come over to butcher them. When I was young, it was a day of adventure spent with my cousins, who were counted among my closest friends. Aunts, uncles, and grandparents all came to work and then were rewarded by taking home cracklings, lard, and fresh pork. The first order of business was to humanely shoot the pigs. Next, they were hoisted on the bucket of my father's tractor and then lowered in a huge tub of boiling water. This cleaned the pig and made it possible to scrape the hair off. The men would then set into them with sharpened skinning knifes. Once they were skinned, we cut the skin with fat into cubes and placed them in a large cast iron kettle that sat in a cradle over a fire. This cooked the fat off rendering the lard. It was an annual tradition for my Uncle Les to send us young boys over to the small country store to get some bottles of soda pop. When we returned, he would have cleaned and cut a pig's heart into several cubes. Skewering the cubes with a piece of bailing wire, he would lower them into one of the huge boiling lard kettles. It took only a few minutes to cook them. Pulling them from the kettle, he would salt them, pray and we would make a meal of the soda pop and fresh pork. It was delicious, more so because we were always so hungry from the bitter cold and our active day.

We finished our barn work by spreading the table scrap slop and grain onto the concrete for the pigs. In typical fashion, they pushed for position to try to consume the most in the shortest amount of time with no thought to anything but their own desires. Every so often a shriek would be heard, as the positioning became more aggressive, and one pig would bite another's ear. After the animals had all been tended to, including Buckshot, Charlie's pony, we headed down the lane back to the house.

During breakfast, I agreed to take Charlie squirrel hunting in the afternoon. We split and stacked wood for the first part of the day. After lunch, we grabbed my shotgun and headed to the woods.

"One of the most important things to remember when you are squirrel hunting, Charlie, is to be as quiet as possible. Let's take our shoes off." I tied my shoes together by their laces and then did the same to Charlie's and handed them to him.

"Here, Charlie, put your shoes over your shoulder. This is something Grandpa taught me when I was your age. Now you will be able to feel a dry stick before you snap it beneath your foot. Step where I step."

Realizing Charlie would have difficulty in quietly moving through the woods, I decided to find a place for us to sit and let the squirrels come to us. I walked slowly with Charlie following in my footsteps. Slipping quietly into a grove of hickory trees, I surveyed the ground until I came across the hull cuttings that had fallen from the squirrels' feeding. Charlie sat beside me quietly looking around to try to spot one. Closing my eyes, I sat back, filled my lungs with the earthy smells knowing it would be many months before I enjoyed them again. As we became still the woods came alive. A chipmunk darted across the top of a large rotting hollow tree trunk that had been blown down in a storm. It would pause, survey its surroundings for threats and then dive inside the log only to reappear elsewhere. A nuthatch landed close to us and started walking down the tree. I could see it had caught Charlie's attention. For several minutes, I sat still with my eyes closed and just listened. Hearing the shrill sound of a red - tailed hawk, I looked up and watched as it circled high overhead searching for its next meal. I enjoyed the break as the war was always just below the surface of my thoughts ready to prey upon my peace. A mosquito buzzed around my ear and landed on my hand. I smeared the pest into a black spot. Looking over at Charlie, I noticed one on his arm. I smashed it, and blood spurted out. Obviously it had been there feeding for a while and was about ready to depart with its meal.

"Look over there. Is that one?" Charlie said with excitement easily heard in his voice. Looking in the direction, I saw a large blue jay jumping from limb to limb. "No, it's just a jay," I said softly. When the sun started settling, Charlie scooted over close to me. I took off my insulated flannel shirt and put it over him like a blanket. He looked up and smiled. Soon enough we heard small pieces of discarded hickory nut hull falling through the leaves. I looked up and scanned the tree until I noticed some movement around some shriveled dead leaves. A large, rust-colored fox squirrel emerged from behind the noisy leaves. I motioned to Charlie and slowly pointed at the squirrel that was reaching to pull a hickory nut from a limb. He became fixated on the squirrel. I motioned to him to quietly get up and follow me so that he could get a clear shot. Using the cover of the trees, we worked our way forward until we were at the base of a large beech tree. Positioning Charlie in front of me, I helped him lean against the tree to steady himself for the shot. We had practiced the routine before, but it was with a stick or some other type of make believe gun. This was much more dramatic. Charlie's face was filled with excitement as I handed him the shotgun and reminded him to hold it tight to his shoulder. When he was positioned for the shot, I gave him some last minute instructions.

"Safety is always first; never forget that," I whispered in his ear.

"Remember to squeeze the trigger; don't jerk because that'll pull you off your target. Hold it tight so you won't bruise your shoulder. You ready?"

He nodded his head, and I pushed the bill of his gray cap over to the side of his head so that he could lay his head on the butt stock and draw a good bead. Charlie's finger slid down and pushed the safety off, and then he slid it to on the trigger. I knew he was experiencing a forever moment and felt thankful to watch the events unfold. The shotgun recoil rocked Charlie back against me, but he held his footing. The squirrel tried to hang onto a branch, but its grip and life were fading fast. It slipped from the limb and made a thump on the forest floor. Charlie let out a whoop and set the gun against the tree. He was grinning from ear to ear, so proud of what he had accomplished.

I smiled at him, reached down, and pushed the safety on the gun. We walked toward the squirrel, but Charlie couldn't contain himself and broke into a run. He picked the big fox squirrel up by its back feet.

"Well done, buddy. I say we ask Mom to fry it for supper," I said to him.

Charlie was so excited that he continued to relive the action as we walked back to the house. During supper, the story was retold with him reenacting the whole series of events and entertaining all of us. When he was finished, he put his hands in his pockets and stood beside my chair.

"Sounds like you've had a memorable day, Charlie," Dad commented as he pulled his pipe from his shirt pocket and filled it with sweet smelling tobacco.

"Uh huh, I did," Charlie said looking down and shuffling his feet.

"Who wants some dessert?" Mother said.

A resounding "I do" was the response even before we knew what it was. Mom stepped into the kitchen and came back with plates of freshly baked persimmon pudding.

"Julia, would you get the vanilla ice cream for me?" she asked as she set the pudding on the table. Mother scooped out a large serving of warm pudding and passed it to Julia, who added a dollop of ice cream on top. I walked to the kitchen and grabbed the coffee that Mother had set on the stove to percolate. Grabbing four thick white ceramic mugs, I returned to the kitchen table. The ice cream was quickly melting from the heat emanating from the pudding. A thick, white creamy coating covered it. I set the mugs down and began to pour.

"Looks like you have one too many?" Dad said. I couldn't keep from grinning.

Charlie smiled as I set one in front of him and poured him a hot mug of sunshine.

"Trying to ruin the boy?" he said in jest to me.

"Better try these to soften it up a bit," I said sliding the sugar bowl and cream towards him. He looked at our father for approval as coffee had been something that only the adults enjoyed.

"Well, I suppose if you're old enough to shoot a squirrel, you're old enough to start drinking this too," our father said. My parents have told me many times how much they appreciate the way I watch over Charlie.

"Julia, what did you do today?" I asked as she had been quiet this evening. She started softly sobbing and slowly her chin dropped.

"I don't want you to go." She had held everything in, and now the dam was bursting with her unable to contain her emotions. The room fell silent as I pushed back from the table, slowly walked around, helped her stand, and put my arms around her.

"Everything will be all right," our father said. His voice helped reassure her and had a calming effect.

"Dad is right, Julia. I'll take real good care of myself and not take needless risks. Before you know it, you'll have to put up with me again." She stopped crying and giggled looking up at me through her tear-filled eyes. I felt her loosen up, and she looked at me. Looking over at Charlie, I could see that he didn't understand the seriousness of what was unfolding as he was distracted with the flowers on the table.

"Please be careful, William," she said, her voice growing stronger. She sat back in her chair, and I helped scoot her under the table as she dried the tears from her eyes. Her fears were understandable as boys that I had gone to school with had been reported as missing or killed in action. The rest of the evening we spent sitting around the table playing Charlie's favorite card games while Mother made a cherry pie and chicken and noodles for the next day.

My last full day at home was a Sunday. We rose early to collect eggs, milk the cows, and complete the other endless chores that have to be performed before church. Once finished, we returned to the house where Mother had placed breakfast on the table. At nine o'clock, the focus of the house shifted from chores to getting ready for church, which is within walking distance of our house.

"William, will you help Charlie get ready?"

"Yes, Momma," I responded, more than willing to help offset the heavy workload she took on every Sunday to make it special.

"Come on, Charlie. Let's get you scrubbed and ready."

With only fifteen minutes before the service, we set out for the church. Our walk led us right in front of the small country store. It was closed in honor of the Sabbath. Others, who lived more distant, drove in and waved when they passed by. The church building is a typical Midwestern style, with white painted slate shingle siding and a steeple that is equipped with a bell. Young boys take turns ringing the bell, which is always done at five minutes before the service begins. The interior of the church has ceiling fans, a pine wood floor, and tall windows with attractive stained glass murals at the top of them. A wide center walkway leads to the pulpit with wooden pews on each side that are attractive, but not comfortable. At the front is a communion table where the bread and juice are set. A thin white cloth is draped over them. Wooden collection plates are set off to the side of the covered communion emblems.

When we approached the church entrance, we were warmly surrounded by friends and family. The conversation and laughter that greeted us was uplifting. I have noticed that the war has magnified emotions and exposed the very worst and the very best in humanity. Upon entering the building, the conversation quieted, and people spoke in hushed voices in holy reverence. Once our preacher had welcomed everyone, we blended our voices in song. With no musical accompaniment, I could clearly hear individual voices singing out around me; the harmony created is angelic. The experience bonds us together as brothers and sisters in Christ. During the service, the babies and youngest of children were passed around among friends and family members. A few of them were less than well behaved and had to be taken out of the service when they became too noisy. The sermon was on the present sacrifices of the young men in service, and our pastor creatively wove in the sacrifice God had made through his son Jesus for all of mankind. After the service, I walked outside and stood on a sidewalk to smoke a cigarette with the other men. Some of them spoke about their experiences in the World War. I shook many hands and fielded many questions about my training and where I would be sent; some of the questions I was not allowed to answer while others I simply did not know the answer. They all wished me well. While walking out of the gravel parking lot, I turned and looked back at the church wondering if I would ever sit in it again. True blessing is fully understood when you are asked to leave it behind. I wished the moments could last longer. It all seemed so special to me. I shook free from the thoughts as they were becoming too painful. As always, lunch was better than any meal a man could have eaten at the fanciest of restaurants. Most of the afternoon, I spent lazily around the house. A few friends stopped by to say goodbye and wish me well. For dinner, Mother prepared all of my favorite—fresh corn on the cob, sliced Brandywine tomatoes, fried potatoes, and steak seared in a hot cast iron skillet. She set out the formal dishes that had been given to her as a wedding present from her wealthy aunt that lived in Chicago; they were only used during special occasions. Julia made a centerpiece for the table from fresh picked daisies and arranged them in a yellow ceramic vase. It helped lighten what was going to be at times a sad emotional evening. As we had done so many times before, we gathered around our worn kitchen table and held hands as my father said a prayer for the nation and my safe return. Mom gripped my hand tightly on one side while Charlie was sitting so close on the other he was nearly on my lap. After dinner, Father and I sat in the living room while Charlie played with marbles at our feet.

Mother and Julia remained in the kitchen cleaning up the supper dishes. When the younger children had gone to bed, I stayed up with Mother and Father. We sat at the kitchen table and drank a cup of warm cider. Mother had added cloves and small slivers of orange peelings to spice it up. I have always appreciated how she could take a little bit of nothing and turn it into something special. Clearly, she had learned to be resourceful through necessity. The Great Depression in the 30s had left a lasting mark on her and it showed. Nothing was ever thrown away, just repurposed. After dinner, we sat for some time talking about nothing and everything. When the hour was getting late, my father pulled his old wooden pipe down off the mantle and sat down in his favorite chair by the fireplace. Taking his can of tobacco, he packed the pipe. Running a wooden match against his blue jean overalls, he brought it up to the pipe bowl. The match flickered as he exhaled. Taking a long draw on it brought a glow from the leafy substance that illuminated his facial features. I have great respect for him. Like many of this world's true heroes, he earned the title over many years of serving those whom he loves. He is a strong man in the most important ways. We don't have excess, but I have never worried about the necessities. As I have grown older, I have noticed the personal sacrifices he has made so that others could have what they wanted. He let out a breath of smoke, leaned back in his chair and Mother moved over and stood by him.

My mother softly cleared her throat. "William, your father and I have been talking about you today—it seems we do every day," she said, with her voice trailing off. Tears started to form in her eyes. "We want you to know how proud we are of you and how much we love you." She softly sobbed as Father reached his hand out to her. Her fear and concern set ablaze the anxiety that had been piled up within me for the last few months. It brought back the burden of my uncertain future that for the last few days had faded into the background. I try not to think of the possibility of not returning, but when I do think about it, it is from a selfish standpoint. I hadn't given much thought to the emotional burden they carry around on a daily basis or the long term impact my death would have on so many people I try to tell myself it won't happen to me, but I know better. More often than not, I try not to think about it. My father maintained his composure. It instilled confidence in me that he believed I would make it through this dark tunnel. He exhaled and the sweet smell of the pipe tobacco filled the room. I took the moment to explain about the intense training I had completed and the talented crew I was a part of, as well as information about our top-of-the-line bomber.

My father finally spoke. "We know you will be alright son. Be careful and remember all that we've taught you."

Mother stood up and picked up the cups. "I suppose I should be getting to bed. The cows are going to expect their feed at the same early hour tomorrow." She bent over and kissed me on the forehead. "Always know that I love you, William," she said.

"I love you too, Mother." My father and I sat in silence for a moment.

"I suppose I should go to bed too, son. Your mother has nearly worried herself sick." He stood and walked toward his bedroom and then turned back around and looked at me. "Take care of yourself, son," he said.

"I will, Dad."

With that, he turned and disappeared into the bedroom. Reaching into my pocket, I pulled out a pack of Camel cigarettes and then fished out my Zippo lighter from my top shirt pocket. Flipping the lid open, I rolled the striker against the flint. The smooth taste of the tobacco calmed me; I have just recently acquired the habit. In the past, I had smoked cigarettes on occasion and never felt the urge to continue past some fishing excursion or hunting trip. However, with the recent mounting tension, it had turned from an occasional treat to a habit. I knew that I would miss the house and the farm, but far more than all of these, my greatest pain would be the separation from my family. After a few minutes of internal reflection, I smashed the glowing end of the cigarette and headed to bed. Since I had returned home, Charlie had been sleeping in my bed with me. When I turned on my table lamp, I noticed he was sprawled out across the bed in such a manner that I would need to move him so I could lie down. When I did, he stirred and sat up.

"I was thinking a while ago, and I'm real glad that you came home to see us."

"It sure is good to be home, buddy," I stated as I tucked the covers in around him. I walked around to the other side of the bed and slid under the heavy blanket that Mother had quilted. Before I drifted to sleep, I heard the puffing of old Engine Number 55 earning her keep by pulling hard on heavy-laden boxcars. With the window open to allow the cool breeze to blow in, I heard the familiar 'clickity-clack' as it passed by in the night. The rhythmic sound had a soothing effect on me. The steam whistle cried out at the crossing, and my mind drifted back to a time when my childhood friend Bud and I hopped the train and rode it to the next town. The boxcar was dirty and smelled like warm creosote. Just before it reached the town and came to a stop, we tumbled out, skinning our knees. Those adventures helped to break the monotony of the hot summer days. The train finally faded, and the only sound left was the mantle clock with its pendulum ticking back and forth in slow rhythmic fashion. The last time I heard it strike was eleven o'clock.

The next morning, I rose early to help Dad with the chores. Mother fixed a hearty breakfast that would stay with me well past lunch. When finished, I changed into my uniform for the long, lonely train trip back to base. Father was going to drive me to the passenger depot in a neighboring city as there is no service in our town. Thus, my goodbyes would be said at the house. I grabbed my green canvas army duffel bag and stepped into the kitchen Mother, Julia, and Charlie were all standing by the kitchen table. They walked me outside where I tossed my bag into the wooden truck bed. Father came over to join us, and I knew it was going to be tough saying goodbye.

"We have a few presents for you before you go, Will," Julia said clearly excited about the gift she had gotten me. She held out a small box neatly wrapped in brown paper with a small tan ribbon around it. I gently shook it and pulled the wrapping off it.

"I hope you like it," she said.

"Julia worked hard doing odd jobs for neighbors and selling eggs to make the money to pay for it," Mother added.

I opened the box and pulled out a gold cross necklace. I had mentioned to her that I liked it when we were at our general store. "Wow—I love it. You didn't have to do that," I said, smiling at her.

Charlie reached for it. "Let me see it," he said.

"Be careful with it," I said gently placing it in his hands. I walked over and hugged her. "Thank you, Julia, I love you," I whispered in her ear.

"Your mother and I also wanted to give you something," my Father said as Mother handed me another present.

I pulled the store bought paper wrapping off and discovered a soft leather bound journal with "Lt. William Alan Pritchet" in gold lettering inscribed across the front. Father smiled at me.

"Don't rely on your memory for any of it, William. Write it all down as someday when you're an old man, you can read your adventures to your grandkids."

"I will."

"We better get going so we won't be late. They won't hold the train for us," my father said, starting towards the other side of the truck.

"Wait," Charlie said. He ran over to me, grabbed my hand, and pressed something into it. I looked into my hand.

"It's a buckeye. They bring good luck. I didn't have any money to buy you something, so I searched and found this," he said smiling proudly. I pictured him searching through all of the buckeye seeds that had fallen from the tree in the back yard and selecting what was the best of the lot to give to me. I bent down on one knee and my eyes filled with tears.

"Thanks, Charlie, I'll take it on every mission."

Charlie wrapped his arms around my neck, tucked his head, and squeezed hard. "Hurry back home," he said. I could feel the warm wet tears flow down my neck from his tears. I knew I had better not hug him much longer or my emotions would break through.

"You know I will," I said.

Father fired up the truck, and I climbed in. With a wave, I began a journey that would take me all the way to the bloody skies of Germany and then hopefully back down this same driveway.

Chapter 4

There are almost a dozen men in our crew. Our pilot is a
32-year-old college graduate named Robert Lane. We call
him Pappy. His nickname was quick to follow the disclosure of
his age. Cool under pressure, Pappy is an All-American guy
who loves to have a good time. He is liked and respected by the
crew. Sitting next to him in the executive office is our co-pilot,
Lew Mason. Lew is more uptight and concerns himself with the
smallest of detail. He is a strict, by-the-book type of pilot, and
mentally notes even the smallest of mistakes that Pappy makes.
He gently points them out in an attempt to avoid offending him,
but he isn't always successful. More than once, I have heard
them in a heated debate after one of our practice missions. I
listen to their points and counter points, but lose interest when
it turns technical and beyond my understanding. Our flight
engineer is Jim Martin. He is responsible for many aircraft
systems and monitoring the engines and the top turret during
battle. Jim knows more about the technical aspects of the
bomber than anyone on board. If we have a breakdown in

flight or suffer battle damage, we report it to him, and he coordinates solutions with the flight deck leadership. Hailing from the state of Texas, he is as proud as any to call it home. We are constantly hearing stories about the enormous size and many other facts about his great state. He let us know that Texas is three times larger than England and Scotland combined. In battle, he is also called upon to operate the top turret. It is no secret that he was the best marksman in his gunnery class. We know because he told us. He said he came by it naturally and claimed his dad was a champion skeet shooter who taught him how to handle guns at an early age. There was disagreement among the crew about where the truth ends and the stories began, but we all agreed we wouldn't want to be on the receiving end of his twin browning 50 caliber machine guns. Hanging from the bottom in the ball turret is Little Frankie Lucas. Spinning around in that little ball, he is all courage. Without enough room to wear a parachute, he has to have nerves of steel. Jack Peterson and Albert Hull man the right and left waist gunner windows. They are inseparable. Wherever one is found, the other is sure to be. I once saw them get in a scrape at the base over someone cutting in the chow line. They worked three fellas over pretty good before the fight broke up. We are all happy to have them aboard as they are natural fighters and bring comic relief to some tense situations. At the beginning of every flight, we are required to verbally check in by stating our names. This assures we are in place and our mics and headsets are working. When Albert and Jack check in, it always brings a round of chuckles. With Jack always stating his name first and Albert making something up that plays off "jack." Once Albert followed with "rabbit"; another time it was "ass." He seems to have an endless supply. Our bombardier is an American Indian named John "Eagle Feathers" Thompson. He is stationed in the nose of the bomber with me. He is trained on the most guarded secret of all the equipment on board, the Norden bombsight. It allows us to bomb from high altitude and hit targets with considerable accuracy. He hails from the Choctaw nation. I find him to be quiet and reserved. We found common ground in having come from strong families. I especially enjoy hearing stories about his ancestors and the bond that they felt with Mother Earth. From his earliest days, he has been taught the Choctaw way of life. He has a long line of warriors in his ancestry, and if born a few hundred years earlier, I have no doubt he would have distinguished himself by counting much coup. His parents and grandparents trained him from an early age to overcome any life test he encounters. He is my best friend, and I am certain our friendship will extend past the war years. In the nose with John and me is Archie Chambers, who operates the nose turret. Finishing out the crew is a tall, lanky fellow from Wyoming, our tail gunner Ben Alexander. Never calling attention to himself, he is cool under pressure. I serve as our navigator. Presently, my duties include plotting a course across the Atlantic Ocean. A miscalculation could result in our missing our destination by many miles or worse yet, put us over enemy held territory. We have trained together for more than a year, and these men are all like brothers to me. I am convinced they feel the same about me.

Droning on through the darkness, Pappy broke the silence. "Anybody thought of a good name for our bomber?"

"How about something that's a good luck charm?" Archie suggested.

"What the hell is left?" Little Frankie asked.

"Yeah, he is right. Pictures of bombers in the war zone show nose art littered with four leaf clovers and horseshoes," Lew said leaning back in his co-pilot seat.

The idea struck me to mention the buckeye that Charlie had given me, but I hesitated, and before I mentioned it, John piped in, "Hey, William, how about your buckeye?" There was momentary silence.

"What's a buckeye, John?" someone asked.

"My people call them *hetuck*, which means 'eye of the buck,' and it translates into 'buckeye.' They're a dark brown tree seed with a light brown spot making them resemble an eye. My grandfather showed me how to grind them into a powder so that it could be thrown into the water to stun fish. They're poisonous," John said.

I added to his comments. "It is something that is thought to bring good luck. My kid brother gave me one as a present right before I left home. It is actually a seed from an Ohio buckeye tree."

"Does it bring good luck?" Jim the top turret gunner asked.

"Oh, about as well as anything else, I suppose," I said.

From the cockpit Pappy chimed in. "Lucky and poisonous—I like the combination. Seems appropriate for a bomber."

"Call for the vote," Lew said in a lighthearted way.

"All in favor of naming her *The Buckeye* say 'I' " came Pappy's voice through the intercom system. An overwhelming "I" came through my headphones. "Motion passes," Pappy said. Using his fist as a gavel, he firmly struck the top of the instrument panel.

The more I thought of it, the more pleased I was it had been chosen. I decided to write a letter home to Charlie as he would be proud to hear about our bomber's name.

"Hey, John, how about meeting mid-ship for some hot coffee?" I asked.

"Sounds good."

Taking off my headset, I bent down on my knees and crawled out of the nose of the airplane. The opening was small and nearly impassable with the crew's bags and bottles of booze jammed around it. Some of the crew had been told the money invested in the booze could be tripled in the war zone. I had to wriggle through the narrowed opening and push over the top of the pile until I reached a spot that I could stand. Reaching the catwalk that spanned the bomb bay doors, I grasped firmly onto the metal structure running along the side of the fuselage to secure myself. Placing one foot in front of the other, I carefully made the crossing. The wind was rushing through the bomber, and the chill seeped in even though I wore woolen long underwear under my clothes and my heavy brown wool lined jacket. Once over it, I passed through a bulkhead and saw that John had beaten me to the spot. The wind whipped his coal black hair around that was protruding from the front of his cap. I sat down opposite him.

"Here you go," I said, extending a cup his way. He held it up to be filled. Prying the cork top off of my thermos bottle, I poured until the cup was half-full. I would have filled it but feared the turbulence rocking the aircraft would splash it onto his hand. I then poured one for myself.

"Thanks. What's in the brown sack?" John asked.

"Some of Mom's brownies with hickory nuts and powdered sugar on top," I said while opening the sack. "She packed them in my duffel bag. I just found them a while ago. Help yourself," I said handing him the sack. John reached into the bag and took out a good-sized brownie that was wrapped in wax paper. I then pulled out one for myself. We sat in silence and ate the brownies while sipping the hot black coffee.

"Homesick yet?" I said in jest.

John shook his head. "Naw," he said chuckling.

"What was that story you promised to tell me about you and your grandfather?" I asked. "My grandfather was always teaching me the ways of our people by creating tests or training me in all sorts of survival skills. When I was a young boy, he started an annual tradition that required me to survive for a week on my own in the woods. I wore traditional buckskin clothes with moccasins and was given a flint, a five-foot piece of heavy string, and a knife. Every year he explained the importance of the training, encouraged me, and then left. During my early years, the nights were scary. There is a lot of nighttime activity in the woods. I would build a good-sized fire and cling to my knife. I fashioned a wooden hook and caught small fish from the river and used the string to snare small game. I also collected edible berries and plants. Between them, I was able to avoid being tormented by hunger pains. When I was young, I considered building a large deadfall, but I knew killing a deer would amount to tremendous waste, which was against our ways. My people have great respect for wild creatures and believe it is wrong to shed their blood without using everything that they offer in their sacrifice. As I grew older, I began to enjoy the experience. One of my fondest memories was sitting on a high bluff that overlooked the river in the evenings and enjoying a cup of hot sassafras tea and smoking a pipe I had made. Every year we would go through the same ritual until I reached the age of sixteen; then he took my knife away. By that time, he had taught me how to make one from stone The next year he took away the string."

"Let me guess. You made some?"

"Well, sort of," John said with a chuckle. "I used thin grapevine, which isn't as limber as string, but if you find it when it's still green, it will work. When I turned eighteen, he took the flint away. I stayed in the woods a full month the last time and built a small, simple wattle."

"What is a wattle?"

"It is a small dwelling built by weaving vines, river cane, and wood together. They are simple in design but can take a while to build. I made a bed by driving forked wooden stakes into the ground, which served as corners. Then I laid long poles between the forked stakes, secured them, and wove a grapevine bottom for the bed frame. Finally, I took straw grass and laid it out on the bed to add some cushion. It wasn't the most comfortable bed to sleep on, but when it rained, it held me above the wet ground. Eventually, I did build a deadfall and took a whitetail deer. I smoked the meat and used the brains to tan the hide. My grandfather and I hauled the rest of the smoked jerky home at the end of my stay. The experiences stirred something deep inside me that certainly traces its roots back to my ancestors. A few years ago, my grandfather admitted that during the first few years, he had stayed in the woods to watch me and make sure no harm came my way."

"So he was nearby and you never knew it?"

John nodded, taking another bite of the brownie. "He has the ability to pass by only a few feet away from others in the woods, and they wouldn't even know he is there. It still amazes me that I never saw him, but he could move through the woods like the wind: silently, effortlessly gliding along. He taught me many lifelong lessons and helped increase my self-confidence.

We sat silently sipping our coffee with the ever-present wind and noise from the engines.

"Hey, William, Pappy wants to see you on the flight deck," Little Frankie hollered while squeezing his way past us.

"Are you staying here?" I asked.

"I am going to find somewhere to get some shut eye," John said as he handed me the empty cup.

As I made my way back through the bomb bay, I had a good idea of what Pappy wanted. I stepped up onto the flight deck and tapped him on the shoulder. Pappy pushed one side of his headset off to hear.

"Frankie said you wanted to see me," I said.

"Yeah, could you shoot some stars and double check our course? The winds have picked up according to the weather reports we are getting."

"Sure thing," I hollered back. I headed to the nose of the bomber to my small navigator table, pulled out the bubble octant from the wooden box, and stood up in the small Plexiglas dome that was built above my station for this purpose. I shot three stars and plotted points on a map. Pulling my headset on, I spoke, "Hey Pappy, I have a course correction. Turn to 035 degrees."

"Roger that," Pappy called back.

"How far out are we?" Lew asked.

After a few more quick calculations, I answered, "About 135 miles."

It wasn't a long wait before we were circling for a landing at Goose Bay, Labrador. Upon landing, Pappy taxied *The Buckeye* to the ramp, and Lew, checklist in hand, methodically went through the shutdown procedure. He assigned one of the waist gunners to sleep on board and guard the aircraft throughout the night. Although he only told one of them to stay, both Jack and Albert slept aboard the bomber.

After a good night's sleep, our crew was awakened in the early morning hours, fed, and sent on our way. Our next stop was Reykjavik, the capital of Iceland. It didn't sound like a friendly place, and at our early morning briefing, we were informed it wasn't. I guess some Icelanders are sympathetic to the Nazis. Cold and barren, it wasn't a pleasant place; the wind never seemed to be less than gale force. Based on the chilly reception we had received from the few Icelanders that we had encountered, none of us cared to venture into town. The next morning we were served our first green eggs and powdered milk. Just as we had been warned, they were hardly worth eating. I remembered that I had one more brownie on board and decided I would eat it once we were airborne. A crew was just beginning to board a Boeing B-17 Flying Fortress as we walked out across the ramp to board *The Buckeye*.

"Look at her," Frankie said. "The B-24 will haul more bombs and fly faster, but still the 17 gets the headlines."

He was right. The Boeing B-17 was the darling of the media. On the other hand, the B-24's brutish looks had attracted an assortment of uncomplimentary nicknames that overshadowed her superior performance.

"I am going to go out on a limb here and say the Germans will shoot down a good looking bomber as well as an ugly one," Lew said sarcastically.

"Yeah, since when did smooth lines and a graceful stance make a hoot in hell's difference as to how good a bomber was?" Pappy added. We continued our rag tag formation out to *The Buckeye*, climbed aboard, and prepared for takeoff. Once we were loaded and Pappy had the engines turning, he called the aircraft control tower. He was told to follow the B-17 that was taxiing to the runway. Truly believing he was in a superior machine, the B-17 pilot heard the instructions given to Pappy by the tower and took the opportunity to flaunt his arrogance.

"Hey fellas, look at that elephant lumbering along behind us," he said on the tower frequency. A few chuckles could be heard in the background. Pappy was not about to let the insult go unanswered.

"Okay, hot shot. How 'bout we race these two tin cans?" he said in reply. "I'll lay $500 on us beating you over to Scotland," Pappy said.

"That ought to shut them up," Pappy said on *The Buckeye's* internal intercom system. Lew rubbed salt in the wound "bock, bock, bock." There was complete silence from the B-17 pilot as he knew better than to wager a nickel, let alone five hundred dollars on such a challenge. The next response heard from the B-17 pilot was his acknowledgement to the tower that they were cleared for takeoff. The bluish gray smoke puffed from the engines as power was applied, and the big four-engine B-17 Fortress raced down the runway until it became airborne. *The Buckeye* pulled onto the runway for departure and rapidly accelerated to rotation speed and lifted off the runway. With sufficient airspeed, Lew eased back on the yoke, and the wheels broke free. I gave Pappy a heading of 145 degrees. Our trip was just shy of eleven hours.

"Anybody want to lose a little money playing cards to one of the best flight engineers in the Eighth Air Force has ever seen?" Jim said on the intercom.

"I thought you were the best gunner?" someone stated.

"I want in," said several crew members who couldn't be discerned as they all spoke at the same time.

"Hey, John, you going to get in on the action or just watch?" I said making my way to mid-ship.

"I am sitting in the bleachers. Little Frankie cleaned me out last time," he said.

It was well known among the crew that Little Frankie had the most experience with cards. He would bet on anything. When his luck ran out, he would play on sheer guts and somehow at least break even; trouble was it was hard to tell, as he had mastered the bluff. I made my way to the game and watched the money swap hands until Little Frankie was pushing it into his wallet with the others looking somewhat sore about their loss.

After the game, John and I headed back to the waist gunner windows to see the view, which happened to be spectacular. We were popping in and out of a layer of cumulus clouds. Periodically, we could see the waves and white caps on the angry sea far below.

"Looks pretty hostile down there," John said.

"Yeah, glad we have four engines," I shuddered thinking of how cold the water would be if we were forced to ditch.

John pulled on the waist gunner's headset, "How high are we Pappy?"

"Seven thousand feet," he replied.

We sat silently, absorbed in our own thoughts. "I'm going to go up and make sure they still have this thing pointed in the right direction," I said as I made my way to the flight deck. The sun was reflecting brightly on a layer of clouds that were above our altitude. I tapped Pappy on the shoulder and motioned for him to remove an earphone.

"How are things going, Pappy?" I hollered. He looked at me and grinned. His square cut jaw and military issued sunglasses gave him the classic look of a pilot.

"There is a drop in the oil pressure on the number four engine," he said with a serious tone to his voice. "I want all those screws out there turning if possible," he said.

Lew was watching the oil pressure gauge with a concerned look. Ahead was a solid wall of clouds that extended well above our altitude. Presently, we would fly right into the great white unknown with an associated risk of flying blindly into a thunderstorm. Everyone knew they were to be avoided at all cost. In addition to the threat, entering the clouds would require Pappy and Lew to fly solely by instruments, which placed a much greater burden upon them.

"Let's see if we can fly below it. You want to take us down?" Pappy asked.

Lew placed his hands on the yoke and gently pushed forward. *The Buckeye* pitched over in a shallow descent, confirmed by the altimeter, which slowly unwound as we proceeded down through the wispy cloud deck. I watched as Lew's vision focused on the instrument panel. His eyes scanned from one instrument to the next to verify the aircraft speed, rate of descent, and the wings remained level. The hours of time in aircraft simulators and training were evident as they methodically settled into flying the big bomber by no other

reference than the flight instruments. While other
crewmembers slept, our pilots were busy earning their pay. I
pulled on the radio operator's headset and listened as Lew and
Pappy talked back and forth.

"Watch your airspeed… looks good… hold her steady
now." Pappy's words were reassuring as Lew eased ten men's
lives down through the clouds. At 800 feet, we broke out of the
overcast. *The Buckeye* held its heading and altitude for the next
couple of hours.

I made my way back to my station and lay against my
rucksack napping intermittently;
I was awoken only when turbulence jostled me.

After flying low for about an hour, Little Frankie came on
the intercom. "Hey Pappy. Looks like a whale on the surface
just off to the right of our course; think we could swing over
and take a closer look?"

I stood up, went, and positioned myself behind the flight
deck to watch. Pappy, wanting to accommodate, kicked the
rudder, changed course by a mere ten degrees to investigate and
eased down to 500 feet above the surface. As we drew nearer,
the whale took on a more mechanized appearance. Something
didn't look right, as it lacked the smooth graceful movement of
a living creature and appeared somehow artificial, similar to a
manikin at a department store. I strained to assemble the puzzle
pieces in my mind to determine what it was.

"Something looks strange about it…" Archie said, while
peering out the nose window.

Lew grabbed his binoculars and pulled them up to his eyes to see it clearer. "Change course and climb – submarine!" he hollered. Quickly setting the binoculars aside, his hand flashed over to the propeller pitch and then throttles for a maximum climb.

"Maybe we can make the clouds?" Lew said hoping for the best. Pappy flung the bomber into a left-hand turn 90 degrees from our previous heading. Lew continued working the engine controls pushing the throttle handles full forward to get maximum horsepower. The altimeter steadily climbed, but the sudden change in throttle setting and the high demand on the engine was all that was needed, and the number four engine started surging out of sync with the other engines. "Shut down number four," Pappy hollered out. Lew's trained hands moved from one lever to the next making adjustments. He continued to scan the gauges to verify his actions and was coordinating his efforts with Jim our flight engineer. Behind me, Jim was busy shutting fuel off and other systems to the engine. I looked out of a side window at the submarine and could see the sailors swinging their deck guns around to bear on us.

"It's not enough. We aren't going to be out of range of their guns in time," Little Frankie frantically screamed.

I cringed waiting to pay the price for our carelessness. Holes were about to be ripped through men and metal. It was then that I heard a burst of gunfire from the stinger turret. I could see the twinkling from the submarines' deck guns and knew that shots were being fired at us. Another burst let loose from the tail, and I could see the tracers tracking across the water until they found their mark and paused on the deck guns. The twinkling ceased.

"Shit! What was that all about?" Archie said.

"We just about cashed in before we've even made it to the war," Lew said with a serious tone.

"That you back there hammering away at them, Ben?" Pappy asked.

"No, it wasn't," Ben replied.

"It was me," John said. "I climbed in the turret about 15 minutes ago."

"You sure certainly saved our asses," Pappy added.

"You can thank my grandfather for that one. He told me a dead Choctaw is one who fails to sense the presence of his enemy."

John's words struck home with us. For the remainder of the trip, the other gunners made sure their guns were primed just in case some other foe should appear. John's ability to react and sense imminent danger was amazing. He later admitted a feeling came over him before the attack, but he doubted himself, so he remained silent. He promised in the future to alert everyone when he sensed any hidden threat.

Our long flight finally ended, and we approached the Scottish coast. We were all happy to be down and looked forward to getting a good night's sleep. The landing, like most of Pappy's, was flawless and left a sense of confidence in us.

We all felt the deck was stacked in our favor with him at the helm.

An aircraft tug pulled *The Buckeye* into a hangar where mechanics diagnosed the problem, located replacement parts, and started turning wrenches. The next morning, she was sitting back out on the apron ready for the last leg of the journey. We would have departed for England early in the morning, but a heavy fog had settled in over the airfield. Therefore, we were forced to wait a couple of hours until the sun had burnt it off. The weather cleared at 9:30, and with a little bit of coaxing and sweet-talking from Pappy, the engines rumbled to life. Our clearance was to our destination, the airbase at Wendling. In just about an hour, we were circling, and I found myself wondering what the next few months held in store for us. I knew there was a little bit of everything in between us and a return flight home, and I expected most of it would be bad.

Chapter 5

"Do you think that's enough for one night?" Tucker said.

"I suppose so," his mother replied. Their curiosity had driven them as far as they could go in one evening.

"Mom, do you think we could find William or any of the crew?" Tucker said as he inserted a bookmarker and closed the journal.

"I don't know. That was a long time ago, and it's possible they were lost in the war," she said as she stood with her coffee cup and headed to the kitchen. Tucker followed her.

"I doubt that he was killed in the war because we have his journal," Tucker said.

"Perhaps," his mother said.

Tucker set his coffee cup in the sink and then headed to his bedroom. The familiar smell of the room he had known as a child still lingered and was comforting to him. He slipped out of his shirt and blue jeans, set his alarm, and fell asleep. Tossing and turning throughout the night, he couldn't stop dreaming about the journal and its story. It began with him as the pilot with no idea how to fly and ended with him trapped in the ball turret with the aircraft on fire. It was a tumultuous dream that robbed him of a sound night's sleep. He awoke several times and was thankful when the alarm finally sounded off at seven o'clock. His mom was already up and had begun preparing breakfast.

"Sunny side up, like always," she said placing a plate before him that held eggs, toast and strips of crispy bacon. A cup of hot coffee to wash it down made him feel as if he could face whatever the day had in store for him.

"What jobs do you have for me around here?" Tucker asked knowing there must be plenty of neglected work without his father.

"How about taking down a tree?" she said. "You remember that old ash tree that Dad hung that tire swing in for you?" she said.

"Yeah, the big one by the creek" Tucker replied while sopping up the remaining egg yolk with his toast.

"It was struck by lightning last spring, and the bark is peeling off the sides. It needs to come down before it falls on the garden shed," she said.

"I'll grab the saw and see what I can do," Tucker replied moving towards the closet to grab his old blue jean flannel lined work coat. He found his father's chainsaw under the workbench with a sharpened blade and full fuel tank. Always careful with his tools, he taught Tucker the same respect. Twice Tucker had to return to the shed, once to grab some wedges and another time to grab the sledgehammer. His thoughts were about the journal. His dad had introduced him to the woods at a young age and taught him how to identify trees by the bark and leaves. While growing up, Tucker had viewed the woods as his classroom, and he was an excellent student. He sized up the tree from a distance and could see that it was leaning towards the creek. It should fall in that direction, but he would have to thread it between a few trees so that it wouldn't be hung up on the way down. Since the tree was dead, there was also the concern of a widow maker limb breaking loose and crashing down upon him. He decided to cut deep into it with the chainsaw and then switch to the wedges when the tree seemed ready to fall. They were his best bet in placing the fall through a narrow opening that he had chosen. The chips began flying the minute he set into the tree with the saw, and after a few minutes spent cutting the backside, he moved to the other side to make a straight cut that would set the general direction the tree would follow. He shut off the chainsaw and kept an eye on the tree, as it could start over at any time. Picking up the wedges, he drove them deep into the cut with the sledgehammer. He could see the tree slowly start to move in the desired direction. Driving them deeper, he heard the telltale popping and cracking as the tree began its descent. As a safeguard, he backed up from the tree and felt a sense of relief when he heard and felt the familiar thump as the dangerous menace was brought down. He wondered how old the tree was and how big it would have been when William headed off to war. Counting the rings on the stump, he estimated it would have been about twenty years old when the journal was being written. Tucker felt the sweat trickle down his back as he set to the task of trimming off the limbs and then hauling and stacking them into a brush pile.

"How's it going?" his mom asked. She had walked across the yard with a glass of ice tea.

"Fine," Tucker said as he sat down on the stump to catch his breath. "I saw you leave a while ago. Where did you go?"

"I just needed a few odds and ends from the store and stopped by a realtor's office to discuss the idea of putting the house on the market," she said.

"What did they say?" Tucker asked.

"She gave me some information that I want you to look through."

They sat in silence, and soaked up the autumn sunshine they knew they would be deprived of in the coming months.

"Well, I suppose I better get back at it—thanks for the tea," Tucker said as he pulled his leather gloves back on. Picking up the saw, he gave it one strong pull and revved the motor. The chain teeth raced around the bar with such rapidity that it became a blur, each tooth indistinguishable from another. He spent the rest of the day cutting and stacking. Physically, Tucker worked on the tree, but mentally he worked on the journal mystery. The sun finally began relinquishing its throne to the moon and started its retreat into the western sky. Tucker gathered up the tools and returned them to the shed.

"What's for supper, Mom?" he asked entering the kitchen.

"How does biscuits and sausage gravy sound?" she replied.

"Awesome," he said. Tucker took a quick shower and then dressed for supper. Once they finished their meal and cleaned the dishes, they headed to their familiar spots to read more from the journal. Tucker opened it and breathed life into a story that was written many years ago.

Chapter 6

Once Pappy taxied to our designated parking spot and shut down, we unpacked our meager belongings. Most of the bags were tossed out the waist windows while the precious bottled cargo was gently lowered down into a crewmember's arms.

"Be careful. It would be a shame to bust it," Frankie said gently handing their treasure through the waist window.

"Boy, would you look at those bombers. Those aren't the old 'D' model trainers; those are dropping bombs on the enemy type," Lew said with an element of awe. He was referring to the latest model of B-24J's, equipped with all of the war modifications. I wondered about the stories these bombers could tell if they could talk. We were about ready to enter the diamond for the big game, and we knew some of the team wouldn't finish the game. The minimum number required before a crewmember would be rotated home, thirty missions, stood between us and the rest of our lives. This was where history was being written, and we realized that we were about to become a small part of it. The base was hopping with activity. There were sounds and movement everywhere; it reminded me of a bustling city at lunchtime. We waited in the shade along *The Buckeye* until a sergeant and private came roaring up in a pair of jeeps. The sergeant looked the part, with the stub of a cigar hanging from his mouth and hands that were so greasy a month's worth of scrubbing wouldn't clean them. The private had his bill bent up in the fashionable way, if it was called fashion, on a wartime bomber base.

"You guys the Lane crew?" he bellowed to anyone who would answer.

"Yep—you're looking at us," Little Frankie stated.

"Load up. We've been expecting you for the last couple of hours," the sergeant said climbing back in the seat. The airbase was already proving different from the regimented training environment that we were accustomed. All of the more traditional salutes and courtesies we had grown used to in training were gone. We loaded our gear in the jeeps and were taken to check in at headquarters. Once checked in, we were shown our Nissen Huts. The huts were located about a mile from the main runway. I am stationed in an officer's hut, which sleeps four. The enlisted crews have a larger hut that holds two crews or 14 men. The hut design is simple, requiring a minimum amount of material and time to construct. Each hut is built by laying a concrete slab, then taking corrugated metal sheets and anchoring them to one side of the slab, and securing them to a metal frame that arched up and over to the opposite side. Finally, they were again fastened to the slab; they looked like miniature aircraft hangars. Inside there are pipes along the sides for hanging clothes and footlockers. The open walls provide space for the men to personalize their small corner of the war. Usually, they were filled with pictures from home or pin ups of beautiful women. In the center of the hut is a small barrel stove that is used for heating purposes. It was a curiosity that our hut has two chimney pipes sticking out of the top. It appears that the hole was originally cut in the wrong location. Our cots are located along the walls one per corner. We weren't the first crew to be stationed in the bunk. I wondered what happened to the last crew and realized there were only three options. They either had been rotated home, were prisoners of war, or were dead. The smell inside the hut is a blend of sweaty socks and stale cigarette smoke. We spent the rest of the day exploring the base. In many ways it is like a small city with a theater, various repair shops, sewage treatment center, recreation center, and a hospital. Most of the buildings, uniforms, vehicles, and scenery are earthy shades of green, brown and tan for the express purpose of blending into the surroundings. The dull colors left a bleak feeling within me. Inside and outside the building everything with form had been designed to follow function with no concern given to the aesthetics. A good example would be the urinals in the latrines. Instead of separate urinals, there is an old rain gutter set about three feet off the ground that slopes to a drain. We stand shoulder to shoulder to relieve ourselves. It has a slow stream of water running from one end to the other, constantly carrying the urine to the drain.

Around four o'clock, all of the base personnel started to migrate to the grass that was in front of the air traffic control tower to watch the return of the bombers. Everyone stopped what they were working on and flowed in that direction. Our crew was carried along in the stream of men, and we found a spot and sat in the grass with the rest of the men. The ground personnel were anxiously awaiting the return of their crews as the firefighters in their trucks sat with the big V8 engines purring ready to race to any accident scene. Some of the rescue personnel were in fireproof suits that gave them the appearance of alien invaders. It wasn't long before the drone of far off engines could be heard. Like an approaching storm, the distant faint sound grew from a tremor to an ominous, thundering roar. I heard some of the ground crews say that the mission was a long one to Hamm, Germany. Several airplanes landed before one arrived that was damaged. When they drew near, they shot off red flares signaling that there were wounded aboard. The emergency personal in their ambulances were alert and ready. On final approach, some of the damage was apparent with part of the horizontal stabilizer shot away and a piece of metal flapping loose along the side of the fuselage. Most troubling was when I saw that the left main gear had not extended and locked into place. We all attentively watched as the pilot landed on the right main gear and then held the left wing up as long as possible. As the airspeed bled off, there was not enough lift to keep it from sinking to the runway. Gradually the left wing settled to the runway with a shower of sparks and a loud grating noise. The bomber swung into a tight turn and departed the runway throwing up dirt and a huge cloud of dust. The fire trucks zoomed toward it. When they were about half way to the aircraft, I noticed smoke and then a small flame growing on one of the engines. Some of the crew jumped out and started running from the bomber. Eventually a man dropped out of the bomber with his heavy flight jacket and pants on fire. He was dragging one leg struggling to move away from the bomber. He tripped and fell.

Our group completely silent watched. I was startled when someone close hollered, "Come on man, run!" willing the unfortunate crewmember to safety with his words. I could sense the group collectively holding their breath for the fury they knew was about to be unleashed. Then came the roar and blast as the fuel tanks exploded. The explosive power of the blast hit the man and literally tore him apart sending body parts flying in all different directions. A few seconds after the blast, I felt the heat from the enormous fireball. A man beside me spoke pure frustration, "Damn this war." Others looked away or stared at the ground knowing that many of the men had been trapped inside the aircraft.

I knew that the tough, battle-hardened men around me were holding back tears. Sickened, I stood staring unable to fully process the gruesome scene that I had just witnessed. It brought about a deep sorrow and loss within me even though I didn't know them. The fire trucks were calming the fire as the stream of bombers methodically landed. The destruction was a visible reminder of what they all feared. I thought of the letters that would be written to the families and the grief that would be felt upon hearing that a son, husband, or brother was gone. I wondered again how my family would take such news. We had effectively been introduced to the war.

During the coming week, our crew scrounged enough money together and threw in some of the booze to get a sergeant, who served as a head cook, to paint the nose art on

The Buckeye. I had heard that he was a skilled artist and had seen some of his work on other bombers. Once he understood what we wanted, he made a sketch on a piece of paper. The crew suggested a few modifications, and then we all agreed on it. First, the Sergeant penciled in the buckeye tree. He then moved to the base of the tree and drew a cartoon character hillbilly with bare feet and holes worn in his bib overalls. The cartoon character wore a tattered felt hat that provided shade for his eyes as he napped against the tree. As if it was not already apparent, he imparted more leisure by drawing a piece of wheat hanging out of the hillbilly's mouth, and a moonshine jug sitting at his side with 'XXX' on it. Falling from the tree was a buckeye that was clearly going to strike the sleeping hillbilly on the head. Above the scene, and following the arch of the tree, he penciled out in large italicized letters *The Buckeye*. Once he finished the penciled outline, he began filling it in with paint. The entire crew was impressed and agreed our money and the booze was well spent. I have spoken to Sarge on a few other occasions and hope to make a friend of him.

After many hours of additional training missions at the base, the time had come to see if the taxpayers' investment in us was money well spent. Pappy brought the news to us one evening. We were all in the mess hall when he strolled in. "We are on the roster for tomorrow," he said. No more discussion about what it would be like to be in battle; here shortly we would all speak from experience.

"Get some sleep because we will roll out for briefing and breakfast at 3:00 a.m."

The early rise wasn't news for us as we had intermingled with so many other crews we knew what to expect, or at least, we thought we knew. I was surprised at how well I slept the night before the mission. With it still well before sunrise, a soldier came to tell us to rise and shine while he shined a flashlight in the face of anyone who was reluctant to get up. I rolled out of bed and dressed. To our crew, it was a monumental day, but it came with no fanfare, no band, and no big hoopla. The whole event was not as spectacular or dramatic as I had envisioned it would be. I had thought about it often for the last year as we had trained continually for this day. For such a big event, with life and death hanging in the balance, it all came rather quietly and was handled and processed in a methodical matter-of-fact-way. We were about to fly into the mouth of the German war machine and see if we could avoid being chewed up, but the magnitude of the event seemed unnoticed but by us. Once dressed, I became part of a long stream of men moving in the darkness toward the shower house to methodically prepare for battle. Since there was no logical way to predict who would perish and who would be spared, some crews clung to silly superstitious rituals as if some random chain of events or event held the keys to such great mysteries. They would attach success to any number of things, from the way in which they performed a simple task before the mission to who entered the airplane first and who boarded last. At the mess hall, I met up with the rest of my crew. We were served real eggs as a treat instead of the typical dried ones. Our nervousness was masked behind much teasing of one another. John was the only one who seemed different. He didn't show the animation or the excitability like the others and had a quiet seriousness about him.

After breakfast, the rest of the officers and I walked over to the mission briefing room. It was a large room with exposed rafters, bench seating, and a raised platform in the front. After we were seated, the room was called to attention, with the commanding officer, the intelligence officer, the meteorologist, and the chaplain walking resolutely down the center aisle and up onto the stage. The chaplain walked to the wooden podium.

"Please bow for prayer." We all removed our caps and bowed. "Our Father in Heaven, watch over all of these brave men who are going into harm's way to protect the freedoms that we hold dear. Give us strength each day to complete our mission and hasten the day that peace is restored on this earth, so that we may return to our friends and families at home. In Jesus' name, Amen."

Even the non-believers lowered their heads. Perhaps they knew that they could be wrong and, thus, were comforted with the thought of protection from a higher power. The chaplain moved to the side of the platform. As he had many times before, the commanding officer moved to center stage. "Men today's mission is to..." we intently watched as the intelligence officer pulled on a cord that slowly moved the curtain back exposing a long red string that stretched from our base to the target. The commanding officer continued with "Gütersloh." A foreign city that, before this day, was meaningless to us but now would never be forgotten by those of us who survived. After we were briefed on the overall mission, we broke up into specialty briefings. Eventually, we all reconvened in the crew room, where we layered on clothing to protect us from the negative forty-degree temperature that we would be subjected too. Each of us donned different attire based on our battle station in the bomber since some of us were more exposed to the elements. The harshest position is at the open waist windows with the extreme temperature coupled with the wind blasting them. The first layer was the standard wool long underwear and then an electrically heated suit. Other layers were added until we finally pulled on wool-lined heavy leather pants, boots, and jackets. Once dressed, we picked up our escape kits and, for the religious, there was mass with the priest or prayers with the pastor. Our crew eventually completed the mission processing and boarded a transport truck known as a "deuce-and-a-half" and made the trip out to *The Buckeye*. Lew inspected the exterior of *The Buckeye* with checklist in hand as Jack and Albert placed their waist guns on their mounts. The rest of the crew loaded gear and double-checked all of their equipment; nothing was left to chance. Eventually, we boarded for additional checks and rechecks. I climbed into the bomber and moved to the nose section to lay out my navigational instruments and mission charts. We waited until the control tower launched a green flare, which was the signal to start engines. After going through a lengthy checklist, Pappy and Lew primed the number three engine, pushed the mixture control to rich, and hit the starter. The same sequence was followed until the other three 1,200 horsepower Pratt and Whitney Twin Wasps were spinning their huge three bladed propellers. *The Buckeye* was now one of many Liberators about to show her nasty side to the enemy. She meant more to me this morning than she ever had before. All of our hopes and dreams of living life past this war were riding on her ability to do her part and safely transport us to and from the target. Pappy carefully maneuvered her out on to the taxiway behind a line of other bombers that were making their way to the runway.

"Where we going Pappy," came a voice across the intercom.

"Gütersloh," he said, and paused for a moment before he continued. "Looks like you guys have been living right, cause according to the senior crews, this is an easy one. What they call a 'milk run.'"

A milk run… I wondered who had come up with the phrase and how any bombing mission could be considered easy. Even if the enemy didn't kill us, there were plenty of other threats that could. *The Buckeye* was finally cleared for takeoff. Pappy smoothly added power to the engines and took us onto the runway. He held *The Buckeye* in place with the brakes and then added full power. The straining engines were causing every loose item on board to shake, which added more noise to the experience. When he released the brakes, *The Buckeye* lurched forward and began its long roll down the runway in search of rotation speed. Once we were airborne, Lew reminded us to be looking for the colorfully striped formation plane. After several minutes, Frankie spotted it. "That thing looks like somebody puked after eating too much circus candy," he said. A few laughs trickled in across the intercom. The formation B-24D airplane was war weary. It had seen many missions and bore the battle scars as a testament to its service. All armament had been stripped as it wasn't needed in its final useful role before the scrap yard. Its sole purpose was to organize the formation. Like an old racehorse, it had been turned out to pasture. Looking around, I watched as first one, and then another B-24 popped up through the cloud layer. After a half hour, our squadron had formed. We then merged into a larger fighting unit and finally into a bigger formation called a "group." The bombers were staggered in a manner to maximize the amount of guns that could be brought to bear on any aircraft that made an assault.

Out over the English Channel, Pappy spoke, "Go ahead and rip off some rounds."

The guns' firing startled me as I was concentrating on calculations at my navigator's desk. We flew with no one speaking for some time. Each man was left alone with his thoughts. Pappy finally broke in, "We are close to crossing from France into Germany, men—look alive. We are unwelcome visitors." Looking out my window, I could see friendly fighters flying high and wide of us escorting us to the target. They looked to be long range P-51 Mustangs.

Never in my wildest dreams would I have guessed that the first time I would see Germany would be flying into battle at 22,000 feet. In fact, I hadn't thought much of traveling outside of the United States. I looked down and imagined the hatred that would be dealt out to me if I ever found myself on the ground in enemy territory. I whispered a quick prayer of protection. Shaking off the thought, I continued with my task and started identifying landmarks. In all actuality, my calculations were unneeded and redundant as we were in formation and following the lead navigator. However, regulations required it, and I enjoyed the distraction.

"Pull'em up tight boys. The closer we are, the more deadly our bombing will be and the more protection we will receive from our defensive firepower," the squadron commander said on frequency. It felt good to know a seasoned veteran was leading us. *The Buckeye* was in the lower box at the rear of the formation, a position known as "tail-end Charlie" or "Purple Heart corner." It was not an enviable position, as everyone knew that it is one of the most dangerous locations in the formation. The other bombers were so close that I could look out the side window and see the waist gunners in them. They were at their post and ready to thwart any enemy attack. I was comforted knowing that I was not alone, but part of a well-trained fighting force made up of other men who were struggling with me to get through this madness and return home.

"Fighters at five o'clock high," came Ben's voice over the intercom.

"Yeah, I see them. They're still well outside of gun range," Albert added.

I knew from my station in the front of the bomber I would not be able to see them.

"What are they doing?" came back Pappy's voice from the cockpit.

"Just back there taking a good look," Ben stated.

"Probably calling all their buddies up for the party," Little Frankie added hanging from the ball turret.

"Keep your eye on them and let us know if they start a run at us, Ben," Pappy said

"Roger that," he replied.

Our formation droned on until we reached the initial point of the bombing run. For the Norden bombsight to be accurate, the bombers have to maintain their altitude and airspeed throughout the bombing run. We feel like sitting ducks as we have no options to evade or escape the German anti-aircraft guns.

"Wow! Look at that flak," John nudged me as he pointed to the anti-aircraft shells bursting up ahead.

The shells were sending out thousands of pieces of metal shrapnel, much like the burst of a hand grenade, only with much greater force and killing radius. I turned to see the black sooty death bursting below the bombers that were ahead of us.

"Looks like they're a little low," Lew said.

"Hope we are out of here before they dial in the right altitude," Pappy replied.

I watched them explode below us and could see a small fireball in the center of the blackness. On we flew until we arrived at the initial point of the bombing run. Pappy flipped some switches that effectively slaved the autopilot to the Norden bombsight controls. In effect, through the bombsight controls, John maneuvered *The Buckeye* to a position that would put the bombs on the target. The bombsight worked out complicated equations that took into account the bomber's forward movement and the wind, which would influence the bombs trajectory, as well as the wind resistance against the bombs as they fell toward the target. I watched him work the adjustments on the bombsight and felt the ship start to momentarily climb when the bombs were released. We flew beyond the black carpet of flak, and a portion of my anxiety subsided. With the reduction in load, our airspeed would be faster, which would mean a quicker trip home. Once we had cleared German airspace, British Spitfire fighters came alongside to shepherd us to our base. Archie wrote on a scratch sheet of paper, "One down and twenty nine more to go." I gave him a thumb up. When we were below 10,000 feet, we were cleared to remove our oxygen mask. I realized this war is going to take everything I have to get through it, and I am not sure that will be enough. We sat in silence and watched the passing landscape as *The Buckeye* carried us over the English countryside. Pappy greased the landing, and our first mission was officially recorded. With a relatively uneventful raid, it was a quick debriefing, and then we received our customary shot of whisky. I passed on the offer and left to check in my gear.

The next morning, I woke to the first frost of the year. I knew it wouldn't be much longer before we were using the pot-bellied stove that sat in the center of the Nissen hut, that is, if we can find coal or anything else to burn in it. Everything is in very short supply. Hoping that the hot water hadn't run out, I headed to the shower. Once I had showered and shaved, I returned to our hut to see if John was interested in getting some breakfast. When I entered, he spotted me in a mirror he was using to comb his hair.

"What's on the agenda today?" John said

"First thing is breakfast."

John finished and grabbed his smokes, and we made our way to the mess hall. Grabbing a couple of trays, we proceeded through the line and found a table. We watched other crewmembers as they passed by our table, sat silently, and ate our breakfast. When finished, I fished out my cigarettes and offered one to John. A mess hall cook walked past and filled our coffee mugs. Our conversation wound around to base life and some of the bands that might visit. The dances would provide a good distraction, and we both were excited about the chance to meet some of the English girls. Rumors were always floating about as to what band would be visiting, and most fellas were hoping it would be the Glen Miller Band. Our conversation slowly trickled to a stop, and for a while, we sat and sipped our coffee and enjoyed the peace.

John finally broke the silence. "I need to get some laundry done and heard there is a widow lady that lives down the road a bit who will do them. You have any dirty laundry?"

"Sure, I have some stuff," I said in reply.

"Let me get some directions, and we will set out. Meet me in front of the chapel in ten minutes," John said as he stood. I finished my coffee and picked up our trays and walked them to the sinks. Arriving at my hut, I grabbed my laundry, stuffed it in my duffel bag, and headed to the chapel.

While I was waiting for John, a chaplain exited the base hospital and briskly walked over to me. Is there something I can help you with son?" he asked. He was overweight and had a kind face and wore his hair in a comb over.

"No, I am just waiting on a friend. My name is William Pritchit," I said, holding out my hand.

"Welcome to the base. My name is Kent Wimbley. I am one of the chaplains here on base."

"Yes, you prayed before our mission yesterday."

"I am happy to see, in your case, my prayer was answered," he said looking directly at me. "The honor of praying for all of you is given to Father McDooley and me. Where are you from, William?"

"Indiana."

"Oh, a Hoosier. That is a beautiful part of the country and wonderful people."

"So you have been there?" I asked.

"Several times. Prior to the war, I preached at a yearly revival at a small country church. I need to ask you a question, William. What are your beliefs?" he said with genuine concern in his voice. "I don't mean to be pressing, but you are in an extremely dangerous business."

"It's okay. I am a Christian."

Chaplain Wimbley smiled, "How wonderful. I am so pleased to hear that."

"I grew up in a Christian home, but I have friends who say they have no beliefs," I said.

"Interesting, well if you think about it 'no belief' is actually a belief with values and actions attached to it. The good Lord did not allow for the option of 'no belief,'" he said pausing to let his words sink in. "Everyone has the right to choose, but all must choose."

"I guess you're right." I instantly felt at ease and was drawn to the grandfather-like warmth of Chaplain Wimbley. I am certain he serves as a calm port during the storm that rages in the lives of the men. He has a tough assignment ministering to men who are facing life and death issues that have come far too early in life. While we spoke, John arrived. I introduced them, and then we started toward the main gate. After walking about a hundred yards, we heard Chaplain Wimbley holler. We turned to see him walking quickly towards us.

"William, how about we grab a cup of coffee sometime? You're invited too, John."

"I would like that," I said.

"Very good, very good. Well I will let you boys be on your way. God bless."

John and I set off again for the nearby village of Beeston. "How far is it?" I asked.

"Oh, about quarter a mile," John said.

We walked along enjoying the English countryside until we arrived at an old farmhouse reminiscent of many back home. The familiarity was comforting. I never knew cow manure could smell good, but it triggered such fond memories of home that I found myself smiling. John stepped up on the front porch and knocked on the door. To my surprise, a young woman answered. She wore a light blue summer dress made of cotton that had a small delicate flower print. Over the dress was a simple white apron. Her dark brown hair was pulled up in a ponytail, but some had worked loose and fell loosely around her face.

After a slight hesitation John spoke, "We must have the wrong house. We were looking for a Mrs. Ward who does laundry."

"You're at the right house. She is my Mum and is out back taking clothes off the line."

"Super, my name is John Thompson."

"I am William Pritchet," I said unable to look away from her.

"My name is Elizabeth Ward. Shall we check in your laundry?" she asked politely.

"Most of the crews use my younger brother for pick up and drop off," she stated while stepping out the front door. "In fact, that is generally preferred by all parties as it gives him something to do, and the men like the convenience."

That explained why there wasn't a line at the house waiting to ask her out. The men at the base were unaware of her.

"I'm sure he would do the same for you if you like," Elizabeth said while smiling at us.

"That would be swell if it's not too much trouble," John replied.

"Thanks for the offer, but I enjoyed the walk," I said setting myself up for future visits.

"You can bring your clothes around back to the laundry room," she said leading the way.

While she was distracted checking in the clothes, I studied her face. Her delicate features imparted a refined eloquence. She contained the very essence of beauty that all men have loved in women from the very beginning. I have seen attractive women before, but never have any of them stirred my heart like her. It is more than just physical beauty; there is something else that I am drawn too. I realized the risks and dangers imbedded in the feelings that swept over me, but I was unable to control them. There is a real possibility I am setting myself up for disappointment, as she could have a boyfriend or be married, for all I know. I looked for a ring and was relieved when I didn't see one.

"Are all of your clothes marked with your names in the seams?" Elizabeth asked.

"Mine are," John replied.

"Mine too," I added.

"Okay, I need you to write down your name and where you wish them to be delivered. Timmy, my brother, will deliver your clothes two days from now. William, if you want to take another walk, yours will also be ready for pickup on the same day."

It was evident from her manners that she wasn't the type of woman that the crews depicted on the nose art of their bombers. I know the war is my primary focus and such a distraction could be my undoing. There are many logical reasons why I shouldn't allow myself to dream, but this is not a matter of the mind; it is a matter of the heart, which is infinitely more difficult to control. It was in those first moments that my heart won out over my mind and I determined, regardless of the risk, I would sacrifice whatever would be required to pursue her.

Chapter 7

Mom yawned. "Do you think that's enough for tonight?" she asked interrupting Tucker mid-sentence. He was so intent on the story that was unfolding that he had lost track of time.

"I suppose so. It is getting late," Tucker said closing the journal and laying it on the coffee table.

"He certainly is a good writer and has my curiosity piqued on how this is all going to unfold," Tucker said as he stretched.

"I hesitate in even guessing as to how this will end," his mom added. "We should try not to get too attached. It's possible that he didn't make it back home."

"I suppose you're right, but it's hard not to feel for what they were going through," Tucker replied. In reflection, he realized he was becoming fond of William and the crew. "Well, we can put a face to a name now. That girl in the picture is certainly Elizabeth," he said. Tucker took the picture from the journal and looked at it.

"So young, alive, and full of hope," he said handing the picture to his mother to examine.

On Sunday morning Tucker awoke to wind and rain. He could hear the large sycamore leaves rustling and the wind whistling and moaning against the window beside his bed. The temperature had dropped sharply overnight. He pulled the heavy blanket up. Knowing that there was miserable weather occurring outside made him feel that much more reluctant to get out of the warm bed. He lay there for a moment until his alarm performed its duty and sounded off. Tucker silenced it and then sat up and on the edge of his bed. When he entered the kitchen, his mother was sitting at the table with a cup of coffee reading the morning paper. She knew it took him a while to warm up to conversation in the morning, so she kept to herself until he spoke to her.

"What are your plans for today?" Tucker asked.

"There are some things I could do, but none of them are urgent. How about you?" she asked.

"I was going to clean the gutters out, but this rain has canceled those plans," Tucker replied.

"I thought it might be a good day to stay inside and read some more from the journal," she said.

He smiled. "I was hoping you would say that."

Tucker started to make French toast for breakfast as he knew it was one of his mother's favorites. He walked to the pantry and selected a large cast iron skillet that was one of many hanging on the wall. Setting it on the stove, he poured some oil in it and turned on the stove to warm. He then broke three eggs, added a small amount of milk, and whisked the ingredients. Once the skillet was warm, he started the sequence of dipping pieces of bread into the egg mixture, placing them in the skillet, and adding a dash of cinnamon on top. When both sides where browned, he placed them on plates and set them on the table.

"So about selling the house, Mom," Tucker paused momentarily, knowing he was venturing into an emotional topic. "When were you going to put it on the market?" She set her coffee down that she had been sipping and looked out the big picture window that they had sat next too.

"Oh, perhaps next spring," she said. "Do you think we could have it ready by then?"

"I think so," he said. They discussed the home sale as they ate. After finishing breakfast, they cleaned up the kitchen and headed to the living room. Tucker picked up the journal, turned to his bookmark, and started to read.

Chapter 8

I awoke this morning to find that we were off for the day as low clouds were covering any potential targets. It was a bit of good fortune. As promised, Elizabeth's younger brother, Timmy, brought John's clothes to the base. He rode his bicycle and pulled a wagon lashed to it. I met him when he dropped off John's clothes at the hut. He is close to the age of my younger brother Charlie, a quirky little fellow who always carries a smile with him. We loaded him up with candy, or sweets, as the British refer to them. His arrival told me my clothes were ready for pick up. Timmy asked us if we wanted him to take our dirty laundry back, and John took him up on the offer. It took considerable patience, but since it was close to lunchtime, I decided that it would be best to eat before I walked to her house for my laundry.

Luckily, John hadn't said anything about Elizabeth to anyone, and I intentionally kept quiet as I didn't want any competition. If word got around the base, who knows how many fellas would be hand delivering their laundry. In the early afternoon, I started down the road to her house. An anxious feeling with accompanying knots in my stomach washed over me about half way there. Above all, I feared this would be our final encounter, or I would learn another man was courting her. My feelings were similar to the ones I felt before a mission: a mixture of anxiety and excitement. It occurred to me how silly this all was in that the missions required I risk my life while the most that could happen with her was rejection. It didn't help. About fifteen minutes later, I arrived at the farm. Pushing open the gate on the picket fence that bordered the house, I started down the sidewalk. At the front door, I removed my cap and tucked it under my arm. I gently knocked on the door and within a few seconds heard soft footsteps approaching. Elizabeth opened the door. Her expressive brown eyes flashed at me, and I wasn't sure I could respond. She was more beautiful than I had remembered.

"Oh hello, Yank," she said smiling at me. I hoped such a smile wasn't handed out to every visitor.

"Hello, Elizabeth. I am here to pick up my laundry like I promised."

"I think Mum has them around back. Follow me," she said, circling around the front of the house to follow the familiar route. Her mother was working hard at the task of ironing.

"Mum, this is William Pritchet. He is here for his laundry. William, this is my mother Claire."

"Pleased to meet you, Mr. Pritchet," she said momentarily looking up from her work.

"Pleasure to meet you too." I momentarily froze and couldn't think of something else to say. I was happy when Elizabeth picked up the conversation.

"William, where are you from?" she asked continuing with her work.

"From the state of Indiana. I live on our family farm. I drove to Indianapolis and signed up for service in the Army Air Force after I completed high school. Until the war, I hadn't traveled outside of the state except on a couple of occasions."

"You will have to excuse us, Mr. Pritchet, but we have a long list of chores. Elizabeth have you been able to tend to the barn?"

"No, I have been mending the fence where the cow busted out last week, so I haven't been able to start on it yet. Once I have finished with the fence, I will see to it."

I could hear the weight of the responsibilities in Elizabeth's voice, and seeing an opportunity, I jumped in. "I have a lot of experience with livestock and would be happy to help you."

"That's very kind of you William, but I am sure there must be many other things that you would rather do than spend time here working, especially in the smelly barn," Elizabeth said.

She couldn't have known how far she was from the truth. I would have flown an extra thirty missions just to spend time with her.

"Actually, I feel more at peace working in the barn than practically anyplace else on earth." Elizabeth looked at me as I spoke. I think she was trying to determine if I was being honest.

She must have believed me or felt overwhelmed by all of the physical labor needs of the farm. "Okay then, let's get started," she said.

We crossed the barn lot and hitched the team of horses to the wagon. Climbing onto it, I took the reins and guided the horses to a point that positioned the wagon in front of the door that led into the animal stalls. Setting the brake, I entered the barn, and the familiar smell of straw, old lumber, and animal manure met me. I closed my eyes and breathed in; memories of home flooded my mind. I was reacquainted with a peace that I hadn't known since I had left. The barn was smaller than my father's but was of the same layout. The center section ground level had a granary while the outer areas were animal stalls. The grain room had additional supplies that hung from the walls or leaned against them. I found a pitchfork in the granary, and opening a small wooden gate, I entered the animal holding areas. It was apparent that it had been a while since it had last been cleaned. The manure and the straw bedding had been mixed and packed from the animals' walking on it creating a woven mess that would take some muscle to pry loose. Wanting to impress Elizabeth and relieve her of the burden of this demanding task, I set into the work. After over an hour of work, the wagon was full. Looking around, I noted that I was about one quarter of the way through the job. Climbing onto the wagon, I took it to a field behind the barn to unload. Cow manure is an excellent fertilizer, and back home we always spread it on the garden. The vegetables thrived and rewarded us with a bountiful harvest. Arriving back at the barn, I again set myself against the work. With my back to the door, I failed to see Elizabeth watching me as I pried and strained against the thatched mess until a part of it would break free.

"You've been working hard, William. How about a drink?" she said handing me a tin cup filled with well water.

"Thank you."

I wiped the sweat from my forehead with my handkerchief and leaned on the long handled pitchfork.

"I am getting there," I said looking around at what was left. I noticed that she had changed into a pair of work pants and boots and had pulled her hair up with a handkerchief.

"I don't know how I can repay you," she said.

Seeing my opportunity, I spoke, "If we get done early, do you suppose we could take a walk?"

"I suppose Mum wouldn't care too much if I took a break when she learns the barn is clean," Elizabeth said.

Walking into the granary, she returned with a pitchfork, pulled on her work gloves, and started in by my side. She didn't have the physical strength for such manual labor, but nevertheless, she struggled against the work with determination. My heart raced being so close to her. The day was playing out better than I could have ever expected. I never would have thought one of the best days of my life would be shoveling manure. We spoke of everything except the topic we were tired of, the war. My initial anxiety about Elizabeth was a distant memory as I found conversation with her to flow effortlessly.

Her English accent and soft nature set me at ease, and I felt defenseless to her feminine charm. We shared much of the same life philosophies with family being important to us. She was curious to hear about my life at home, and I asked her to explain British customs and currency. Several times we laughed as we shared stories and let the ugly reality waiting beyond the barn door retreat to a faraway place in our minds.

A few hours later, we had finished the task, and before I took the final load to the garden, we started filling the hay bins. When I bent over to pick up more hay, the cross necklace Julia had given me fell out from behind my shirt and dangled from my neck. It caught Elizabeth's attention.

"That is a beautiful necklace. Is it from your steady?" she asked.

I felt she was wondering as much about my status as I was hers. "Oh no, I don't have a steady. It was a gift from my kid sister, a present when I left home." I leaned back against one of the bins and told her the story of my last morning at home.

"How about that walk you promised me?" I said. She smiled at me.

"I know a pleasant place. I will change and tell Mum we are leaving. If you want another drink, the well is just outside the barn lot."

"Okay, thanks."

As Elizabeth walked to the house, I unloaded the manure and stabled the horses. Outside the barn lot, I found a small tin cup hanging on the side of an old rusty cast iron pump. After priming the well, water came gushing out. A couple more pumps to make sure it was clean and then I filled the cup. The water was cool and refreshing. Washing out my handkerchief, I then took the cool cloth and cleaned my face and neck. As I stood and surveyed the farm, it occurred to me that for a short while I had completely forgotten about the war. I felt recharged. "What a blessing," I said to myself. It was the first time that I would have chosen to be in England instead of at home. After a few minutes, Elizabeth reappeared, and I started towards the house to meet her.

"Everything set to go?" I asked.

"All ready. Mum said to tell you thanks for the help. Let's head down the road and cut off at the creek," she said. "It winds through some shady areas and makes for a relaxing walk."

"Sounds pleasant," I said as we started down the road.

"You know, I wouldn't want you to think my Mum…It's just been such a heavy load with Dad gone. She is doing her best, but even when both of them were here to work on the farm they barely kept up. Now the burden overwhelms us at times," she said.

"It must be terribly difficult for you both." Stopping in the road, I turned towards her. "I enjoyed working with you today. It brought back memories of home. I hope there will be other times that I can help out again around the farm." After I spoke, I feared that I might have come on too strong.

We walked until we arrived at an arched cobblestone bridge. Leaning against it, she removed her shoes and socks.

She tied the laces together, pushed her socks in them, and set them against the edges of the bridge. I did the same and then followed her down a worn path that dropped off in the creek. Wading up it, we took in the serenity of the scene. The limbs of the mature trees were swaying from a gentle breeze, and the creek held all types of secrets that we discovered as we explored. Arriving at a sand bar, we sat and talked until the sun started to approach the horizon.

"I better get you back," I said.

"I suppose so," she said.

Arriving at the bridge, we climbed the path and put our shoes on. Elizabeth sat on the bridge and slowly turned towards the creek. We sat side-by-side, talking and staring down at a large pool of water.

"It was so kind of you to help, and I enjoyed hearing the stories of your family," Elizabeth said. Periodically, a bug fell from the trees onto the water. Seconds later, trout emerged from the dark deep pool to lightly break the surface and snatch the dainty morsel. We sat silently watching. The afternoon sun was fading fast as we started back to her house, and the dread of the next mission started to cast its shadow in my mind.

When we arrived at her house, she turned towards me. "I would be happy to hold you to your promise to help out around here," she said.

"I would be happy if you did." I tried to imprint the image of her standing there in my mind as I knew I was about to descend into hell again.

"I'll come back for my laundry when I am free."

"I will make a list," she replied. She started to walk into the house and then turned back.

"You will be careful?" she said.

"I always am." I started missing her the moment I took my first step back toward the base. When I arrived at the base, Albert came by and said we were on the mission schedule for the next day. I headed to the chow hall and caught up with John. He shared how he had spent half his day at the pub, and I told him about my day with Elizabeth.

Our fifth mission was a deep one to Brunswick, Germany. We had a full bomb load and had been told that we would get our fuel tanks topped off after we taxied from the hard stand to the runway. This meant we would be in the war zone more than enough time for the Germans to work us over with flak and fighters. *The Buckeye* had never gone on a mission so deep into enemy territory, and the anxiety was evident in the crew, who after completing four missions, had a better idea as to what horrors awaited us. I sat at my table going through my before-flight checklist. I could see Pappy and Lew methodically going through the engine startup procedures. Clearly, Pappy had it memorized, but as expected, Lew had his checklist and was assuring nothing was missed.

Finally, Pappy's voice came through the headset, "Alright, men, this is a long one. We have trained hard. Let's show'em what we're made of."

Pappy always gave pep talks before our missions. It helped, and the superstitious crewmembers expected him to continue the ritual. "We will come out fine. Besides men, we have *The Buckeye*. The best bomber in the 8th Air Force," he said. The talk eased our nerves and reminded us that we were not going into this alone.

"Hold on fellas, here we go," with that Pappy added power to the four powerful engines, and we started down the runway.

I reached down in my pocket and felt the buckeye that Charlie had given me. I had kept my promise and took it on every mission. Once we had climbed to altitude, and Pappy had maneuvered *The Buckeye* into its assigned position in the formation, I started to track our course.

"Looks cold down there," Ben said looking down through his bombsight as we crossed the English Channel.

"I don't care to find out," Jim said from the top turret.

Those who had duties tended to them while the others waited their inevitable turns to contribute in their unique ways.

"I see one falling out of formation and turning back," Jack said.

"Anybody see who it is?" Pappy asked.

Albert answered from his position in the left waist window, "Looks like *Old Glory*."

"Hate to lose them from the formation," Little Frankie said. "They have some experienced gunners on board."

"Yeah, especially that tail gunner. I heard he was a marksman back home, even won some competitions," Archie said.

"I heard he rabbit hunts with a 22 caliber rifle and can hit one on a dead run with beagles in hot pursuit," Frankie said as he climbed into the ball turret.

"Hell, I heard he could shoot the eye out of a starling in a gale force wind," Jack added.

"Don't forget he had his eyes closed, and it was at night," Albert said.

The story continued to grow more and more ridiculous until most of the crew was laughing.

"All right knock it off you wise guys and get back to work," Lew said.

The huge formation of bombers droned on minus the six thousand pound bomb load that *Old Glory* would have delivered.

"Friendlies at two o'clock high," Archie said.

"We have more back at seven o'clock high," said Ben from the tail turret.

We were happy to see our little friends join us. I continued to plot our course on my sectional chart until I heard, "Enemy fighters at three o'clock high." Peering out one of the small side windows in the nose off the bomber, I could see a group of about twelve fighters that were circling around to the rear of the formation. They continued to track us like hawks above, waiting for the correct time and position to make their deadly dive on the slower formation of bombers.

"More enemy fighters at two o'clock swinging to the rear," Lew said.

"Watch'em boys and don't shout into the intercom," Pappy instructed.

"Here they come," Ben warned from the rear of the plane.

The fighters came in hard and fast presenting multiple targets for the gunners. When they drew close enough, I could see the flashes along the wings from their guns and feel the vibration of our guns answering. "*Double Trouble* has the number two engine smoking, and it looks like they're falling out of formation," Albert said watching them from the waist window. We knew what that meant. Once the bomber fell back from the defensive firepower of the formation, it would be swarmed. The fighters would prey upon it like a wolf pack on a wounded caribou and eventually take down their prey. We had strict orders about falling out of formation to help a straggler. "No reason to sacrifice the lives of another crew on a doomed bomber," was the theory from the top brass. They may have been right in theory, but it was a cold response to a personal matter. Doing nothing while another bomber fell behind the formation was sure to leave them to a slow bloody death. It was troubling to think about and much more difficult to watch. I noted the time and location in my navigator so that I could provide it at our debriefing. The deeper we penetrated Germany, the stiffer the resistance became. Eventually there were multiple formations of fighters mounting attacks from many different directions. While writing down details of the mission, my sectional chart jumped off the table. Picking it up, I found a bullet had pierced it. I traced the hole through the table and saw where it had entered the bomber. An enemy had either slipped past the gunners watchful eyes or courageously pressed his attack to the point of scoring some hits on *The Buckeye*. I looked around and couldn't see any further damage. It was fortunate that I hadn't been leaning over plotting our course when that bullet passed through.

"Any damage from that attack?" Pappy asked.

"A few holes down here, but no significant damage," I radioed back. No one else reported hits. The formation droned on toward the target. A few minutes later, the next warning was heard.

"They're forming up out front again for an attack," Lew said.

"I see them at about one o'clock high," Archie said, determined not to give them another shot at us without a vicious reply from his guns. I could hear the electric nose turret whir as Archie tracked the target. He stayed on them as they began their dive at the formation. Once they were within range, he cut loose with his twin browning 50 caliber machine guns. The tracers arched out towards the incoming fighter. Flashes could be seen on the enemy aircraft, and then it started shedding small pieces. A wing separated, and the once lethal enemy was reduced to man and metal falling to the earth. When we were within ten miles of the target, all of the enemy fighters disappeared. The next hell we knew as flak was about to be unleashed upon us and it was even more feared as no skill in the world could combat it. Hundreds of deadly 88mm gun began firing up at us. Their shells exploded and sent hot metal shrapnel in all directions. One close hit could kill a crewmember or bring a bomber down. I could see aircraft in front of us entering the dark cloud of destruction. When we entered the flak, it subdued the sunlight. The acrid smell of the explosives' charges permeated the interior of *The Buckeye*. Everything around me took on an eerie pale green color much as I have seen prior to a thunderstorm. Time itself seemed to slow down, and my senses were all in tuned to the extreme danger that surrounded us. The German guns had our altitude and were accurately placing shells. Looking out a side window, I could see a fighter paralleling our course and communicating our range and direction to the anti-aircraft batteries below. "Bomber going down," Jack said. I glanced out the side window and saw a bomber rear up on its tail with the center section on fire.

"Come on you guys get out," one of our crew said.

I watched as it flipped over on its back and started into a tight spinning dive. The centrifugal force would hold the crew tight against the interior of the bomber dragging them to their deaths miles below.

"Anybody get out?" Archie asked from his position in the nose turret.

"Not that I saw," John replied.

"Another bomber in our formation is going down," said Little Frankie. I started counting the men coming out of the plane and saw at least six.

Finally, I heard John call out, "Bombs Away," and Pappy immediately took evasive action to avoid the remaining flak. Friendly fighters were seen attacking the stalking aircraft. It looked like a pair of P-51 Mustangs, but I was unsure as they were quite distant. While I was watching, I noted that our fighter escort had returned to escort us back to England. We were all happy to see them. They would ride in position until a threat appeared and then would dive toward it like a mad swarm of bees. I watched several times as a melee played out in front of the formation. The enemy fighters would, at times, make it through our fighter cover and get strikes on the bombers. It was a sickening sight to see a bomber begin smoking, and crewmembers silenced with their guns hanging limply in turrets. I personally witnessed six bombers shot down with the loss of sixty men. The last page had been written in their lives. A short story where a novel should have been. No warm hugs from their children, no more laughter with friends, no romantic evenings with a lover. It was an end to all things they had hoped for in life. Such great loss is hard to understand.

We fought off numerous attacks as we headed home from the target and flew across several hot flak areas. After hours of fighting, we came upon the *Double Trouble* still struggling to survive. She was down to two engines and had been shredded from enemy attack. I watched as the formation of German fighters sat back out of gun range and would send one lone fighter in to attack. It appeared that less experienced pilots were being trained using the Double Trouble as a real life target much like a cat might teach its kittens with a wounded mouse.

Jack summed up what we all were feeling. "Stupid German bastards are toying with her."

As we drew near, I could see that half of one of the vertical stabilizers had been shot away. It was a testament to the ruggedness of the aircraft design and a crew that they were still in the air.

I was overcome with emotion and spoke. "We can't just leave them."

There was silence for a moment and then Pappy spoke. "Any objections to assisting them?"

"Let's get'em," Little Frankie said with a clear view of what was transpiring.

Others spoke their agreement.

"Heads up men. This may get a little bumpy. Jim, Frankie, and Archie: we will come in straight behind that gaggle that is trailing them. Jim: Once we are within range, you open up. When he does, everyone else let loose. Our advantage is going to be surprise," he said.

Pappy banked the aircraft out of formation and dove turning altitude into airspeed. It came as a surprise that *The Buckeye* had such nimbleness and grace.

The enemy pilots were so intent on this training session that they had stopped checking behind them, a fatal mistake for a fighter pilot. *The Buckeye* was rapidly closing the distance. Closer and closer we flew.

"Cut'em down boys," Jim said.

With that, three different turrets simultaneously opened up. I could see a stream of tracers streaking toward the enemy aircraft. *The Buckeye* spit fire like a dragon in medieval times. Two of the enemy aircraft burst into flames and started to smoke. One of the canopies pushed back on another, and the pilot rolled out. Our gunners weren't done and struck additional aircraft with great effect as we roared through their broken formation.

"Pappy pulled the power back and did a sweeping turn out in front of *Double Trouble*. Once completed, he slid *The Buckeye* into formation alongside them. Looking over at the bomber, I could see the extent of the damage. The sides were riddled with bullet holes and black burn marks ran back along the number two engine.

"You fellas want some company?" Pappy said.

"You are more than welcome to tag along," came back the reply. No more had the conversation ended than Ben spoke excitedly into the mic.

"O God, more fighters are forming up behind us. I count at least six."

The two bombers huddled together to present the most formidable defensive firepower.

"Here they come," said Little Frankie from the ball turret. The crew tensed as we knew the ferocity that was going to be unleashed upon us. As with other encounters, we worked like a professional ball team, calling out enemy aircraft and handing them off when they were entering another's field of fire. A few strikes were made on *The Buckeye*. The enemy aircraft continued to chip away at us, and each pass seemed to draw us closer to destruction. After several attacks, they struck the number four engine on *The Buckeye* causing a loss of oil pressure. Lew rapidly worked to cut the fuel to the engine and feather the propeller. Pappy brought up the power on the remaining three engines to make up for the loss. We started to feel the fatigue of the continuing battle and were very low on ammunition. The situation was becoming dire.

"I am not sure how much more of this we can take," Lew hollered over at Pappy.

"Just keep your head down and keep fighting."

"Pappy, I see another formation directly above us," Jim said from the top turret.

"And they are forming up in the rear again," Ben said from the tail.

"Were running low on ammunition back here," Albert said.

"I hate to add to the misery, but three are swinging around for a frontal assault," Archie said from the nose turret.

"Here they come six o'clock high," Jim said.

All available guns were tracking them ready to greet them whenever they were within range. I watched them draw closer and closer. Looking closely, I noted twin tail booms. Only one fighter could create that silhouette.

"Don't fire! They're friendlies! P-38 Lightning's! " I yelled.

When the P-38's were close enough, half went after the enemy trailing us, and the other half tore into the ones forming up in front. Several enemy aircraft were hit as bullets squirted out of the Lightings and found their mark. We started cheering them on and, for a few seconds, chattered unrestrained into the microphone. Slowly we moved away from the air battle, and the enemy threat was no more.

"How far out are we, William?" Pappy asked.

"About one hour," I replied.

After what seemed an eternity, we were crossing the English Channel. Arriving at the airbase, *Double Trouble* shot a red flare and took the lead to land. "Most of our panel is shattered. Would you all mind paralleling our course and calling out speeds for us?" their pilot asked. He was amazingly calm.

"Will do," Pappy responded.

Flying a few hundred feet along side of *Double Trouble*, we matched their descent. Lew called out the airspeed to them while Pappy delicately maintained our position. We too had suffered damage. I heard *Double Trouble's* pilot inform the tower that they would be making a wheels up landing, "Our hydraulics are shot to hell."

Although we were at least an hour overdo, I could see all of
the men still waiting for us in front of the air traffic control
tower. I watched out the side window as *Double Trouble* sat
down and created a huge tail of sparks. It was a rough landing,
but the crew, who hadn't been wounded, would walk away.
Pappy poured the power to the remaining three engines and
banked *The Buckeye* a little to the right flying directly over the
men gathered in front of the control tower. Looking down, I
could see them cheering and saw some hats waving as others
were tossed in the air. Pappy circled around and made a smooth
landing. After shut down, we exited *The Buckeye* and started
lighting cigarettes as we piled on the transportation that had
been sent for us. When we hopped off the jeep at debriefing,
we were swarmed with men who had already heard part of our
heroic story. There were cheers and much backslapping as we
made our way to the debriefing room. The sun was just starting
to settle when I looked across the airfield at *The Buckeye*. Men
were hooking a tug up to move her to the repair shop. She had
carried us through. I entered the debriefing room and supplied
them with my mission notes. My information would be gleaned
for intelligence information and to write the Missing Aircrew
Reports that were completed when an aircraft failed to return.
As was standard procedure, we were given our glass of
grapefruit juice and a shot of whiskey. I usually drank the juice
and pushed the whiskey to another crewmember, but today I
drank it. Everyone knew the questioning wouldn't end in the
debriefing room, which was why none of us were surprised
when Pappy and Lew were told to report to base headquarters.
We could hear loud voices, but the two had already worked out
their story about losing an engine, falling out of formation, and
luckily taking our spot alongside the *Double Trouble*. Although

the individual pieces were true, they were not in the correct order. It was either believable or senior officers found a story that would cover them too if they were questioned by their superiors. In the end, they received far less than we feared.

The next morning, I was awakened by the sound of the bombers roaring off to hit another target. I had seen Elizabeth some over the last few weeks, but I was ecstatic when I remembered my three-day pass. It seemed like I had lived a lot of life since the last time I had spent considerable time with her. I had to put her out of my mind during my mission days as it would be too distracting to me. It was wonderful to let her fill my mind again. Sitting up, I scratched my head and looked over toward the other bunks. Based on last night's stumbling around and laughing, I knew that the partying had started early for them. Heading to the showers, I was pleased to find that the big push on them was long over. After enduring the long cold temperatures at altitude, it felt good to let the hot water wash over me. Arriving back at the hut, I saw John still in his bunk.

He rolled over, looked at me, and groaned. "Morning, Sunshine," I said tossing his hat at him.

"I feel like I was hit by a Mack truck," he said.

A little too much celebration last night?"

"Guess so. What's planned for today?" John said as he sat up on the side of the bed with the heavy army issue green wool blanket pulled around his shoulders.

"Well, I am supposed to help at Elizabeth's house, and if it warms, she spoke about going on a picnic," I said. "How about you?" I asked.

"Some of us are planning to head to London."

"Sounds swell," I said not envying him the least bit.

John finished dressing, and we headed to the mess hall. Upon entering, I spotted Sarge, the head cook. He extends a warm greeting to everyone, which makes him popular among the men. He also jokes often about the food to keep them laughing. His mess hall is kind of like the base living room with men gathering there often for smokes and coffee.

"Hey, Sarge, fill'er up," I said.

"Sure, a double helping for anybody from *The Buckeye* crew," he said raising his eyebrows in jest.

John and I walked over and sat at a corner table that allowed us to watch people coming and going from the mess hall.

"How is your family?" I asked.

"My grandfather wrote to me the other day," he replied.

"And how is he doing?"

"Good. He took a six-point deer a few weeks ago with his bow and said the family is doing well."

"You still going to show me how to make a bow when we get home?" I said.

"Sure. I know where there is a stand of Osage orange trees we can use," he said.

Archie entered the mess hall and looked around until he spotted us. He walked directly to our table

"Hey, John, you coming?" He took one last drink of his coffee and stood.

"Take your tray?" he asked pointing at mine.

"Yes, thanks," I replied.

John grabbed our trays and took them to the counter where they were picked up by a corporal and placed in the automatic washer.

"Be seeing you, William," John said as he disappeared with the gang.

I looked around and saw Chaplain Wimbley seated with his back toward me. Grabbing my coffee cup, I walked over to his table. He was reading and failed to see me approaching him.

"Mind if I take a seat?" I asked catching him by surprise.

"Hey William. Of course, have a seat," he said while closing his Bible with his finger stuck in it to hold his place. "It's good to see you. How is life treating you?"

"Some of the best and the worst times I have ever experienced," I said.

"Well, I know about the worst, so tell me about the best."

I smiled. "Her name is Elizabeth." A thrill passed through me just speaking her name.

"Oh, a girl. And I assume British?"

"Yes, and she is wonderful."

"I can see that," Chaplain Wimbley said taking a drink of his coffee. "That is great news, William. I am so pleased to see the joy this brings you. You know, most of my work is on the heavy issues and seldom do I hear about the good parts of life over here. It is nice to be reacquainted with joy."

I proceeded to tell him about where she lived and my day on the farm.

"Well, it sounds like you are off to a wonderful start. You may have noticed everything moves a bit faster over here. I have seen this in matters of love too. With the uncertainty that the war brings, people are in a hurry to live life," Chaplain Wimbley stated.

"What passage in the Bible are you reading?" I asked.

"I have been going through the Book of James. It is practical and gives me direction on how to live life on a daily basis," Chaplain Wimbley stated. "You know, William, back home I take my time in sharing the gospel and my belief, but over here I don't have that luxury. I hope the men don't think I am being too pushy, but where they spend eternity hangs in the balance. There is more than a physical war going on here." We sat for a moment in silence. "I have a box of Bibles that were sent by a church back home for the men. Would you take this

Bible, give it to a friend, and encourage him to read it?" he asked.

"I would be happy to."

"Well, I need to make my daily rounds starting with the hospital," Chaplain Wimbley stated as he stood up.

I stood with him. "May I take your cup?" I asked.

"Thank you. We will talk later."

Stopping by the hut I sat the Bible on my side table. Moments later, I started out for Elizabeth's house. While walking down the country road, I passed my crew on a truck headed for the train station. They were rowdy as I expected. I could hear them hooting and hollering out the window to harass me but could not make out what they were saying over the noise of the truck engine.

I continued my journey and enjoyed the quiet countryside. Occasionally kicking rocks, I traveled past the familiar sites meandered down the winding road to Elizabeth's house. The sun was beaming, and a light breeze was blowing. Butterflies and honeybees were working the enticing colorful petals that the wild flowers extended to them. An occasional songbird would flush from a bush and fly ahead burying itself back into another secret hiding place. As I knocked on the front door, a fear overtook me that her feelings could have changed for me. Timmy swung the door open wide for me, and I entered the hallway.

"Got any gum, chum?" he asked. I reached into my trousers, pulled out a pack of Double Mint, and handed it to him.

"The whole pack?" he said with excitement. I nodded and winked at him. He bounded off through the house calling for Elizabeth and then raced back to me and grabbed my hand.

"Come on. She is this way."

As we approached, I could hear her speaking to her mother. She looked at me and smiled.

"Hello Will. Are you ready to work?"

Any trace of my anxiety instantly melted away. "I thought the day would never arrive," I said.

She wore a tattered pair of tan pants, a heavy work shirt, and rubber barn boots. Her hair fell loosely past her shoulders.

"What's on the agenda?" I asked as we passed through the family room and into the kitchen.

"Mom ask me to dig up the rest of the potatoes and store them in the fruit cellar."

"Sounds like that will keep us busy for a while. Do you have a spud fork?" I asked.

"I know where it would be if we do," she said.

Proceeding out the back door, Elizabeth walked over to a weather worn shed, unlatched the door, and swung it open.

"It would be in here," she said.

Inside was an array of garden tools. Picking through them, I located one. Elizabeth grabbed a couple of wooden crates that were stacked along a wall in the shed. With tools and crates in hand, we headed toward the large garden that was located in the back yard. An old fencerow ran along one side of it. I could see various types of vining plants with large melons as well as green beans, tomatoes, and sweet corn.

"Hey, Elizabeth, what is that one there?" I said pointing at a tall dark green vegetable with what looked like small cabbages growing off the main center stock.

"Those are brussel sprouts," she said. "I will fix some for you if you think you would like to try them."

"Sounds swell. Looks like more than just the potatoes need harvested," I said.

"Yes, the garden has been neglected as of late," Elizabeth said.

Arriving at the row of potatoes, I set the spud fork in the ground at the base of one of the mounds, stood on it, and sunk it deeply into the soil. Pulling back on the handle, several potatoes boiled up with the dark rich English soil. We gathered them and moved to the next hill.

"Tell me about your crew?"

I spent the next fifteen minutes telling her about each of the crewmembers. I ended by telling her that earlier they had all passed me on their way to London.

"I hope you didn't miss a trip because of the work around here," she said.

I think she knew I was right where I wanted to be, but like me, she needed reassured. I could have told her how much I had thought of her since our last day together but feared it might overwhelm her.

"What? And miss another hot day sweating on the farm with you?" She laughed.

We hauled potatoes to the cellar for about an hour and then started on a new task: cutting down the corn stalks. We piled them, bound them, and then carried them to the barn so they could be used as bedding during cold weather.

"Are you getting hungry yet?" she asked.

"Yes, but let's get all this cut and stacked in the barn before we eat."

We finished in the early afternoon and walked to the house to gather our supplies for the picnic. I watched her as she pulled items from the icebox and finished packing it all into a basket.

"What have we forgotten? Oh, a blanket," she said answering her own question and walked to the hallway closet to pull one out.

"Anything else?" she said turning and smiling at me.

"Nothing I can think of," I said. With that, we headed out the door.

"Where do you want to go?" I asked as we strolled down the quiet country road.

"I have a place in mind," she said.

"Hmm, a mystery huh?"

Arriving again at the cobblestone bridge, we removed our shoes and waded down the creek until we stood at the edge of a large lake. Working along the edge of the bank, we came to a grassy spot that offered a beautiful view of the lake. Elizabeth spread the blanket under a large oak tree and placed the picnic basket down beside it. She sat on the blanket and invited me to sit beside her.

"When I was young, we used to swim here often. There was a rope tied high in that tree and we would swing out and drop into the lake," she said pointing to a large smooth grey beech tree.

"Sounds fun," I said imagining her family enjoying a hot summer afternoon at the lake. "The lake reminds me of a reservoir that my best friend and I used to spend a lot of time at when I was young. It is within walking distance of my house. We didn't have permission to fish it, but that didn't stop us. The railroad company had built it by damming up a hollow. It provided water for the big black steam locomotives. A man was paid to help the trains load water and police the reservoir for trespassers. We would get to laughing and horsing around while fishing, which would invariably attract his attention, and he would start across the lake towards us. Fortunately, for us, his old boat had squeaky oarlocks, and we would hear him coming while he was still some distance away. Sometimes we would taunt him by dancing around on the bank and laugh the entire time. That would really get him to pulling hard on the oars. When he was close to our bank, we would grab our gear and fish and take off running. We could hear him cursing as we ran away. It was exciting for us, and we would be panting as we walked home retelling the adventure.

"Did he ever catch you?" she asked.

"No, but he came close once on a soggy spring day. The rain lubricated his squeaky oarlocks, and instead of coming straight across the lake, he worked along the shoreline out of our sight. He was nearly upon us when we finally saw him. We grabbed our stuff and took off but couldn't get up the muddy clay bank. He actually grabbed my foot. I was a muddy mess by the time we clawed our way up it. I could hear him laughing loudly as we made our escape.

Elizabeth giggled, "I can just picture you scared to death and scrambling up that bank." Our conversation trickled to a stop as we sat side by side looking out across the lake. I reached over and slid my hand under hers. She laced her fingers in between mine.

"Peaceful isn't it?" she said looking out across the water with the trees reflecting off its surface. The colorful leaves dropping onto the lake were gently pushed along by the slightest of breeze.

"Yes, it certainly is," I said taking in a deep breath of the woodsy smells. "I wish I could take some of this serenity back to the base."

"I worry about you, Will," Elizabeth said softly while looking down at the ground.

I turned toward her, reached over, put my hand under her chin, and raised her face up to look at me. "I'll get through this, Elizabeth."

"I know," she said looking away and struggling to regain her composure.

We spent a considerable amount of time sharing stories and dreaming about life after the war. Eventually, Elizabeth reached down into her basket and pulled out some sandwiches wrapped in wax paper and unwrapped one and handed it to me. She then pulled out a thermos filled with hot tea and poured both of us a cup.

"Sorry I don't have more to offer but with the war and all," she said

"This is perfect," I said.

She smiled, "I guess it is a bit wonderful considering the times and all."

We sat silently eating our sandwiches and sipping on hot tea and watched the ducks float lazily around the lake. They were loafing with their heads turned around resting on their backs. They too were being pushed about by the gentle breeze and only paddled when they were made uncomfortable by drifting too close to the bank. Elizabeth slid her hand back under mine.

"Thank you for helping me with my work."

"Oh, you know I enjoy it."

"Me too," she said softly.

"The separation from my family is difficult," I said.

"You have me here."

I turned toward her, placed my hand onto her cheek, and gently our lips touched. It seemed surreal, much like when the fighters were attacking us in battle. I could feel intense emotions welling up in me that I had never felt before. She lay back on the blanket, and I followed kissing her. Eventually, we lay side by side speaking softly. Once we were silent for a while, she pulled close to me and laid her head on my chest. I closed my eyes wishing the moment would never end. With the afternoon slipping away and not wanting her mom to be concerned about her, I spoke.

"We should be getting back. It will be dark in an hour," I said. The sun was slipping below the treetops with the warm air leaving with it. Once everything was secured in the basket and we were ready to walk back, I took my leather flight jacket and placed it over her shoulders. Picking up the picnic basket, we made our way back to the bridge. Arriving at her house, we entered the back door, and I placed the picnic basket on the table.

"Can I see you tomorrow?" I asked.

"I would like that," she said.

"What time would you like me to call on you?"

"How does nine o'clock sound? I was thinking we could go visit the children at the orphanage."

"That sounds like time well spent."

When I arrived back at the base, the last light was fading from the sky. I stopped by the latrine to wash up and then headed out for some chow. Most of the discussion in the officers' club centered on the day's mission. The hell they had endured and the heaven I had experienced were polar opposites. While Elizabeth and I had walked down a peaceful creek, men were dying. I avoided the discussion as I wanted to block out the war as much as possible and hang on to the peace I felt from the day with her. After enjoying a coke, I made my way over to the recreation center and played some table tennis against some tough opponents. Once I relinquished my paddle, I sat in a rocker to smoke and watch several games. At a little before 10:00, I headed to the showers. When finished, I dressed and walked back to our hut. Without the other crewmembers around, it was empty, quiet, and lonely. Even though sometimes we annoyed each other, we were a surrogate family; ours isn't a blood bond, but it is just as strong, one that develops between men who protect each other's hopes and dreams. Laying back the covers on my bed, I noticed the Bible that Father and Mother had given me on the day I was baptized. I opened the first page and read what she had written: William, you are a gift from God, all our love July 15, 1934. My mind was taken back to that day. A few of my cousins and I had answered the invitation song and made our confession of faith on the last day of our summer revival. The day was stormy with a low gray overcast sky. Church members had driven to Alma Lake and stood on the sloping bank and sang hymns as we followed the minister down into the water. When the baptism ceremony began, the sunrays broke through and shone down on where we were being baptized. As it ended, the clouds closed up again. When I climbed the steep bank, my uncle hugged me and whispered "The angels are rejoicing in heaven." My mother was smiling though her tears.

Reaching over, I turned on my reading lamp and then walked over and shut off the overhead light. I lay on my bed, picked up the Bible, and started to read. I woke several hours later with the side light on and the Bible beside me on the bed where it had fallen. Placing it on the table, I lit a cigarette. Looking around the hut, I began to think about how none of my belongings are private. I decided to try to find a concealed place to hide my most treasured documents. I built a compartment on *The Buckeye* where I keep my journal. If found, it will be confiscated as any written record by us is forbidden. For multiple reasons, I need to find a hiding place in our hut, but the problem is there are no rafters or crawlspace. Everywhere I look is either arched wall or ceiling. I crushed out the cigarette and decided to search for a spot the next morning.

I awoke early to the sound of the bombers departing for a mission. The temperature was the chilliest I had experienced while at the base. "Guess I will be the first to try this thing out," I said to myself as I wadded up some old newspaper, grabbed some small kindling sticks we had gathered, and lit the combustible mixture. Once I knew it would take, I dove back under my blankets and quickly fell into a dream. It was a familiar scene. We were camping at a gravel pit that was owned by my father's best friend. Bluegrass music was ringing off the hills that surrounded the lake as my father picked the banjo and his friend accompanied on a guitar. It was just starting to get dark. Fishing top water baits for bass, Charlie and I worked the boat around the peaceful lake. I was popping a hula popper while Charlie's jitterbug added a splish-splash from its back and forth motion. He had fished all afternoon and had nothing to show for it while I had landed several decent fish. I knew that Charlie had his heart set on a trophy size largemouth bass. He told me he had prayed for one. I felt bad for him and was coaching him on where to cast the lure.

"Pitch it up under those tree limbs that are overhanging the water."

Charlie did as instructed and had just started retrieving his lure when the water erupted. "Whoa," I cried out and instantly started coaching him on how to fight the fish.

"Lift the tip of the rod and keep the line taut. Don't give him a chance to throw the lure from his mouth." Charlie raised the rod and stood up in the boat. The fish dove for the bottom and his reel squealed as the drag slipped and let out line. Moments later, it shot up to the surface and broke water. It shook back and forth struggling against its unknown master.

"It's a real whopper bass," Charlie hollered.

I became concerned that it would wrest free and his excitement would quickly turn to tears. The bass tried every trick it could including racing under the boat for deep water only to then turn and head for the brush. Eventually Charlie had worn it down and was able to bring it alongside where I slid the dip net under it and brought it aboard. I swung the dip net around into the middle and set it directly in front of Charlie.

"Oh my! Look at that one," Charlie hollered. He was so excited to show his catch to our father that he begged me to start for the bank. Father must have heard our excitement as he had stopped playing and was watching us. I set to work the oars, and we quickly reached the shore and beached the boat. We headed up the bank so that Charlie could show them his fish. Just when I was about to reach our father, I heard a strange buzzing noise: it was my alarm clock. As the dreamy fog exited my mind, the anxiety of the war and a longing for home settled in on me. I felt like a cruel trick had been played on me as the dream had been such a high only to be slapped in the face with the cruel, cold reality of separation and war. I rose and started my morning. After stopping off at the latrine, I headed to the mess hall for some food, and most importantly, a fresh cup of hot black coffee.

"Morning Sarge, have anything good for breakfast?"

"Sure. How about two eggs, sunny side up, with some fresh bacon, and toast smothered with black raspberry jelly?" he said. All the while, he was stacking up some rock hard biscuits and topping them with some greasy looking canned sausage gravy. "That will send you trotting to the latrine when it hits bottom," he said laughing.

"It's that good huh? Why don't you take a break and join me?" I asked.

"Sounds good as long as you don't expect me to eat any of this stuff," he said laughing.

Sarge grabbed two coffees and followed me to the table. We talked until I had finished my meal. "How about a smoke?"

147

I said as I pulled out a pack of Camels. He took one and had his Zippo lighter sparking before I could fish out mine. The coffee, mixed with the faint whiff of lighter fluid, set the mood for a much needed and enjoyed smoke. Sarge took a deep drag off his cigarette.

"What did you do before the war, Sarge?"

The smoke exhaled as he spoke. "I spent several years working in a coal mine in a small town in Virginia. I tried to enlist as a gunner, but the Army had other plans for me."

"Oh yeah," I said.

"How about your artwork. Did you major in art in college?"

"Naw, I started drawing in high school."

"Oh, in a class?"

"More like classes," he said

"So you took a lot of art classes?"

"Who said anything about art classes? I used to doodle while bored in my math, English, and history classes," he said laughing. "My family was large and my father was a drunk, so as the oldest son, I quit after the tenth grade and made money for my family so we could eat. One job I had was designing and painting custom signs in our small town. I enjoyed it, and I hope to start my own business back home after the war is over."

The more I learned about Sarge, the more I admired him.

"How come you didn't go with the rest of the guys to London? They say it's a crazy place," he added.

Pulling out a cigarette, I tamped it against the pack and thought about how to respond. I still feared that if some of the other guys found out about Elizabeth they might start showing up with their laundry.

"I have other things that I would rather do," I said.

"Such as?"

I decided to trust him "I have a girl that I have been seeing. She lives about a mile from the main gate."

"You talking about that hot little number whose mother does laundry?" Sarge asked.

"Yeah that's her, but don't say anything to the other fellas about her, Sarge."

"Tell any of them. Hell, they all know about her," he said. "Most of them tried to pay her a visit, but she wouldn't have anything to do with them," he said. "She gained a reputation around here. They started calling her the Ice Princess. Guess her mom is kinda chilly too."

"Wait a minute. You mean to tell me that a lot of the guys know about her?" I asked.

"Sure, but like I'm telling you Lieutenant, she wouldn't have nothing to do with them. She scolded a couple of them, and, you know, I think the whole lot of them are half scared to approach her. She has a reputation. You must be working some kind of magic if you melted her.

I laughed when I thought about Elizabeth getting after them.

"What do you two have planned today?" Sarge said while noticing some of the kitchen staff staring at him.

"What you all chatting about? Can't a person have a few minutes with a friend?" he bellowed at them. "I'ma gonna peel you all like a sack of potatoes if you don't knock it off." Once he re-exerted his authority, they returned to their work.

"We are going to the orphanage today."

Sarge smiled. "I been there. Sad sight to see all those kids without any parents, but at the same time, it's heartwarming to see others step up to the challenge of caring for them." A smile broke across his face, "Wait here, Lieutenant," he said and rose from the table disappearing through the kitchen doors. He emerged carrying a large white flour sack that was stuffed with goodies.

"Take this for them. I think Uncle Sam would be proud of us being so generous to those who have less."

Looking down into the sack I could see assorted cans and vegetables as well as candy treats on top.

"I put an extra something in there for Elizabeth and her family too," he said.

"Thanks Sarge, I appreciate it, and they will too."

"Would you do something for me?" Sarge asked.

"Sure."

"Tell the lady that runs the orphanage that I said hello."

"Will do."

"I better get up before these bums around here start complaining about me stretching my break time. Nice talking to you, Lieutenant," Sarge said as he rose from the bench. I heard him holler a couple of threats towards the cooks as he worked his way deeper into the kitchen. Actually, I knew he wasn't angry with them. There was a lot more bark than bite in him. It was his odd way of showing his affection for them. He watches over them as a pilot watches over his crew. There wasn't anything he wouldn't do for them. I still had 45 minutes before Elizabeth would be expecting me, so I pulled a pack of Camels from my pocket and shook one from the pack. I lit it and sat pondering why Elizabeth hadn't shut me out along with the others. With no clear reason emerging in my mind, I decided to ask her if the opportunity presented itself. Snuffing out the cigarette, I stood, pulled on my brown leather flight jacket, and headed out the door enroute to her house.

Chapter 9

His mother rose and pulled back the curtain of the front door. "It's still raining. Are you getting hungry, Tucker? We need to be thinking about what we're going to have for lunch."

"Yes, I am, and my eyes are a little tired."

"Why don't we take a break and pick it back up after we eat?"

"Sounds good."

"How about something simple like grilled cheese sandwiches and tomato soup?"

"That'll do the trick. I'll do the sandwiches if you start the soup," Tucker said walking to the kitchen. His mother followed and started the soup as he assembled the sandwiches. With cheese placed between the slices, he applied butter to both sides, placed them in a heavy cast iron skillet, and turned the heat on medium. His mother had just completed setting the table and sat down.

"I wonder how he became separated from his journal?" Tucker said.

"Perhaps he made it through the war, and you can return it," she said.

"He has a lot of admirable qualities," Tucker said flipping the hot cheese sandwiches.

"Yes, he does," his mother said.

Once the sandwiches were a golden brown, he sliced two big slabs of tomato, opened and laid them on the melted cheese. Closing them, he sprinkled some Tabasco sauce on his.

"Tucker, I believe you would read the journal while eating if I asked you to?" his mother said.

"I have a lot of questions: do they get married, does he make it home? Maybe we can find him and return the journal."

"I have thought about many of the possibilities but most have a sad ending," she said.

They sat quietly eating their sandwiches.

"Care for some more milk, Tuck?" his mother asked.

"Sure," he said positioning his glass for her. After she filled it, he picked it up, stood, and headed into the living room.

"Guess lunch is over," his mom said laughing. She pulled a warm heavy quilt off a rocking chair that sat in the corner of the room and sat down on one of the couches.

Tucker set the milk down in front of him on the coffee table. Opening the journal at his bookmark, he started to read aloud.

Chapter 10

I had just cleared the air base perimeter fence and turned down the road when I heard the low slow moan of the air raid siren. It grew louder and louder until it started to wail. Scanning the horizon off to the west, I spotted two German BF-109 fighters diving toward the air base. I noticed their guns twinkling as they started their fearsome strafing run. I watched in disbelief as I saw them raining down destruction on what had just a few minutes before been a safe haven. Being on the open road, I decided I might become one of their targets, so I jumped into the tall grass that was growing in a ditch beside the road. The fighters circled around for a second pass. By that time, the airbase antiaircraft gunners were coming alive, and on their second pass, they hit one of the fighters. At first there was smoke and then flames spread down the sides of the cowling. The fighter passed low over the top of me in the direction of Elizabeth's house. It dove below the trees, and then I heard a thunderous explosive thump and watched as debris flew high into the sky. A terrifying thought entered my mind, and I started running towards her house. There was dark oily smoke from the burning wreckage. The final curve in the road blocked my view of her house. I knew it struck close by and fought against the horrible thoughts that preyed upon my mind. Finally, rounding the corner, I spotted the house and could see that the fighter had crashed about a half mile away in a field. When I arrived, Elizabeth was standing on the front porch with Timmy. He was crying and had his arms wrapped around her waist. She was visibly shaken. I walked up the steps onto the porch and put my arms around both them. It took a while before I caught my breath and could speak.

"I was so worried," I said between heavy breathing.

"Oh, it was horrible, William. The pilot tried to get out at the last minute, but his clothes were on fire, and he fell from the aircraft," she was sobbing onto my shoulder. I couldn't think of any comforting words, so I just held her.

"Timmy, are you alright?" I said looking down at him. He had stopped crying and looked up at me but remained silent. I was concerned that he had witnessed the horrible scene. "Did Timmy see the crash?" I asked.

"I don't think he saw anything, but the loud explosion and my scream scared him," Elizabeth said. We stood there for a few minutes until we saw the authorities headed down into the pasture to secure the wreckage and locate the body for a proper burial. After we had settled down, Elizabeth spoke "Why don't we go inside, and I will brew some hot tea?" Timmy let loose and opened the door. Elizabeth took my hand and led me into the house. She set a small kettle of water on the stove to boil and turned to the cabinets to select some teacups. Setting the cups on saucers, she turned and carried them to the table. The cups rattled on the saucer as she set them on the table. I reached for her hand to settle her. She stopped and looked at me.

"We're all right," I said.

New tears filled her eyes as she looked at me. Finally composed, she spoke. "William, I contacted the orphanage and told them we would be stopping by today."

"Swell. Timmy will you be going with us?" I said in an upbeat manner.

"Can I, Elizabeth?" he pleaded.

"Absolutely. In fact the children would be sorely disappointed if you weren't with us," she said as she bent down and hugged him.

"Mr. William, what's in the bag that you set on the porch?" Timmy asked.

In the excitement I had completely forgotten about the package that Sarge had sent with me.

"Well something for you and for your friends over at the orphanage."

"Wait here and I will get it," I said. Returning to the kitchen, I sat on a chair and placed it between my legs on the floor. Timmy came over, climbed on my lap, and started looking through the sack. "Pull out that one there," I said pointing to one of the packages. Lifting it out, he held it up for Elizabeth to see.

"What is it?" Timmy asked as he turned it over repeatedly and finally handed it to her.

"I am not sure. You will have to open it to find out," she said.

"May I?" he asked her.

"You will have to ask Will."

"Mr. William, may I open it?" he asked.

"Yes, it's for you," I said smiling at him.

Timmy unwrapped it and found a Mars bar. "I will eat a lot now and save a little for later," he said. His comment made us laugh. The steam finally started to whistle from the kettle, and we sat around the kitchen table and enjoyed the calming effects of a hot cup of tea.

"Are you ready, Timmy?" I said reaching over and tousling his blond curly hair. He stood and handed me my heavy leather, cotton-lined jacket that was hanging on the back of my chair.

"Get your heavy coat too, Timmy," Elizabeth said while writing a note to her mother. Timmy disappeared into the other room to do as he was told. I sat and watched her as she continued to clear the table. She stopped and looked at me when she noticed that I was staring.

"What are you looking at?" she said.

"The prettiest girl I have ever seen," I replied as I felt a rush from the thrill of telling her.

"William, I am sure you have seen your share of pretty faces in America."

I stood up and walked over to her. "None as beautiful as you," I said as I cradled her face in my hands. She set her dishtowel aside and put her arms around me. We gazed into each other's eyes for only a moment as we heard Timmy approaching.

"Mr. William, would you help with me mittens?"

"You bet. Come here, and I'll button up your coat too." Once finished with bundling him up, I pulled on my coat and scarf.

"Put your boots on, Timmy, and, William, where is your cap?" Elizabeth asked while pulling on her coat.

"Aw, I forgot it at the base."

"Now I won't have you catch a cold," she said while turning back towards the coat closet. She dug in a wooden box and produced a hand knit stocking cap. "You need to put this on," she said.

"Yes, Mother," I said while winking at her.

"Come on Elizabeth," Timmy said while tugging at her hand and pulling her towards the front door. I walked behind her and pulled the door shut.

"Oh wait, I need to grab the donations I brought for them," I said. Quickly, I walked back into the kitchen and grabbed the sack. As I exited the house, a cool breeze met me, and I was thankful for the hat.

As we walked down the country road, Elizabeth spoke about the children and what they had endured. They all had their own unique story with a common element of tragic loss. It was heartbreaking to hear how the war had caused the children to suffer.

"The orphanage was originally the home of a wealthy merchant who had taken great pride in maintaining its beauty. Unfortunately, subsequent owners had let it go, and it was in need of major repair when purchased by the local Lutheran church. With a sense of urgency, the congregation generously provided material and time. Everyone contributed in some way. The elderly covered the cost of purchasing material, while young strong backs poured in the physical labor. Prior to the completion of the renovation, congregational members kept the children. The whole house continues to operate on donations. The Americans supply a lot of food and personal items that are nearly impossible for us to obtain in Britain," Elizabeth said.

While walking between us, Timmy reached over, held my hand, and then put his other hand in Elizabeth's. "It is a sad sight to see all of those children with no Mums, so I try to come over as often as I can and bring them something if possible. Just bringing Timmy puts a smile on their faces as he has many friends here," she said.

"How many children are at the orphanage?" I asked.

"About twenty."

We continued past the Wendling train-depot and into the small city of Beeston. On the outskirts of the town, we approached a large two-story house with a wraparound front porch.

"There it is," Timmy said with excitement. It was well kept with a large playground that had clearly been constructed with salvaged material. Looking toward the city, I saw a high brick steeple and wondered if it was the Lutheran church she had mentioned. Several children were watching out the tall windows as we approached the gate.

"We're here," Timmy announced as he ran up to the picket fence gate and unlatched it. He held it open until we walked through and then properly shut and latched it. Clearly excited to play with his friends, he hurried past us and bounded up on the large wide steps that led to the front door. We had just started up them when Timmy stood on his tippy toes and reached high for the old brass lion face doorknocker. Just as we reached the door, it opened.

"Hello Elizabeth," the young woman looked to be about our age. Her outfit was built for service. She wore a towel over her shoulder and an apron with many pockets to hold an assortment of medicines, toys, and diapers. With so many children to watch over, she certainly had no time for superfluous accoutrements. She was the embodiment of functionality. Necessity dictated that thrift be her constant companion.

"And Timmy and a guest too. It's always nice to see you," she said while Timmy pushed past her to run towards his friends.

"It's good to see you too," Elizabeth said.

"Penelope Whitaker, this is my beau, William Pritchet," Elizabeth said.

"How do you do, Mr. Pritchet?"

"Very well, thank you," I said.

"Come in out of the cold."

"May I get you some hot tea?" she asked. I removed my hat and followed Elizabeth through the doorway.

"Oh, none for me," Elizabeth said.

"Mr. Pritchet, how about you?" she asked politely.

"No, but thank you," I said knowing that the resources were scarce. "I brought this on behalf of the men at the airfield."

"Oh my. You Yanks are so generous. Thank you so much," Penelope said.

"You're welcome, but I can't take credit as I am only the deliverer. A friend of mine that works in the mess hall put the package together. He said to tell you hello and said he knows you." She smiled and looked in the sack.

"Yes, I know him," Penelope said laughing. "He doesn't give…" One of the staff interrupted her before she finished.

"Miss Andrews, would you come and check on Sarah? Her temperature has gone up."

"I'll be right there. Please excuse me," Penelope said as she hurried off to the latest in her endless stream of tasks.

"Certainly," Elizabeth replied.

"What did she mean about Sarge?" I asked.

"He is interested in courting her, but she just hasn't shown any interest."

"Hmm…now I understand," I said.

"Let's go find Timmy," Elizabeth said. Proceeding down a long hallway, we passed several doors before we arrived at a large open playroom.

"Elizabeth!" Several children sang out in unison as she walked into a large room. There were children scattered about the room. Some were playing alone while others were huddled in small groups. There were chalkboards, homemade wood toys, and boxes that were decorated and made into a fort. They swarmed her as she sat down on a large area rug that covered the hard wood floor. I sat down beside her, and Timmy came over and sat by me. Elizabeth leaned over to me. "I don't think he is interested in sharing you." A small girl that was sitting beside Elizabeth rose up on her knees and cupped her hands over Elizabeth's ear. While she was whispering to her, Elizabeth glanced over at me. "Yes, he may have. Why don't you ask him, Rosemary?" Elizabeth said aloud while looking at me and smiling.

The little girl who looked to be about three years old walked over and stood before me. With her hands held behind her and slowly twisting back and forth, she spoke in a hushed little voice. "Do you have any sweets?" she asked as she brushed her long hair out of her face. I was so glad that I had stashed some candy bars and treats for the kids in my pockets.

"Hmm, well let's see," I said. Rummaging through my pockets, I started piling the candy on the floor. Her eyes lit up as she gazed down at the treats. I opened the packets of gum and pulled out individual pieces so that each child could have something. "Since you asked first, Rosemary, you can take first pick," I said quietly so none of the others would hear. She bent down with her knees on the floor, placed her hands beside them, and studied the pile of treats. She looked so grateful and happy. Finally, she extended her hand and chose a candy bar.

"Thank you," she said looking at me. Then, unexpectedly, she put her arms around my neck and hugged me. I looked at Elizabeth and smiled.

"They win your heart quickly, don't they?" Elizabeth said.

"Timmy, why don't you tell the others about the goodies?" I said.

"Just a moment. Let's use your hat as a grab bag so we avoid any disagreements," Elizabeth said.

"Good idea," I said handing it to her. After a short time, the sweets had disappeared. Some of them couldn't wait and started to eat or chew it right away while others sat and talked about the moment later in the day that they had chosen to enjoy their treasure. Elizabeth then showed me how to make puzzles for the children. She browsed through an old magazine and then carefully pulled a scenic picture from it. Smearing paste, she then placed the picture on the cardboard, pressed down firmly in the middle, and worked towards the edges. Next, she took scissors and started cutting out irregular shapes. Once done, she invited the children to work the puzzle. Several children gathered around her and started piecing it together. We then enjoyed a simple lunch with them. When finished, Elizabeth held the smaller children on my back as I acted like a wild horse bucking around the floor snorting and puffing. They wore me out, and this would have gone on for much longer, but Elizabeth explained that they needed to put the horse out to pasture to rest. While I was still breathing hard in the corner, Elizabeth started to read a story titled *Five Children and It*, one of their favorite stories. Her maternal nature acted like a magnet and drew more and more children in as she brought the characters to life. I sat peacefully and leaned against a wall and admired the many dimensions of her beauty. They sat engrossed by the story of a group of children who were granted wishes by a sand fairy. They giggled and were amazed as the children in the story chose what seemed to be wonderful wishes only to have them turn out to be bad choices. The youngest children eventually lay down on their blankets, and by the time she finished reading, many of them had fallen asleep. She looked over at me and quietly asked if I would carry them to their beds. I started delivering them to the bedroom as Elizabeth pointed to their individual beds. She then tucked the covers in around them and gave each a kiss on the forehead. She paused at Rosemary's bed.

"Isn't she just wonderful?" Elizabeth said.

I came alongside her. "She certainly is," I said softly. Walking down the long hallway, Elizabeth stopped at Penelope's office to say goodbye. Talking on the telephone, she held her hand over the receiver. "We will visit more next time," she said and then resumed her conversation. Elizabeth looked around and found Timmy behind her.

"Timmy, are you ready?" she said.

"Yeah, I guess so," he said noticeably saddened by the news of our departure. We walked to the front door, turned, and said goodbye to the children that were following us.

"What a wonderful bunch," I said.

"You're good with the children, Will. I am sure they would love to see you again," Elizabeth said.

When we arrived back at her house, her mother was busy with the laundry. "We're home Mum," Elizabeth said.

"Would you mind helping with the laundry?" she replied.

"I am sorry, Will, but I better help out Mum. She has a lot of work," she said with an apologetic look on her face.

"Of course," I said starting to move towards the door as she followed.

"Will you be over tomorrow?" she asked.

"Sure, if you think you can put up with me for three days in a row."

"I think I can suffer through it," she said laughing at my comment. With my heart racing, I pulled her close to me. When she pressed against me, the heat from her body wafted up out of her shirt, and I could smell her delicate perfume. It was intoxicating. I stared into her eyes, and then we kissed. I knew at that moment that I loved her. Not a love like any I have previously known. It is an all-consuming, uncontrollable fire. She dominates my thoughts. From the moment I left her company, I missed her. It scared me to think I might lose her or she might lose me.

My walk back to the base was, as usual, very lonely. Elizabeth and the kids had filled my morning with happiness and distraction. For a while, I completely forgot about being thousands of miles from home and the ugly aspects of the job I had volunteered to do. I walked deeper into loneliness with each step I took away from her. A cold, merciless wind blew and chilled me. The sun was settling in the sky, and I knew that most of the men would have eaten supper, but I hoped there might be a friend to share the meal. As I came within sight of the base, I thought of the stark contrast of Army Air Force life. One day I am fighting for my life in the skies over enemy territory while the next I was holding my sweetheart in some peaceful setting. It brought about an undesirable cycle where I would momentarily forget about the war and become caught up in my personal life, and then with an ugly fury, the realization that I must go back into battle would rush upon me. It would take my breath away like a blast of cold artic air in the winter. I combat the anxiety with positive talk by telling myself that I am going to make it through.

As I approached the entrance gate of the base, I realized I only had one more day, and then I would be called upon to once again wage war. Arriving at my hut, I found just as I had left it: empty and cold. I turned on my bedside lamp so it wouldn't be dark when I returned later and grabbed a new pack of smokes. Before I left for chow, it occurred to me that I had forgotten to find a hiding place for my personal items. Investigating every corner of the hut, I was about to give up when I found a suitable hiding place that I believe would go unnoticed by the most determined inspector. Upon entering the mess hall, I heard a gruff voice holler out, "Would you looky over there?" Sarge was still at it, cooking and cleaning. He never seemed to stop.

"Hey Sarge, got something good to eat?" I said looking over at the serving line.

"Good no, something yes," he said, putting some mashed potatoes on a plate. Excess water drained from them. "How are the kids at the orphanage?" he asked as he topped the potatoes with meat and a thick slice of bread and then spread gravy over all of it.

"You mean how is Miss Whitaker, I mean, Penelope?" I said as I set a glass of ice tea on my tray. Sarge smiled when I mentioned her name.

"Miss Whitaker, who is she?" he said knowing that I was on to him.

"The one that you won't quit bugging for a date," I said setting the tray on my usual table.

"Did she say anything worthwhile about me?" he asked hungry for the slightest morsel of information about her.

"She was busy, so we weren't able to speak much to her." I told him about the experience and what Elizabeth had told me concerning Penelope. I wished I had something more positive to tell him. Once finished with supper, I walked back to the hut to tend to the delicate matter of writing some letters home. I provided some details to my family about my experiences, but there is so much I didn't share. There is no reason to worry them by telling them how dangerous the missions are and how many crewmembers I have seen maimed or killed. Instead, I remained upbeat and focused on the positive. I told them about Elizabeth and inserted a page for Charlie to explain how we had named our bomber and one for Julia about the orphanage. I finished, shut the lights off, and lit a cigarette. After I finished it, I fell asleep while I reviewed the day's events in my mind.

I woke again by the sound of the bombers departing. Looking over to my nightstand, I saw the Bible I had for John. Picking it up, I turned to where Pastor Wimbley put the bookmark. It was a passage in Corinthians where the apostle Paul was giving advice on marriage. I pondered verse eight and nine: "I say therefore to the unmarried and widows, It is good for them if they abide even as I. But if they cannot contain, let them marry: for it is better to marry than to burn." The verse struck home with me in light of my relationship with Elizabeth, and I knew the longer I knew her, the closer we would become. My desires would only burn hotter within me. I set the Bible back on the table and started into the morning routine eventually making my way to breakfast. The rush was over and preparations for lunch were under way. After filling my plate, I found my seat and sat down.

"Hello young man. Care if I join you?" Chaplain Wimbley said as he slid the chair out across from me.

"Please do"

"So tell me about your family back home, William."

"Well I have a younger brother and sister. My father farms about 160 acres and raises some livestock." I explained in detail about growing up in Indiana and my future plans to attend college after the war. Chaplain Wimbley listened attentively and occasionally sipped his coffee.

"Sounds like you have been blessed with a wonderful family. I wonder, is there anything I can do for you?"

"I have been reading from my Bible and I do have a question for you," I said.

"Wonderful. What would you like to discuss"?

"Well, I am curious. Why do you believe in a creator? I want to have a good explanation when others ask." Chaplain Wimbley explained in depth evidences from personal experience to science, all of which supported the validity of the Bible. He then wove in how he found the Bible to be full of wisdom such as the way it explains why there is evil in this world. The Bible certainly explains the origins of all of the present pain and suffering.

"It has been my experience that God reveals himself to people through various mediums. Some people see God in nature, while others find their way to Him from an emotional heartache. If you look for Him, you will find Him regardless of what lens you use. Personally, I can't see how anyone could draw any conclusion other than that there is a creator. Consider that there will never in the history of man be another man like you. None will look exactly like you, and none will have your life experiences; you are unique. William, you are simply a miracle," Chaplain Wimbley said as he patted my hand. Reaching over, he picked up my spoon. "Look at this spoon. We don't know who made it, but we know someone did. No one would say that random chance and time created it, and yet men will claim that something as wonderful as you has no creator. How can they draw such a conclusion? God can be seen, but it takes an open mind and willing heart. He will not force himself on anyone, but he clearly wants his children to be restored to him. Many paths lead to him. However, I am not saying that all religions lead to God. Jesus clearly eliminated that when he said in John 14:6 'Jesus saith unto him, I am the way, the truth, and the life: no man cometh unto the Father, but by me.' In the end, as God intended, it comes down to faith. He is separating the wheat from the chaff through this experience we call life. Nobody can be absolutely sure, but remember, William, as I said before, we live within a forced model. The good Lord does not give us the option of not making a decision. We live out what we believe every day by the decisions we make, and those decisions are either leading toward or away from God. For me, when I see all of the evidence in the Bible and the natural world, I feel confident in my belief. Even the evil of the present age is evidence of the fall and curse of man. Everything points toward God whether it is the birth of a baby, a death, or some wonder in the cosmos. Good or evil, it all speaks to his existence. Once a person understands there is a creator, then the natural inclination is to find the creator. A logical next step is to look at the religions and search for the truth. Most are 'works based' where you do enough good to earn your way to paradise. My experience is that all men have a dark side and could never fully recompense their transgressions. Thus, we need someone who can pay the debt for us: Jesus. Christianity is unlike any of the others as our king died and rose for us; other religious leaders are still buried. That is how I reason with someone who either questions my faith or is looking for answers. Does that help?"

I was impressed with the depth of his response. "It does. You have not only given me evidence for others, but you have bolstered my faith too," I said.

"Very good, very good. Just keep reading, praying, and living for him," Chaplain Wimbley said with a smile.

"Thank you. I would love to talk some more, but I better head to Elizabeth's if I am going to be on time."

"I enjoyed visiting with you," he said as we stood. I picked up our trays and walked them to the sink. Exiting the mess hall, I started towards her house.

The last day with Elizabeth was wonderful. The first part of the day was spent raking leaves of which Timmy enjoyed running through. Next we mowed the grass and then repaired and cleaned the gutters. I relished the work as it gave me an opportunity to show her how I felt about her. She fixed me a

British wartime meal called the Oslo. It consisted of two pieces of whole wheat bread with a little butter, a small block of cheese grated over some lettuce leaves, salted vegetables, and a cool glass of milk. The milk was especially good as I hadn't enjoyed any since arriving on base. At home I would typically have at least one glass a day. During the afternoon, we walked down to the market and picked up some essentials. The rationing is severe, and I have a better appreciation of just how hard the war has been on the British civilians. Everything that she selected required a stamp, which effectively limited the amount and controlled what she could buy. She introduced me to several friends and neighbors. I never grew tired of being introduced as her beau. When we arrived back at the house, I set into mending the fence around the barn lot while she helped her mother with the endless laundry. I had to wrestle loose rotted fence posts and replace them. Next was stretching the fencing back around the post. It was physically demanding, and once I had completed the task, I helped Elizabeth hang laundry. Conversation is never a challenge for us. We talked and teased each other throughout the afternoon. We heard the drone of bombers as they returned to base, and one was trailing smoke. Elizabeth stepped close to me and slid her hand into mine as we watched one bomber after another pass overhead.

"Wonder how it went?" I said. We stood in silence for a moment until Elizabeth spoke.

"Let's get some supper, love."

Once we had eaten, we moved into the living room and sat on the floor playing games with Timmy until his bedtime. After we had him tucked in, we sat on the front porch swing.

"What are you thinking about?" Elizabeth asked as she slid close to me.

"How much I have to live and fight for."

Elizabeth pulled her legs up on the swing and leaned over on me. I placed my arm around her and she laid her head on my chest.

"When will I see you again?" Elizabeth said.

"Well, I have to complete five more missions, and then I will be issued another pass."

"I would like to see you before then. Perhaps you can come over for supper sometime in between missions," she said optimistically.

"That may be possible, but I won't know until the day before. Would short notice be okay?"

"Of course, dear," she said.

We sat resting in the swing taking in the night sounds and enjoying each other's company.

It was dark when I left her home. When I was about half way to the base, I was nearly run over by a drunk on a bicycle. He was heading back to base and most likely had been at the local pub called the Dog and Pony. I watched him weave down the road until I saw him lose control. He flew over the handlebars, and the bicycle went careening into the ditch. When I reached him, he was rubbing his leg and starting to stand. I retrieved his bicycle and straightened the handlebars.

"Let me push it for you," I said. We talked on the way back to the base, and I learned that he was a mechanic whose bomber failed to return from the day's mission.

"There were some real good men on that airplane. The returning crews said they saw a few parachutes, so maybe some of them made it," he said.

We walked in silence for the rest of the way. It was an ugly reminder of the cruel reality of war and the price it required of the unlucky ones.

Upon arriving at the base, I walked to the mess hall to see if my crew was back.

"Hey, William over here," Little Frankie said.

They had stories from their trip to London. The stories weren't a surprise to me as seasoned crews had been sharing them for weeks. Wild stories about a city filled with excitement for young men who had no moral constraints and could fulfill all of their carnal pleasures. Nonetheless, the crew was wound up as they had just experienced it firsthand. I sat silently and listened to their stories of women, fights, and booze. Jack and Albert had bruises from one encounter. They told a story of some drunks picking on Little Frankie, which didn't set well with them. Luckily, they all made it out before the MP's arrived. The crew didn't question why I hadn't gone with them to England, as they knew I was a Christian. They respected my decision but felt I had missed a great time. From my perspective, nothing could have been further from the truth. Wanting to wring every bit of pleasure from their three days off, they headed to the recreation hall to squeeze as much fun out of the little time that we had left. Everyone knew we were listed on the mission board to fly the next morning.

I sat and drank a cup of coffee until I saw Sarge working behind the counter. "Hey Sarge, do you have a minute?" I hollered.

"You trying to pull me away from all this fun?" he said as he headed over to my table.

"I was thinking today about how you might be able to get a date with Penelope."

"Is this one of those practical jokes that is funny to everyone except for the poor sucker that is the butt of it, and this time it would be me?"

"Naw, I am serious"

"Okay, you have my attention," he said.

"Maybe Penelope would be more at ease on a double date. The base dance is coming up."

"Keep talking. I'm listening," he said as he sat down at my table.

"Perhaps she would be more comfortable if Elizabeth and I were along."

"You may be right. I hadn't thought about that. Yeah, sounds good. But I gotta tell you I am gonna be mad as hell if you get your ass shot off and this whole plan falls apart," Sarge said.

"Glad to see you're so concerned about my wellbeing." I said. As I ate, Sarge and I planned the perfect date with the girls.

"Now all we have to do is get her to say 'yes.' When do we put this plan in motion?" he asked

"I will mention it to Elizabeth next time I see her."

"You know this might just work," Sarge said patting me on the shoulder as he rose from the table. He began whistling as he started wiping off the tables again.

Chapter 11

The lights in our hut flashed on. "You guys are on today. Up and at it," were the words that I awoke to on the morning of my eighth mission.

"Come on coach, can't we sit the bench today," Pappy said as we started rolling out of bed.

Typically, I couldn't turn off my thoughts before a mission, but last night was different. I had slept soundly. I was thankful as I had a feeling that this might be a long haul since we hadn't experienced one since our third mission. They could last as long as eight hours with temperatures at bombing altitude registering negative forty degrees. The short ones left me drained. The deep ones left me completely exhausted. Once dressed, we all stumbled out of the hut and into the cold morning air. The routine was monotonous, but there were so many critical details needing our attention. Our lives depended on our ability to leave nothing undone, so we paid attention to everything. Complacency could kill. At breakfast the stories of their wild times in London emerged. The city had been transformed by the war. The Red Cross had purchased a building and worked hard to make it into the typical drug store that the men knew at home. It was called "Rainbow Corner" and stayed open 24 hours a day. The crew had spent considerable time there.

"Hey, William, you missed a good time in London," Albert said for all to hear.

"That so," I said sensing a teasing was about to be delivered.

"Yeah, what did you do while we were away?" Jack asked.

"What say, ye?" Albert said pushing me for an answer.

"I heard he was visiting some girl down the road," Archie said.

"That's right. I met a girl," knowing they weren't going to stop, I just wanted to get past the inquisition.

"Tell us all about her and include the juicy details," Albert said grinning and leaning across the table.

"She's not like that. Her house is about a mile off base. I met her when John and I dropped off our laundry," I said hoping that would suffice.

"Why, you ole dog. I heard she wouldn't give anyone the time of day, but you thawed her out, huh," Little Frankie said grinning at me.

"Cut it out. She is a nice girl. I just helped her out as her father was lost at Dunkirk, and they are overwhelmed keeping up with the farm."

"You know, the Army frowns on British war brides," Jack added.

"Yeah, I know, but they can mind their own business."

"Oh, so you're getting married," Albert said seeing the opening for another jab.

"We're just steadies, but who knows," I said somewhat surprising myself.

The lively conversation paused for a moment until Ben picked the discussion back up. "You should go see London with your next pass. The city has been pounded by the German bombings, but their spirit is unbroken, and there is a lot of excitement."

"Perhaps, next time," I said knowing I wasn't going. With that, the conversation returned to the excitement they had experienced in London until we broke up to move on to our next processing station.

I walked into the briefing room with the rest of the officers who were on the roster. The commanding officer, base meteorologist, Father McDooley, and the intelligence officer entered. We all stood at attention. The commanding officer turned to Father McDooley. "Father," he said as he swept his hand slowly toward the podium inviting him to go first. He moved in front of the podium. "Let us pray. Invincible God and righteous warrior, we entreat thee to extend thy protective covering to your sojourners here below as they set out to liberate and secure those who are persecuted; safe guard them from all evil that threatens to prevent them from completing their mission and being reunited with those whom they love and love them; rescue your humble servants from the desolate solitude of war and restore in them a holy place of communal love, and when their journey, is complete lead them into thy eternal kingdom that is filled with everlasting happiness and thy eternal presence. In Christ holy name, Amen."

Once finished, Father McDooley moved from the podium and stood off on the side of the raised platform.

"At ease men," came the expected order from the commanding officer. He stood before a large map that was covered. The destination shown behind the covering would determine the fate of men's lives. The longer the string stretched into Germany, the greater the likelihood of our undoing. "Today's mission is one deep into enemy held territory," he said with a seriousness befitting of the dangers ahead. All eyes were fixed on the map as he explained our target was the airfields at Bernberg, Germany. Like most of the others, I had never heard of the place. Not surprising though, as I had never heard of many of the cities in Germany that now held more meaning to me than any other cities on Earth. The briefing continued with various facts about the raid, form up times, formations, and bombing altitudes. I scribbled down notes and checkpoints that would be used going and returning from the target. Heaven help us if we were separated from the rest of the formation. With everything being on a tight time schedule, the last detail was synchronizing our watches. Finally, after being thoroughly briefed on the mission, we were released to our bombers. We climbed on a truck called a 'deuce and a half' and headed to *The Buckeye's* hardstand, which was about a half mile from the briefing room. The sun was clearly up, and as we drove around the huge perimeter road, we passed crews prepping their bombers for battle. The deuce and half came to a stop, and we piled off.

"Hey, this isn't *The Buckeye*," Jim stated.

"Yeah. What type of joke you trying to pull?" Little Frankie added.

I saw Pappy approach the driver and discuss the situation. The truck pulled away, and Pappy walked over to the crew.

"I was informed at my briefing that *The Buckeye* has been pulled off of the line for some upgrades," he said.

Most of the crew were looking down at the ground or off in the distance. None of us made eye contact with him as we were angry.

"Well listen, one Liberator is the same as the next, right?" Pappy said wanting to restore morale.

"You don't believe that any more than we do, sir," Jack replied.

"I suppose you're right, but we are going to have to do the best with what we have, and today the best we have is O*le Number 60*," he said, pointing to the tail number of this soulless bomber.

"Let's get going, men," Lew stated.

"Top it off, Earl," Pappy hollered to the Crew Chief.

"Already have. Rumor mill has it's a long one today," he said.

"Your mills a reliable one," Pappy replied without divulging where we were headed.

"Give'em some for me while you're out there," he said.

Pappy and Lew walked around the bomber going through the preflight checklist while the gunners assisted in pushing the propellers through.

"Cycle them a few more times. We don't want to blow a cylinder when Pappy lights the fire in them," Lew said.

With our gear loaded, we meticulously inspected our respective areas. The first flare was fired, and the field started to rumble with the sound of huge radial engines coming to life. Pappy taxied *Ole Number 060* into the stream of bombers that were taxiing to the end of the runway for takeoff. We all plugged into the intercom, and Jack asked what all the crew wanted to know.

"Where are we heading?"

"Bernberg, Germany," Pappy said.

Albert asked what is always the follow-up question. "Where in Sam Hill is that?"

"A long way from home, Dorothy," Jim said.

Pappy, realizing they weren't after a geographic location, told them what they wanted to know.

"It's going to be a deep mission into the meat grinder," Pappy said. Multiple sighs could be heard across the intercom. Conversation trickled off as we all were seized by the usual fear that preyed upon our minds.

"Shake it off men. *Ole Number 060* won't let us down," Pappy said. Everyone assumed their takeoff positon. I sat by others on a bench that was behind the cockpit at a lower level. The bomber squatted under the heavy load as it worked its way to the runway. Out the side window, I saw some familiar aircraft trundle by ahead of us in the takeoff line up. Some of the crews I knew; others I was glad that I didn't. If they were lost it was sad, but less personal. Ben was calling out some of the names as they passed by: *The Briar Patch, Our Gal, Axis Grinder*, each with their own nose art. The last one to pass was *Shangri-La*. The nose art was of a woman dressed in lingerie leaving little to the imagination. Her breasts were exposed, and she had a mischievous look that hinted to the fact that she would be a willing partner to some late night activities that are better left unspoken. Twenty minutes after the engines were started, *Ole Number 060* was pulling onto the runway ready to take us to whatever fate awaited.

"Okay, everyone secure for takeoff," Lew said.

I silently said my takeoff prayer asking God to protect us. After a long roll chewing up most of the available runway, *Ole Number 060* broke ground and headed for our assigned altitude.

We all searched for the gaudy formation ship that served to get the group into formation for the mission.

"There is the old Judas goat at 11 o'clock high," Archie said.

A Judas goat was the nickname given a goat that was used to lead sheep to the slaughterhouse. The sheep went to the slaughter while the goat was returned to the barn.

"That nickname sure doesn't impart confidence," Ben said. We joined a formation of bombers that British civilians on the ground said took an hour to pass overhead. When we were over the English Channel, we started to transform into a fighting unit.

"All right men, you know the drill. Test fire those guns and check in on the intercom," Pappy said.

One by one the crew checked in on the intercom. Next was the familiar test firing of the guns, coupled with a hundred other familiar sights and sounds that always give me the surreal feeling of impending doom. Flying into battle was the toughest as we knew it was going to get worse before it would be better. With each turn of the propellers, we flew farther from safety and closer to danger. I tried to focus on my duties to avoid thinking about the unknowns that lie ahead. The flak, enemy fighters, and friends' dying, coupled with the stress of our being shot down are mental burdens I carry on every mission. Each mission is the same nightmare all over again.

"Hey, William, want to shut the door behind me?" Archie asked as he climbed into the nose turret. Once he was seated, I closed and latched the doors.

"Looks like our little friends are on time," Lew said.

I glanced out the window and saw a formation of fighters flying past us headed to the front of the bomber formation. Looking around, I could see gunners in the waist windows of the other bombers and an occasional turret spin back and forth searching for the enemy.

Pappy broke the silence, "Keep looking boys. They're not far away now."

With that, we strained to detect the smallest spot in the sky that could be the beginning of our end.

Five minutes later, the warning came. "They're forming up at six o'clock level," Ben said from his position in the stinger turret.

I could hear the whir of Jim in the top turret spinning toward the target in case an attack materialized. The fighters hung just out of range, and I wondered why they didn't start their attack.

"More at three o'clock high," Jack said from his waist window.

"Looks like a mass assault men. Conserve your ammunition. Give them short burst," Pappy instructed.

Pappy tucked *Ole Number 060* even closer to the other
bombers in the formation so that we would obtain the greatest
possible protection of the defensive firepower. The bombers
were huddling together like a herd of wild animals that were
about to be attacked by a predator.

"How far out are we, William?" Lew asked.

"At this speed about two hours," I replied

"Here they come," Ben said.

I heard Ben's guns firing and knew they were now within
range. At the same time, the Bf 109 single engine fighters that
had been paralleling our course broke over and started a
coordinated attack meant to overwhelm the gunners of our
formation. The action was continuous and made it impossible
to take in everything that was happening. An explosive flash
out the side window caught my attention, and I watched as
Yankee Rose started spinning down. I noted it in my navigational
log and counted six parachutes. As the attacks persisted, the
crew efficiently and smoothly announced targets and handed
them off to each other. It was an impressive coordinated effort.
The enemy aircraft were savage in their attacks.

"I made some hits on that one," Little Frankie said.

His ball turret was constantly whirring around as he picked
up one target and then another and gave them short burst.

"They're line abreast diving from 10 o'clock high. You see
them Archie?" Jim asked. Archie brought his nose turret's twin
fifty caliber guns to bear on the enemy, and they barked their
defiance at the threat. Jim started cussing at them and poured

lead into them as they flashed by at tremendous speed. His foul language was directed at those who tried to lead us to our destruction. He found his mark on one of them, and the fighter cartwheeled overhead on fire and plunged down between the bombers in the rear of the formation. Just as quickly as the attacks started, they ceased. We all knew what that meant, a thrashing by the German 88 millimeter anti-aircraft guns. The bombers had to fly straight and level to the target. Any evasive action would make it impossible for the bombardier to hit the target. I glanced forward and watched as bomber after bomber entered a wall of black exploding shells. Our turn was finally at hand and *Ole Number 060* entered the iron overcast. I could hear the thumps and occasional sound of small pieces of metal peppering the sides of the aircraft.

"We have oil streaming out of number one," Lew said.

"Watch the oil pressure on it," Pappy replied as he tried to hold the bomber level through the explosive metal storm. *Ole Number 060* was pitching and bucking violently from the turbulence created by the bombers ahead of us. It was like being in a boat on a very stormy sea.

"Cripes, *The Paper Doll* has a huge hole through its left wing, and the number two engine is on fire," Little Frankie said from the ball turret.

We watched as the flames started streaking back along the side of the bomber until it pitched over on its back and started a dive to the earth five miles below. We were silent as we watched 10 men meet their death.

"Bombs away," John called out.

Within a minute, *Ole Number 060* exited the storm and was free from the shackles imposed by the bombing run. Pappy turned in formation with the other fortunate ones who emerged with us.

"How is the engine?" Pappy asked.

"Holding in there, but I doubt it will be turning when we get back to England," Lew replied.

"I don't want to become a straggler. Those damn fighters will swarm us."

About 10 miles from the target, the fighters started in on us again. Banking, weaving, and at times, running straight through the formation with guns blazing, we methodically fell back on our training. A hotshot group of Bf-109's pressed their attack to nearly the ramming point, and then broke away at the last possible moment.

"Those guys with the yellow spinners are from some crack outfit," Albert said.

"They seemed to have singled us out for destruction," Jack said.

"Looks like we are going to need to feather the number one engine. The oil temperature is rising, and the pressure continues to fall off," Lew said.

"Do it," Pappy said as he maintained our position in the formation. Lew methodically followed the engine shutdown procedure and feathered the propeller.

"We're going to need to draw more power from the others if we are going to maintain our position in the formation," Pappy said. "Bring up the power on the others to 80 percent," Pappy said. Lew pushed the throttles forward to maintain our airspeed. I could feel the noose starting to tighten around our necks.

"Where are those fighter escorts?" Jim said.

Just then I heard the heavy thump of 20 mm cannon shells ripping through the ship. They made a sound like large rocks being thrown on a tin roof. After the strikes, we heard the dreaded, "I'm hit."

"Who is it?" Pappy asked. Everyone turned to the man nearest him.

"It's Jack," Albert said. "He's been hit in the arm." I grabbed a first aid kit and headed to the rear. Jack was still tracking and firing at fighters as they zoomed by. Blood could clearly be seen running down his torn leather bomber jacket. As he worked the gun, I pulled back the torn jacket to expose the wound. There was a long gash in his forearm. Pulling him from the gun for just a moment, I was able to shake sulfa powder on it and then wrap gauze around it. The freezing cold air and the sulfa powder had the desired effect and the bleeding stopped.

"How you doing, Jack?" Pappy asked as he tried to hold the damaged bomber in formation.

"It hurts like hell, but I think I can man my post," Jack said grimacing as he started to swing his swivel mounted waist gun back and forth to make sure he could defend the ship if need be.

"Pappy, we have another issue. That last attack severed several high pressure lines," Jim said. We assessed the damage while the fighters hung just out of range and planned another coordinated assault.

"Here they come again," Pappy said.

I looked out and could see the flashing on the wings of the aircraft while *Ole Number 060*'s guns were sending out a belligerent reply. Watching Ben's nose turret latch onto a formation of enemy fighters, I saw one of the aircraft take the full devastation as hundreds of rounds shredded it. The crack outfit of FW-190's started another strafing pass, and with a loud explosion, the top turret Plexiglas exploded. Jim fell limp out of the turret, and I rushed over to him. The glass had slashed open his scalp, and I could see part of his skull. Blood was streaming down over his face. His oxygen mask had been knocked off, and he looked at me and then went unconscious. Grabbing one of the portable air tanks, I placed the mask on him. I dressed his head wound, gave him a shot of morphine and made him as comfortable as possible. Climbing into the turret, I found that it was still operational although wind was rushing in around what remained of the Plexiglas top. I put on his facemask and checked the microphone.

"Can you hear me, Pappy? Jim was hit. I am covering the top turret."

"Loud and clear. How is Jim doing?"

"He has a head wound that I dressed. It doesn't appear too deep," I said intentionally not telling him the extent of the wound as I knew the whole crew was listening.

I had some gunnery training to prepare me for an emergency such as this. Spinning in the turret, I saw the fighters once again assembling for another line abreast attack.

"Here come our little friends," Ben said.

I watched as four beautiful P-51 Mustangs dove into the unsuspecting Germans. They scattered. I continued to scan the sky, but no other threats appeared.

"John take over for William so he can plot and report our position," Pappy said.

I handed off the turret and returned to my table. After some calculations, I informed Pappy that we were about 40 minutes out.

"Okay men, this old crate has a few more holes than when we took off, so once we are on final approach to land, I want you to assume your crash positions." After another 30 minutes, we spotted the airfield. Once we were in close, John fired a red flare out the waist window to alert the emergency personnel that we had wounded. This also gave us priority to land. Pappy peeled *Ole Number 060* out of the formation and with Lew started through a lengthy checklist to prepare the bomber for landing. He flew a wide pattern to allow more time to identify and correct any problems that emerged. Constantly aware of the dangers of flying with only three engines, he gently reduced power. Once we turned onto final approach, he called for the wing flaps to be lowered.

"Flaps full down," Lew replied.

"Gear down," Pappy said.

"No good, Pappy. We only have two green lights and one red."

"Which one is red?"

'It's the left main."

"John, we need you to try and manually lower the left main gear," Pappy said.

"Will do," John replied.

"Listen men, we have several issues and some that we may not have discovered. I don't want a surprise on the brakes when we need them, so Albert and William, I need you both to post at the waist windows with parachutes. Secure them to the gun swivel mounts. Wait for Lew to give the order to deploy them if we have no brakes. How are we doing on the gear, John?" Pappy asked, anxious to eliminate the problem.

"It's no good Pappy. I have tried to manually extend it, but it won't budge." A few minutes later we were passing over the runway numbers. Pappy pulled the throttles to idle and started a gentle flare onto the right main gear. He held the left wing up and balanced the bomber on the right main tire as long as possible. Eventually, when enough airspeed had bled off, the nose gear touched down, and Lew reached up and pulled the mixture control.

"Shut off the fuel valves to the engines." Pappy ordered.

The heavy bomber rolled down the runway balanced on two wheels.

"Brakes are no good. Dump the chutes," Lew said. The parachutes blossomed and added tremendous drag to slow our speed. Pappy continued to roll the yoke to the right to hold the left wing off the ground as long as possible. When at full deflection, the wing started to settle toward the runway.

"Hold on fellas" were the last words he spoke before the wing sat down and the bomber spun turning the aircraft into the grass. I could see the ground crews watching as grass and dust flew into the air, and *Ole Number 060* finally came to a stop. With lights flashing, the ambulance raced up to us. Ben and I helped load Jim onto a stretcher while Albert assisted Jack in exiting the bomber. Pappy was the last one off. We moved to a safe distance and then turned to look at the bomber. The damage was severe, and it would be a while before *Ole Number 060* would be back on the line. We loaded onto a jeep that took us to the debriefing room where we all gave accounts and drank our whisky ration. I provided specific information for the missing aircrew reports by stating latitude and longitude of bombers that had gone down, as well as a record of the number of parachutes seen. We were wiped out after the mission. The first stop was the showers and then the mess hall for some supper. I entered the mess hall, located my crew, and took a seat along Lew. Pappy gave us an update on our wounded crew.

"Jack received stiches and may be on our next mission. They stitched up Jim's forehead, and they think he suffered a concussion. They're holding him for observation. It may be a while before he is back," Pappy said.

"I hope that was our toughest mission," Lew stated.

"That makes two of us brother," Pappy added.

"I had a bad feeling when I saw that we were assigned that old crate. Hopefully, the rest of our missions will be flown in our ole sweetheart," I added.

"She certainly is the eleventh crew member. I have been told that we will be training tomorrow and then be off the next day," Pappy said.

With that, we broke up and headed to our huts. When I finally lay down, I saw my Bible on my side table, and I fell asleep thinking about the deeper meaning of life and what my purpose might be.

I was sleeping soundly the next morning when I was rustled out of bed by Lew.

"Hey sleepy, you gonna rise and shine? We're on for a training flight today," Pappy said.

Turning over in bed, I woke to find John handing me a hot cup of coffee.

Wow—what a treat.

A coffee pot was one of few luxuries we had in our hut, and Sarge kept us well stocked in coffee. Once I had cleaned up, I headed over to the mess hall to eat with John and ask a favor of Sarge. Although the mess hall was busy, it didn't take long to locate Sarge. He was giving firm directions to one of the cooks in a loud voice. I proceeded through the line until I attracted Sarge's attention and motioned to him to come near.

"I am heading over to Elizabeth's later, and with the war ration on here in England, it would be nice to take her something. It might encourage her to try to persuade Penelope," I said.

"Say no more. I have just the medicine," Sarge said.

"I thought you might," I said winking at him.

"Come by after your day is over, say about 3:00, and give three quick knocks on the side door," Sarge said in a hushed voice.

"Will do," I replied.

After filling my tray, I followed John to two open seats, which were a challenge to find. While speaking to him about the day's training flight, I was interrupted by a familiar voice

"These seats taken men?" Chaplain Wimbley asked.

"Hello, Chaplain, you remember John?" I said standing out of respect.

"Of course," he said, as he set his tray down and extended his hand.

The two shook and once basic pleasantries were extended, our discussion migrated to the day's agenda. We spoke over the course of breakfast with much laughter and comradery.

"William, I have a few things to take care of," John said as he rose from the table.

"Okay, see you in a little while."

"So what do you have planned for the next hour, William?" Chaplain Wimbley asked.

"Nothing specific, what do you have in mind?"

"Would you like to accompany me on my hospital rounds?" he asked.

The thought made me a little nervous, but I knew it was the right thing to do and thus agreed to go. We walked over to the base hospital, a long rectangular building. When I entered, I saw a long row of beds on both sides with a wide center aisle. Nurses and doctors were coming and going as they tended to the wounded men. I surveyed the broken warriors, and my heart was heavy for the immense physical and mental suffering they were enduring.

"Good morning, Chaplain," one of the nurses said as she passed by.

"Top of the morning to you too," he said in a chipper manner.

I followed him as he proceeded down the aisle to greet the men. Jim was among the first ones we visited. He was in much better condition than many of the others who had far more serious wounds. For those, he would kneel beside their bed, place a hand on them, and pray. When they could speak, he would ask if they had any requests, which he would write down in a small paper tablet. Each of the men appreciated his concerns and willingness to share in his suffering. I was especially moved when we came across an airman who had been blinded. He was barely a man at nineteen years old. After some discussion about his baby girl back home, and what this meant to his future, he broke down and with trembling hands reached out like he would have to his own father. Chaplain Wimbley didn't hesitate and hugged him assuring him that God would not leave him and that the doctors had said there was a good chance he would regain his sight. Knowing I was a Christian, Chaplain Wimbley turned to me.

"Will you pray with us?" he asked. I reached over and took both of their hands.

After an hour working through all of the beds, we exited the same door we had entered.

"I am so moved each time I visit with them. They represent the best of our country and humanity," Chaplain Wimbley said. "William, you can help. Will you continue to pray for them?" he asked.

"Of course," I said.

The rest of my day was spent like many of the last year— aboard *The Buckeye* on a training flight honing my battle skills. Flying in her felt like pulling on a well-worn pair of gloves. Her subtle differences and unique smell imparted confidence in us as the morning and afternoon training flights were without incident. I packed my laundry in a duffel bag and kept my 3:00 appointment with Sarge. Shortly after knocking at the door, he appeared with a cloth sack filled with goodies that are readily available on base but are luxuries in wartime England.

"Don't forget the dance," Sarge said.

"Operation double date about to be implemented—thanks for the goodies," I replied. I set the sack in the top of my duffel bag and headed toward the main gate.

Hitting the open road, I was flush with excitement and joy, a rush like I had not felt since childhood overcame me. It was hard to believe that I was on my way to see her and that tomorrow I would eat supper at her house. I restrained myself from running as I knew other base personal were coming and going down the road and this could lead to embarrassing questions. However, I did stretch my gait to decrease the time it took to arrive. The thought occurred to me that I should get a bicycle. Reaching the picket fence gate, I unlatched it, bounded up the porch steps and nearly ran into her mother who was coming out the front door.

"Oh, excuse me," I said, barely avoiding the collision.

"Hello, William."

"Hello, is Elizabeth home?" I asked regaining my composure.

"I believe she is around back," she said.

"Okay, thank you," I replied.

Walking around the side of the house, I saw her hanging up clothes to dry. Before I approached her, I leaned against a large tree and watched. The sunlight behind her was highlighting her figure in her light cotton summer dress, and her brown wavy hair was hanging just past shoulder length. As always, her physical beauty struck me. Oblivious to my presence, she glided about with a certain grace and ease. When she had her back to me, I snuck up behind her. I could hear her humming a song, but could not make it out.

"Guess who?" I startled her, and she jumped quickly turning around

"William," she said with much excitement.

She threw her arms around my neck and hugged me. Her soft hair brushed against my face. Knowing we had a moment of privacy, I kissed her and held her tightly against me. Letting her fall back in my arms, I gazed into her eyes.

"I have some good news. I am free tomorrow night."

"Oh Will, that is wonderful news. Won't you come for supper?" she replied.

"I thought you would never ask."

"Elizabeth, you look beautiful."

With a rush of emotion, I pulled her in for one last hug and swung her around gently lifting her feet off the ground.

"I have something for you. Come around front."

She never let go off my hand as I led her to the front porch where I had set down the bag. Undoing the cinch top, I pulled out the cloth bag and opened it.

"Okay, close your eyes and hold out your hands," I said.

I would set something in her arms and then have her guess what it was only then allowing her to open her eyes to see the surprise. She nearly dropped the heavy ham when I placed it in her hands.

"William, this is wonderful. Mum will be so pleased, and Timmy will be excited too. Let's take it all inside and show her," she said.

I gathered the remainder of the gifts and followed her in the front door. It was the first time I had seen her mother smile. Her voice quivered when she thanked me.

"We are so pleased. Won't you come and eat supper with us? We would love to have you," she said.

"Thank you. I would love to," I said not mentioning that Elizabeth had already invited me.

"Well, I am sure you both have much to speak about. Let me put these away," her mother said.

"I could make some tea for us, and we could sit for a while," Elizabeth offered.

"That sounds nice."

"I think so too," she said.

Elizabeth disappeared in the kitchen, and I found a seat. The living room had two chairs, one straight back and another that matched the couch. There was a coal fireplace, the focal point of the room, with tile around the opening and an old wooden mantle. A family picture was on the mantle. I walked over and stood to see who was in the picture. It was of her parents. Her father was in his uniform standing behind her mother with his arms draped over her. Elizabeth entered the room carrying a tray with a china teapot and two cups and saucers. They had an attractive pink floral design on them. She set the tray on a small table in front of the couch that I was sitting on.

"What has caught your attention?" she asked.

"The picture of your parents."

"It was taken about a week before my father was sent to war," she said setting the tea down on a table.

"You must be very proud of him."

"I miss him dearly," she said.

I looked over at her and was concerned knowing my comment had saddened her.

"Let me put on some music, Beth," I said.

I walked over and wound the gramophone. Placing the needle on the record, the soft melody played. Elizabeth walked over and sat on a seat near the table. Lifting the lid off a small matching bowl, she scooped out tea and placed it in a small metal tea infuser. She then placed it in a cup and poured boiling hot water over it. While allowing the tea to steep, she then performed the same careful sequence brewing another cup. Once both cups were complete, she placed each on a saucer and handed one to me.

"Would you like a little milk to soften your tea?" she asked politely.

"Yes, that would be nice," I said fascinated by how much time and effort she put into this treasured British pleasure.

While sipping on the tea, we shared stories about all that had happened since the last time we had spoken. Elizabeth told me about the children at the orphanage, which followed by my sharing stories about life at the base. I spared her the troubling details about our recent bombing raids.

After sitting and talking for over an hour, her mother entered the room. I think it was a subtle clue she needed Elizabeth to help.

"Well, I better get back to the base for chow. What time shall I arrive tomorrow?"

Elizabeth collected the teacups and set them on the tray. "Three o'clock would do nicely," she said. I reached over and took the tray

"Let me help you with these," I said. I proceeded to the kitchen where I set the tray by the sink. Knowing that I may not have an opportunity to kiss her goodbye outside, I reached for her hand and drew her in. Cupping her face in my hands, I felt a rush of passion as we gently kissed. Passion raced through me, and I felt the desire to experience so much more with her. I looked deep into her eyes for a moment and then spoke. "I realize this is all very fast, but I am developing strong feelings for you."

"And I for you darling," she said softly.

She walked me to the front door, and I started the lonely walk back to the base. When I was about half way, a couple of guys went speeding by in a jeep. The driver locked up the brakes and created a huge cloud of dust. Throwing it in reverse and spinning the tires, he backed up to me.

"Going our way soldier?" I recognized them as some of the crewmembers from a bomber called *Liberty Belle*.

"Sure am," I said climbing into the back seat.

As soon as the Jeep was underway, I reached into my shirt pocket and pulled out my pack of cigarettes. I leaned forward. "Care for one?" Both of them took me up on the offer. Reaching into my pocket, I brought out my Zippo lighter and offered them a light. Slouching in the rear seat, I gazed up at the sky and thought about her.

"Here is your palace sir," the driver said as he stopped outside of my quarters.

"Thanks for the chariot ride," I said in reply. The men waved as they drove off. Grabbing a new pack of smokes, I headed to the chow hall. Afterwards, I strolled over to the recreation hall and shot some pool as other members of my crew gambled or enjoyed a game of bowling. I wrapped up the evening with watching a hit movie titled *The Ox-Bow Incident*. Arriving back at my hut, I read from my Bible, said my prayers, and fell asleep thinking of her.

The following morning was a Sunday, so my day started at the chapel. I was welcomed at the door by some crewmembers whom I had not met. Upon entering, I was pleased to see that the seats were full. Proceeding to the front, I found an open spot on a pew and sat down. Chaplain Wimbley moved to the front and started the service by praying a blessing for all of those in attendance. After Pastor Wimbley's prayer, a crewmember led us in several hymns. Our common belief wove a strong bond between us. My mind drifted back to my small country church and the well-being experienced when amongst friends and family. I felt an internal peace sweep over me. A special song had been selected to prepare our hearts for communion. The communion emblems were passed around, and then we sang one additional song before Chaplain Wimbley stepped to the podium. His sermon was built on the greatest commandments: "Thou shalt love the Lord thy God with all thy heart, and with all thy soul, and with all thy mind. This is the first and great commandment. And the second is like unto it, Thou shalt love thy neighbor as thyself." He is an eloquent speaker effortlessly weaving in personal and humorous stories that held our attention as he deposited his key points in our minds. After the sermon, he extended an alter call. Several men went forward and knelt. Others came along side and prayed with them. It was a moving scene to see these battle hardened men showing genuine concern for each other. Each of them knew the pain of separation from friends and families and the stress of going on mission after mission and the worry about which one would either kill or maim him or a friend. They carried a heavy physical and mental burden out of love for their country. When the last prayers had been offered, Chaplain Wimbley asked that a collection be taken. He explained the money would be used to buy presents for the British orphans when they attended the base Christmas party. The men were very generous. After the service, Chaplain Wimbley greeted each of us at the door.

"William, how are you today?" he asked.

"Very well."

"I am hoping to meet Elizabeth sometime," he said.

"I would like that and have been meaning to speak to you about her. Shall we walk there or would you prefer I invite her onto the base?"

"I would enjoy the walk," Chaplain Wimbley said.

"Okay, I will let you know a good time," I said. As it was approaching noon, I headed to the chow hall for lunch. While in line, I spotted Sarge. When he was close enough, I spoke to him.

"Thanks for the goodies. They were very appreciative."

"I am happy to hear that," he said.

After lunch, I saw some of the crew playing a game of baseball on our ballfield. I stopped to watch and saw Pappy knock one deep into centerfield. He was fast and put pressure on second base before he checked up and returned to first base. Watching a game sounded relaxing, so I climbed onto the bleachers and found a seat. Most of the men were rooting for one side or the other not because of friends on the teams, but based upon their wagers. When Pappy's team was well in the lead, I lost interest and walked back to the hut for a nap. I set my Big Ben alarm for a quarter past two so I would have plenty of time to get ready. I could hear the men hollering from the diamond and the occasional crack of the bat and cheering. Drifting off, I took a nap before my alarm roused me.

At 2:30, I stepped off for Elizabeth's house. She was sitting on the front porch when I arrived. Opening the gate, I walked up to the porch and sat beside her. She was dressed in a cotton summer dress with a thin ribbon adorning her hair and short white dress socks and cloth slippers. It was clear she had spent extra time on her appearance.

"Hello dear," she said planting a kiss on my cheek. I stared at her for a moment.

"What is it, Will?"

"I am just thankful to be able to spend this time with you,"

"What have you been busy with today?" she asked.

I told her about the church service. She sat and listened as I spoke of the scriptural passage and retold the highlights of the sermon.

"Hmm, that sounds thought provoking," she said.

"Chaplain Wimbley asked to meet you," I said as we swayed gently back and forth in the swing. Soon the screen door opened, and Timmy came out.

"Hey, Mr. William," he said as he climbed onto my lap.

"What have you been doing today, young man?" I asked.

"Helping around the house and playing out back," he said in response.

"Would you like to see something?" Timmy said looking up at me.

"Sure"

"Come with me," he said taking my hand. He led, around back and proceeded through the gate and to the barn door. He unfastened the latch and stepped inside. Unsure of what he was so eager to show us, Elizabeth and I followed him.

"Stay here and wait for me," he said.

He reappeared holding a tiny yellow baby chick. His hands were cupped over it with only the little fuzzy head showing.

"Oooh, it's so cute," Elizabeth said.

"This morning when I came out, I found two chicks," Timmy said.

I squatted down to see the chick "Have you named it?"

"No, not yet. I better take him back to his Mum so he won't be frightened," Timmy said.

Once Timmy had set the chick back with the hen, we exited the barn.

Elizabeth looked at me. "Would you like to take a walk?"

"Yes, I would," Timmy said.

I laughed. "Me too, Timmy."

"Let me tell Mum," Elizabeth said.

Timmy and I waited outside for her. Once her mother was informed of our plans, we set off down the road toward town. When Timmy saw the orphanage, he pleaded to walk in front of it to holler to his friends. It was warm, and many of the children were in the front playing. When we passed by, several of them hollered to Elizabeth and Timmy. I was surprised to hear some call out my name. When we arrived back at the house, it was near dinnertime.

"Let me see what Mum needs help with," Elizabeth said disappearing into the kitchen. I sat on the couch with Timmy and waited.

It wasn't long before Elizabeth came back in the room. "Timmy and William, you may get washed up for dinner," she said standing in the doorway. The lavatory is down the hallway on the right. "Will you show him, Timmy?" she asked.

"This way, Mr. William."

I watched as Timmy wetted his hands and started for the towel. "Hey, wait a minute. We need to add some soap to that routine," I said in a gentle way. After we both had properly washed up, we walked to the table. The ham was the centerpiece. There were colorful vegetables in multiple steaming bowls and fresh baked bread. It was laid out on the best dishes and considerable time had been spent in preparing it. Mrs. Ward came in carrying drinks, and Elizabeth was right behind her.

"Hello, William, I trust your day has been a good one," she said setting the glasses on the table.

"Yes, it was, but the second half has been the best part."

"Well, we better start before it gets cold," she said.

I stepped to the side of the table, pulled out Mrs. Ward's chair for her, and then helped her as she scooted it up to the table.

"Thank you. It has been some time since I have received such attention," she stated. I then walked around the table and did the same for Elizabeth.

"Thank you, dear," she said. I sat at the head of the table.

"Would you like to carve the ham, William?"

"Yes, I would, but first would it be okay if I offer a blessing?" I asked.

"That would be nice," her mother said.

I reached out and took Elizabeth and Timmy's hands and her mother did the same to complete the circle. My prayer included a request to bless the family and for the men at the airbase. Once done, I carved the ham and the plates were passed around and filled. Conversation was easy, and we had many laughs.

"Would you like some more, Timmy?" Elizabeth asked.

"No, I am about to pop," he said slouching in his seat. We all laughed.

"William, if you and Timmy would like to move to the living room, Mum and I will clear the table," Elizabeth said.

I entertained Timmy by telling him the story of Charlie's first squirrel. At eight o'clock, her mother tucked in Timmy, and since the evening was pleasant, we moved to the front porch swing.

"There is a big base dance coming up, and I was wondering if I might escort you."

"That sounds so exciting," Elizabeth said.

"I also have a favor to ask. Do you think you could speak to Penelope to see if she might come with us?"

"Just the three of us? Do I have to share you?" Elizabeth asked.

"No, you know who else wants to go with us," I said laughing.

"I will be at the orphanage in a few days and will ask her then," she said.

Kissing and quietly talking, we became lost in our own private world. Suspecting that we would be on the board for a mission the next day, I extended my stay as late as I dared. It was about nine o'clock when I headed back to the base. When I arrived, the rest of the crew were getting ready for lights out. I fell into the routine with them and we heard what we knew was coming. We were on the mission board for the next day's raid. I ended my evening lying in bed reading my Bible. I selected Psalms, as I found the rhythmic poetic verses soothing on the evening before a mission. Setting it aside, I enjoyed one last cigarette and then shut off the light.

The Buckeye was back on the line the next day much to our delight. Mission nine was a no ball mission, the name given for a raid sent against V1 rocket sites. The tenth mission before my next three-day pass was to the marshalling yards at Bingen. After the mission, at supper, I noticed many of the original crews we had meet when we arrived at the airfield were gone. The vast majority hadn't completed a tour of duty. The base took in new crews at a rate equal to the amount lost. The huts and their beds were never left empty. As soon as a crew was shot down, their hut was cleared. They know how demoralizing it is for us to come back and see the empty bunks. As a crew, we no longer reached out to new crews, as it would only increase the pain if they were lost. This experience has created an appreciation in me for even the smallest of moments in life. I take nothing for granted.

We didn't know when my next pass would be, and unfortunately Elizabeth had volunteered to help at the orphanage on my first day off. If she backed out, it would leave Penelope overwhelmed. Neither of us were happy about it, but we agreed it would be best if she keep her commitment. We did make plans for Chaplain Wimbley to come over with me sometime, and the third day would be the day of the base dance. Since I was unable to see her the first day, I worked as a volunteer getting the main hangar ready. The Red Cross workers needed help in setting up the stage, as well as a hundred other jobs. The morale was lifted just in preparing for the big event. I put in a solid day's worth of work helping and ended my day eating supper with Chaplain Wimbley. "Would you have time to walk to Elizabeth's house tomorrow?" I asked.

"I believe so. What time were you thinking of?" he asked.

"How does early afternoon sound, say one o'clock?"

"We will plan on it," said Chaplain Wimbley as he patted my hand.

"Excellent, how about we meet at the chapel?" I asked.

"I will see you there," he said. I retired to the hut and felt genuine excitement about the next day's events.

The next morning was strangely quiet. There was no mission or training as the bomber crews were all grounded on account of a low overcast over the target area. I rolled out of bed and made breakfast by eight o'clock. The chow hall was busy with men coming and going. The base was being transformed, and the war started taking a back seat to the much-anticipated party. The scuttlebutt was that Glen Miller and the Air Force Band were coming. At noon, the gossip was proven true when the band arrived on the base. After a few hours of work, I took a break to eat lunch. Sarge found me and took an open seat beside me.

"Exciting day huh, Lieutenant?"

"Yeah. This is going to be some party. I put operation GI bride into play," I said and grinned at Sarge.

"You think it will work?" he asked with a hint of hope in his voice.

"Best chance we have. That's for sure," I replied.

"Well, I gotta be going as Chaplain Wimbley wants to meet Elizabeth," I said.

As planned, we met at the chapel and then walked over to her house. We sat for an hour in the living room talking with Elizabeth and her mother.

"Well, we better get back to the base as I need to make my afternoon rounds," Chaplain Wimbley said.

"William, would you help me carry these dishes to the sink?" Elizabeth asked.

"Sure," I said as I gathered some of them and followed her into the kitchen.

"I didn't need help. I just needed to speak to you privately," she said.

"Penelope said she would go to the dance," Elizabeth said smiling

"That is swell news. Sarge will be so happy," I said setting the dishes in the sink.

"Would it be okay if we arrive tomorrow at 6:00? The dance begins at 7:00."

"That would be fine."

"I will walk back to the base with Chaplain Wimbley and then be back to help around here," I said.

When we entered the living room, Chaplain Wimbley stood.

"Well, shall we head back, William?" he asked.

"Thank you for your hospitality. It was so kind of you to have me in your home. I have a gift for you," he said handing Elizabeth a Bible.

"Oh, how wonderful. Thank you so very much," she said.

"I wrote a few of my favorite verses on a piece of paper and slipped it in there," he said smiling at her. Elizabeth saw us to the door, and we started down the road headed back to the base.

"May I ask you a personal question, William?"

"Certainly."

"What are your plans with Elizabeth?"

"I plan on marrying her if she will accept."

"Splendid. She is a fine young lady, and I am pleased to hear of your honorable intentions." Arriving back at the base, we found it was buzzing with activity. Typically, the frenzy was for an upcoming raid. Today was the first time I had seen it a buzzing for a happy occasion and not in preparation for another bombing raid. Everyone was in a celebratory mood. Before I walked back to Elizabeth's house for the afternoon, I dropped by the mess hall and told Sarge that he needed to rent a tuxedo.

"Well, you ole dog. You mean she agreed to go?" Sarge said.

"That's what I have been told," I said. Sarge came over to me and gave me a bear hug that nearly squeezed the breath out of me.

On the day of the dance, the base was on stand down so that everyone could attend. I headed over to Elizabeth's house early in the morning. She fixed me breakfast, much of which Sarge had supplied. Then it was straight to work. I patched the barn roof, and Elizabeth set into the endless piles of laundry. At noon, we stopped for simple sandwiches and tea in mason jars made cloudy with milk. We sat under the large old tree that is beside their house. We worked until two o'clock, and then I returned to the base so that she could start preparing for the dance. It was awash with patriotism. The stars and stripes and all variations of red, white, and blue were making the base take on the appearance of a town back home during a Fourth of July celebration. The transformation to the main hangar was amazing. Round tables had been set up as well as a removable wooden dance floor. The tables were decorated with white table clothes and patriotic decorations sat in the center, and tiny sparkly silver stars were cast about the tabletop. Streamers and banners were hanging from the rafters and on the walls. On the backside of the dance floor, placed against the rear of the hangar, was a raised platform with seats for the band members. I stood and took it all in. Excitement washed over me when I thought about the evening, and everyone I spoke to was in a festive mood. With no more work left to do in the hangar, I walked outside and sat in the bleachers to watch a ball game. The base cooks had popped popcorn and were passing it out along with hot dogs and lemonade. I saw John sitting in the stands and took a seat beside him. Munching on hot dogs and sipping on lemonade was exactly what we needed. The score was close and thus brought about much cheering and exaggerated silliness in the stands. To our disappointment, our team did not win.

"I told Elizabeth I would pick her up at six o'clock, so I better go get ready."

"Sounds good. Save a dance for me," John said laughing as we left the bleachers.

I walked to the chow hall to finalize plans with Sarge. "They're expecting us to pick them up at six o'clock," I said.

"I'll be done here in about half an hour. How about I swing by your hut at a quarter till?" Sarge asked.

"That should give us plenty of time," I said.

Arriving back at my hut, I pulled out my dress uniform. There was considerable jostling around in our cramped hut as other crewmembers were going through the same routine.

"Hey, Romeo, are we going to finally meet your mystery girl?" Pappy said.

"Yes, she will be there," I said.

"I should hope so with as much time as you have poured into her," Lew said.

"You'll know it was time well spent when you meet her," I said.

"Tell her to save a dance for me," Pappy said.

"Right, I think your girls are being trucked in from London," I said countering their teasing.

Getting back to my preparation, I spent extra time making sure everything was pressed and in place so I would look my best for her. Sarge showed up on time, and we set off for her house. The trip that typically took me 25 minutes to walk took only a few minutes in the Jeep.

"You ready?" I said as we arrived.

"How do I look?" Sarge replied.

I looked him over. "Pretty darn good. That dress uniform is working its magic," I replied. Sarge reached in the back, grabbed two corsages, and handed one to me.

"Why Sarge, I didn't know you felt like that about me," I said.

"Real funny," Sarge said as we climbed out of the Jeep and headed to the front door.

I saw the curtains move and Timmy came out. "Mr. William," he said as he ran and grabbed my hand.

"Hey buddy, how are you?"

"I am fine. Elizabeth said to watch for you. She is getting ready for the dance," Timmy said.

"Timmy this is Sarge," I said.

"Hello, Timmy."

"Pleased to meet you," Timmy said holding out his hand. "Follow me," he said leading the way into the living room. "Elizabeth said you should wait here." He then ran toward the bedrooms announcing our arrival. We sat patiently with our military caps in hand. The late sun was streaming in through the large windows and warming the room. A few minutes later Timmy came back.

"Here they come," he announced.

When Elizabeth first entered the room, Sarge and I both stood. Elizabeth was wearing a cream-colored dress with a row of small pink and red dots sprinkled across the front starting at her right waist angling down to the bottom left side. Her dark brown hair was pulled up into a loose woven bun and loose hair was failing down the sides of her face.

"Well, what do you think?" Elizabeth said as she slowly spun around.

For a moment I didn't think I would be able to speak.

"Darling, you look absolutely breathtaking," I said.

Elizabeth looked down the hall and with her hand at her side motioned for Penelope to join her. I could hear her soft footsteps on the hard wood floor as she came down the hallway. When she entered, I heard Sarge exclaim, "Oh my."

Penelope had on a mid-length light pink skirt with a fuzzy pink sweater. Her white dress shoes and small purse drew it all together. We walked over to our dates and presented them with the corsages. Elizabeth looked into my eyes. "Thank you dear. It's beautiful," she said.

I smiled at her and gave her a quick kiss on her check.

"Well, shall we head to the big event?" Sarge said.

"Mother, we are leaving."

Her mother came down the hall. "Well let's see what our hard work produced," she said sitting on a footstool with her legs folded to the side. The girls modeled their dresses for her. "Very lovely. You men had better watch that others don't cut in during the dances," she said smiling.

"Thank you for everything, Mum," Elizabeth said as she leaned over and placed a kiss on her check.

"Have a wonderful time, dear."

"Bye, Mr. William," Timmy said.

"Take care of your Mum while we are out," I said.

Sarge slowly drove us to the base and stopped at the security gate to show his identification.

"These men bothering you, ladies?" one of the guards asked.

"Not yet, but we will let you know if they get out of hand," Penelope replied.

"Knock it off fellas or no breakfast for you," Sarge shot back smiling at them.

"Don't make any promises you won't keep" the other guard stated.

"You both are a couple of real wise guys," Sarge said chuckling.

"You know we love you, Sarge," one of them said as he opened the gate.

Making our way to the main hangar, we drove on the perimeter track and passed the bombers parked on their hard stands.

"William, which one is yours?" Elizabeth asked.

"I will point her out to you. She is sitting down a bit farther. There she is," I said as *The Buckeye* came into view.

"Sarge, will you stop so we can see her?" Elizabeth asked.

"It looks so intimidating," Penelope said as we came to a stop in front of *The Buckeye*.

Sarge stopped, and we all walked around the bomber as I pointed out the various crew positions. After circling the bomber, Sarge and Penelope started walking back to the jeep. I started after them but noticed Elizabeth was trailing behind us. I turned to wait and was close enough to hear her whisper. "Please take care of him."

"The best one on the field huh, William?" Sarge said as we drove away.

"Yep, that's right. We sure baby her so when we need her best, she will deliver. I should also state that Sarge feeds us the best food to keep us in trim fighting condition."

"Oh boy, if mine is the best, I would hate to taste the bottom of that list," Sarge said laughing. Sarge continued the slow drive around the perimeter track to the hangar. The air was cooling fast with the afternoon sun quickly fading in the sky. Elizabeth snuggled over close to me and sat forward so I could put my arm around her. Looking over at her, I was nearly overcome with passion. I kissed her. Sarge pulled the jeep as close as possible to the hangar, and we helped them out. We walked past a couple of buses that had brought in local British girls who were escorted by chaperones. The huge hangar doors were open, and the light from within was flooding out onto the ramp. As we approached, it was clear that the party had started early. The glitter from the decorations and candle arrangements placed on the tables made it all glow and sparkle. The mood among the men and the decorum created the desired Cinderella feel to the girls.

I leaned over to Sarge. "It doesn't get any better than this," I said.

"You said it, brother," he replied taking hold of my arm and patting me on the back.

A set of straight tables with white table clothes and decorations was along one of the sides of the hangar. They were covered with sandwiches, cookies, chips, cupcakes, and punch, all luxuries that the British hadn't seen in the last few years. We escorted Penelope and Elizabeth deep into the hangar to a table that gave us a good view of the dance floor. The band was playing "In the Mood," a favorite dance song. In the background was Glen Miller, who at times jumped in with his trombone while at other times he played the role of conductor. The floor was hopping with young couples whose energy made the floor vibrate. At the moment, they were jitterbugging with some of the men showing off their solo moves, while others were wildly swinging their girls around. A bawdy muted trumpet jumped in, and a group of girls straightened their shoulders and shuttered across the floor. This brought hoots and hollers from the men in the crowd. Then the brass faded, and the woodwinds came in with the musicians standing and swaying to the music. Some of the dance moves were well known while other dancers were pulling off some impressive improvisation. There was a cleared center section for the best to strut their stuff. One couple would move into and then out of the section with another couple then taking the spotlight. Sarge and I cheered when we saw Little Frankie take center stage. We all stood and clapped to the beat and watched him swing a British girl around to the delight of all who looked on.

When the song wound down, Sarge spoke "Ladies, would you like something to eat?" They looked over at all that was laid out on the tables, but were too modest to make a request.

Seeing their hesitancy, I stepped in. "How about a little of everything including drinks?" I suggested.

"I suppose we could be persuaded to try it all," Penelope said looking over at Elizabeth and giggling.

Sarge and I left the girls at the table and then worked our way across the crowded hangar floor. Loading up two plates and taking two drinks in hand, we made our way back to the table. When we drew close, I could see two fellas had moved into our seats.

"Okay, boys, up and away. These two are escorted," Sarge said in a gruff voice.

"I don't see rings on any fingers," one of them said as he moved closer to Penelope.

I knew that was the wrong thing to say to a guy who had certainly brushed plenty of teeth with his knuckles. Sarge probably invented the knuckle sandwich.

"There are a few things you may want to ponder before we head down this path," Sarge said. With that he leaned down and quietly whispered into the man's ear. I could see a very intimidating street tough look come on Sarge's face that was indicative of the message he undoubtedly spoke. I set the drinks I was carrying on the table just in case this turned ugly.

The man slid his chair back from the table. "Come on, Harvey, let's get something to eat," he said.

"That's sounds like a splendid idea," Sarge said with a smile.

Sarge and I took our seats. The plates were piled with roast beef sandwiches and an assortment of finger foods and cookies.

"You first, sweetheart," I said as I moved the plate towards Elizabeth. Across the table, Sarge was offering up items to Penelope as they sat and shared in a private conversation. I pointed out various friends and commanding officers as we ate the sandwiches and then started into the sweets. The lights were turned low and the band started to play "Smoke Gets in Your Eyes."

"May I have this dance?" I said as I stood.

Elizabeth took my hand, and I led her onto the dance floor. I held her close as we danced. We spoke to other couples on the floor as we passed them while at other times we spoke softly to each other. Elizabeth laid her head on my chest as we moved about the dance floor. When the song faded, we made our way back to the table. Sarge and Penelope were close behind as the band picked up the beat.

"You all about ready to shake and jive?" Sarge asked.

"I am not about to let that fun pass me up," I replied.

"What do you say, Elizabeth?" I asked.

"Lead the way," she said smiling.

The band picked up the tempo with the song "American Patrol," and Sarge and Penelope were ahead of us heading to the dance floor. We followed and soon were part of the mass of dancers. Sarge and Penelope ended up in the center of the floor and put on a good show. After dancing to several more tunes, we sat down to catch our breath and relive the experience through conversation and much laughter. After a few hours of swing songs, the energy slowly drained from the group, and a more relaxed atmosphere pervaded. The size of the crowd had slowly diminished as the men took the party into the local village of Beeston and others disappeared with their dates. The last I had seen of Sarge and Penelope, they were mingling through the remaining crowd. The final dance was "Moonlight Serenade." Taking Elizabeth by the hand, I led her onto the dance floor.

"It seems Sarge and Penelope are enjoying their evening," I said. "Why was she reluctant to let him court her?" I asked.

"Her fiancé was killed in action a little more than a year ago, and the pain nearly broke her," Elizabeth said. We held each other close as we swayed to the music. I stopped, and she looked up at me.

"Darling, what is it?" she said.

"What do you dream of Elizabeth?"

She spoke softly. "A man that loves me and a house full of children."

"I want to give something to you that is dear to me," I said. Reaching to the back of my neck, I undid the clasp on my gold cross necklace.

"Oh no, William, it is too precious," she said.

I didn't hesitate, but reached both arms around her neck and fastened the necklace. Elizabeth took the cross, centered it on the outside of her dress, and then kissed me on my cheek.

I caught my breath and looked into her eyes. "I love you, Beth."

"And I you, dear," she said.

I held her close and softly kissed her as we danced. The song faded away, and although neither of us wanted it to end, the evening was winding down.

"Well, I suppose we should locate Sarge and Penelope," I said. We found them at the entrance to the hangar.

"Sarge, do you think we should take the girls home?"

"Aw, c'mon Dad, how about a few more minutes?" he said smiling at me.

After a slow ride around the perimeter track, we arrived at the main gate. Reaching Elizabeth's house, we walked them to the door and said our goodbyes. On the ride back to the base, Sarge and I were flying high with reliving the evening's events. He dropped me off at my hut.

"Hey, thanks for what you did. I owe you one," Sarge said.

"It was a memorable evening, wasn't it?" I replied

"Best time I have had in a long, long time," Sarge said.

"See you tomorrow," I said as I opened the door and entered the hut. As usual, she was the last thought in my mind before I fell asleep.

The next day the base was again on stand down. Everyone was required to stay on base and assist in cleanup. Pappy informed all of us that we were on the roster to fly a mission the next day. At 3 a.m. the following day, I was awakened by a flashlight shined in my face. After our briefings and preparation, we were shuttled out to *The Buckeye*. We made the final preparations and boarded. The day was overcast with a low cloud layer and plenty of fog.

"It always feels better to have our gal back," Pappy said.

When our time came to taxi off the hardstand, it was nearly impossible to see. While slowly inching the heavy bomber out, Pappy slipped one of the main gear off the side of the hardstand and the tire sank in the soft earth. We were stuck. Adding power was not going to move the overladen bomber and get us back up on to the asphalt surface. Pappy called for a tug, which took some time to make its way around the perimeter track. Once it arrived, the ground crew hooked cables onto the gear and started to slowly pull *The Buckeye* forward. The whole ordeal took forty long minutes, and our squadron had already rallied and were heading across the channel to the target.

"Lew, will you hop out and check the gear?" Pappy said.

Lew unbuckled, pulled off his headset and disembarked. Within a few minutes he was back in his seat.

"No damage, just a little dirt," Lew reported.

"Well men, by now the formation will be well ahead of us. I need to know if you are all willing to make a hard run at catching them. We will be on our own in enemy territory for quite some time," Pappy said.

Everyone agreed to press forward with the mission. Pappy received clearance from the tower and positioned us on the runway. *The Buckeye* shook and bucked, begging to be unleashed on an enemy that threatened the free world. She was bustling with energy like a thoroughbred racehorse just before the gates are opened for a race. When the brakes were released, she lurched forward and started the long takeoff roll. With three quarters of the runway behind her, *The Buckeye* lifted off, and we started our long climb to our altitude of twenty-two thousand feet. We were still climbing when we crossed the channel.

"Okay you wise guys, let's hear from all positons," Pappy said.

We sounded off, and as we had come to expect, we heard "Jack" and shortly thereafter "in the box," from Albert.

"William, get me a good heading to target and work with Jim to determine what power settings we will need in cruise flight to catch them prior to the bombing run."

As we were off our assigned course, I immediately set to work with the E6b Flight Computer and an aeronautical sectional to plot a course and determine a wind correction angle. In under five minutes, I had a course heading and distance to the target.

"Steer for 080 degrees, Pappy, and I calculate with 85% power we will make 180 knots and catch them before they strike the target, but it's going to be close," I said.

Pappy turned the bomber slightly to pick up the heading.

"Jim, calculate the increase fuel burn at 85% power on the engines and let me know if we will have enough to make the return flight home," Pappy said.

Jim checked the performance tables, noted the winds, and then responded, "It will be close, but I believe we can make it Pappy."

"Doesn't sound like we have much choice if we are going to make this work," Pappy replied.

"I see their contrails," Lew said after we had been long over enemy territory. I informed Pappy that the headwinds were stronger than forecasted and that at our present ground speed, we would not catch the formation before they hit the target.

"John, how do you feel about making the bombing run on our own?" Pappy asked.

"Oh, hell yeah. No one wanted to dump our bombs over the countryside with no effect. Let's finish the job," John said as cheers came in from all stations.

"Let's set this up as a solo bombing run then," Pappy said.

When we drew closer to the target area, the familiar black sooty flak could be seen.

"Pappy turn left to 120 degrees to pick up the initial point of the bombing run," I said.

"You ready, John? I am going to hand off the controls to you," Pappy said.

"Yep, everything is dialed in here," John stated as he turned the knobs and worked the Norden Bombsight.

"Looks like they hit short of the primary factory, Pappy. I am going to adjust for a stronger wind," John reported.

"Okay, she's all yours," Pappy said.

John fine-tuned the Norden bombsight, and at the precise moment the bombs were released, he called, "Bombs away." With that, Pappy resumed control and took drastic evasive action to get clear of the flak. I watched as John continued to peer through the sight at the target.

"Boom, boom, boom. Oh man, we clobbered it," John said excitedly for all to hear.

Cheers erupted out around *The Buckeye*. Pappy poured on the power to catch the retreating bombers. A half hour later we finally tucked in to the rear of the huge bomber formation. There were a few brief fighter attacks before we arrived over the channel, but we didn't see any serious damage to any of the bombers. When we landed and disembarked, we were again heralded as heroes for our extra effort. At the debriefing, we described what we saw upon arrival at the target and our bombing results. Later reconnaissance photographic evidence supported our story.

The following day we were off the mission roster. Most of the crew spent the day relaxing at the base playing ball or enjoying the recreation hall. After lunch, Chaplain Wimbley, Sarge, and I went over to Elizabeth's house.

Chapter 12

Tucker turned the page. He looked up at his mom. "That's all there is. It looks like the next few pages are missing. I can see the remnants of paper where they were torn from the journal," he said, as he inspected more closely. He laid the journal down on the coffee table and stared into the fire.

"So what do you think happened to him?" Tucker asked.

"All our old theories are still possible. I don't think we are any closer to answers than when the questions first emerged. Tucker took the picture and looked intently at the couple.

"I feel like I know them, Mom. I want to find him to return the journal," Tucker said.

"I know what you mean," she said.

"There must be some military records. That bomber I rode on must be *The Buckeye*," he said.

"Yes, it must be."

"Maybe he just chose to stop writing for some reason or became separated from the journal," Tucker said.

"Well, we may never know," his mother said.

Tucker didn't want to think of that possibility as he desperately wanted to know the rest of the story and was hoping it would lead to a joyful reunion.

"Mom, the pilot told me about an old man suffering from Alzheimer's disease who came up and repainted the nose art. I wonder if that could have been Sarge. He thought the man had originally painted the nose art. If he is right, then it has to be Sarge. Locating him may be a start in finding answers," Tucker said.

"Is the bomber at the airport all weekend?"

"I was told it was leaving tomorrow. I will go speak to the pilot to see if I can obtain additional information," Tucker said. "That would be a start," his mother said. "Let's discuss it over supper. Are you hungry?"

"Perhaps for something light. How about you?" Tucker said.

"I could make us some salads, and you could broil us some chicken to shred on them," his mother said while rising from the couch.

"That's a deal," Tucker said. Moving to the kitchen they prepared the meal and then moved back into the living room.

On Monday morning after eating breakfast with his mother, Tucker headed back to work. As usual, there was a flurry of activity all focused on printing the best newspaper by the day's deadline. With the journal in hand, Tucker sat outside Mr. Timmons office until he had finished a telephone call. Gently knocking on the door, he entered the office.

"Good Morning, Mr. Timmons," Tucker said.

Mr. Timmons looked up. "Is there something I can assist you with?"

True to his demeanor, he didn't seem to be in good spirits. Tucker began explaining the assignment and how he found the journal. He handed him the picture and began telling him the story about William. Mr. Timmons sat in silence listening. Mr. Timmons's expressions rose and fell with each twist in the story. He patiently let Tucker describe in detail the contents and only interrupted for clarification. He even let his telephone ring without answering it. When Tucker finished, Mr. Timmons leaned back in his oak roll around chair. Turning from Tucker, he gazed out the window. Finally swiveling back around to face Tucker, he spoke.

"You realize this has the ingredients for something much bigger than just a small story in the back pages of *The Daily Reporter*," he said.

"I was hoping you would say that," Tucker said.

"Here is how we will play this: I want you to try to find the author and return the journal to him. We will run a new story every few days that carries the reader along with your attempts. Of course, your first task is an initial article that packs a real punch and draws the reader into the drama. I am thinking this will generate several stories. The first will be how you found the journal and of you and your mother reading it, followed by one that tells the story that is in the journal, and the final one or ones will be your journey to return it to him. Remember, you are part of the story so weave in your thoughts and pour your heart into it. This is more of an emotional story, than a documentary. The reader must feel what you experience. *The Daily* will cover your expenses; just keep me abreast of what is needed. I am going to give you the rein on this one, and one thing is for sure." He paused for a moment and then looked Tucker in the eyes. "We are about to expose your talents or the lack thereof. Every good reporter can trace his breakout moment back to an opportunity that catapulted him into the spotlight. This story has the key ingredients—suspense, drama, and an emotional hook. The gamble I am taking is not in the story as it is remarkable. The gamble is on letting you manage this assignment and writing the articles. I am going to speak honestly with you: if you weren't already imbedded in the story, I would give the assignment to a more seasoned reporter. Doing so would increase the possibility that we would wring every bit of success out of it."

"I understand," Tucker said. As Mr. Timmons continued to explain, Tucker became more aware of the possibilities.

"Like I was saying, we will try to make a big splash with your first article, and it will be on the front page tomorrow.

Your immediate challenge is to have your first piece ready by today's deadline. After the first two articles, I want you to start the search to unravel the mystery. Your ongoing challenge will be to provide well-written, timely articles so that you build and hold readers over a sustained period of time." Tucker listened intently. "If we are successful, your articles will gain momentum and the attention of the Associated Press, which will grow your readership beyond just *The Daily*." Like powerful waves coming in on a beach, a wide variety of emotions swept over Tucker while he listened. He knew that Mr. Timmons could care less about the people in the story. His concern for others had been sacrificed on the altar of success many years ago. Fortunately for Tucker, that fact would not slow him down in his pursuit of getting the journal back to William.

"Bridget, would you come in my office?" Mr. Timmons barked out. She appeared at the office door. "Please give Mr. Tucker an advance of fifty dollars for expenses. That should cover the short-term need, and if this leads further, *The Daily* will cover the cost. You have a sizable challenge before you Tucker. I would suggest you get started as I imagine this is going to call on all of your unpolished talents to pull it off. If greatness is in you, this will find it."

Tucker was intimidated, but at the same time extremely excited. Sitting at his desk, his head was still spinning as he mentally began processing the last thirty minutes. He pushed aside the fear, pulled out a sheet of white paper, and instantly set into adding black text to the page. The words poured onto the page, and by lunch, a rough draft was complete. He spelled out in detail the emotions and feelings that had been bottled up in him over the weekend. Grabbing the draft, he stepped out to the local diner for lunch and carefully read the text. Using his pencil, he methodically scratched and added to the copy. Once he had finished his lunch and the edits, he looked out the window and smiled. Back at the office, he returned to his desk and set to typing up the corrected copy.

"Well, here goes," he softly said to himself.

He took a deep breath, and at two o'clock, he found himself again knocking on Mr. Timmons's office door.

"Where are you regarding the article? We have a deadline to meet," Mr. Timmons stated, as Tucker walked into his office.

"I have a rough draft sir," Tucker stated and handed him the copy.

Mr. Timmons slid his glasses down from his forehead and took the copy, laid it on his desk, and started reading. His pencil was striking and adding as he read the article. Tucker's heart sank as he imagined the disappointment that was to follow the editing session. Once finished, Mr. Timmons looked up.

"Not bad, but needs some work. Make the changes and bring me another copy for final approval."

Tucker knew this was high praise and instantly his spirits were lifted. After another hour, he had retyped the article and was back in front of Mr. Timmons. When he finished reading the article for the second time, Tucker could have sworn he noticed a slight grin on Mr. Timmons's face.

"With any luck, the story will catch like a grass fire on a windy day. Submit it for print. They are expecting it." Tucker was grinning as he left the office. He turned it in and then walked back to his desk. Picking up the telephone, he dialed his mother and told her what had transpired.

"That is wonderful news! I am so proud of you," she said.

"Thanks, Mom. Tomorrow I will write the second story, and then I will attempt to unravel the mystery. I plan on trying to find the man whom we believe to be Sarge," Tucker stated. Once he was off the telephone, he stopped by Bridget's desk and informed her that he was headed to the airport.

Walking into the terminal, he looked out at the apron and saw that the propellers were spinning on *The Buckeye.* He watched as Bob marshalled them out of their tie down area and saluted as they headed toward the runway. Tucker had just missed them and had no idea where they were headed. He envisioned a long drive to some distant airport, which would cost him time and result in a delay between his articles. Standing at one of the large picture windows, he stared as *The Buckeye* lined up for takeoff on the runway. It was hard to believe that the bomber he was looking at was the one William had written about so many years ago. The stories the bomber could tell if she could only talk. Once Bob made his way into the terminal building, Tucker approached him. "Hello, Bob," he said. "Hey, how you been, Tucker?" Bob said warmly.

"I've been better. I needed to speak to the pilot."

"Well, that's unfortunate," Bob replied

"I would appreciate it if you could tell me where they are going as it looks like I will be heading there too," Tucker said.

"I will do one better than that," Bob said as he made his way over to the radio. "Lib 177, this is Mitchum Field," Bob said.

They listened intently before he made the same call again, but still no reply.

"Most likely they filed an IFR flight plan and have already changed frequencies. Let me make a telephone call to the FAA to see if they will allow them to change back to our airport radio frequency," he said. Bob picked up the telephone and placed a call to the FAA. Shortly thereafter, Tucker heard the pilot on the radio "Mitchum Field this is Liberator 177." A smile flashed on Bob's face as he reached for the radio microphone.

"Liberator 177, this is Mitchum Field. A man here needs some information from you," Bob replied and handed the microphone to Tucker. He suffered momentarily from microphone phobia, but finally stumbled through his request.

"The airport was in northern Tennessee. Give us a minute. We need to pull out an aeronautical chart to find the name," the pilot replied. Tucker had a pencil and paper ready. A few minutes later the pilot called them again.

"Mitchum Field this is Lib 177. The airport name is Peach Tree. It's in the northwest area of Tennessee. The associated city is Kingston."

"Thanks for the help Lib 177 and safe journeys," Bob said as he set the microphone down. Walking over to a huge aeronautical chart of the United States, he took a string on the map that had one end anchored on Mitchum Field and stretched it to Peach Tree Airport. Looks like it would be about a 400 mile drive or about 8 hours one way."

"Thanks for the help, Bob. I sure appreciate it. I have a long drive ahead of me tomorrow, so I better get going," Tucker said as he headed for the door. He stopped briefly by the newspaper office to explain that he was heading to Tennessee and then walked over to the library to get as much information as he could about anyone who lived in the Kingston area with the initials B.L.M. It was an old limestone building built with a Carnegie foundation grant. To impart a feeling of awe, it had two impressive white pillars and a large set of stairs leading up to the oversized oak door. The door was trimmed with brass hinges and brass door handles that over the years had tarnished. Tucker pulled back on the heavy door and entered. Finding Ms. Simms, the librarian, he explained that he needed to locate a man in the Kingston, Tennessee, area with the initials of B.L.M. She provided Tucker with telephone numbers, addresses, and a series of maps. In the end he had five leads. Walking back to his apartment, he planned the trip, and knowing he had a long drive with an early departure, he went to bed early. Well before the sun was on the horizon, he was in his truck headed south to Tennessee. If his calculations were correct, he should arrive at Kingston around noon. It was a long trip with a lot of time to think. His only entertainment came from the trucks AM radio. Periodically, he broke the monotony by digging into his snacks or enjoying some of the coffee from his thermos. He spent considerable time thinking about what he would ask if he found the man who repainted the nose art and what riddles he could solve if the man turned out to be Sarge. Even if he found the man, he wasn't sure he would remember anything as his disease was most likely a real obstacle to communicating with him. He ended up in Kingston a little ahead of schedule. Locating a telephone booth, he started calling the numbers he had been given. Dialing the first three numbers, he was successful in speaking to someone and eliminating him from the list. The fourth number he called was for a Bert Manning. It rang a few times, and then he heard a recorded message that the number was no longer in service. The fifth call was answered and eliminated.

"Now what?" Tucker said to himself.

He realized that in his rush to find answers, he had made a mistake: it would have been best to call the numbers before he had made the eight hour drive. Determined to find him, he considered the possibilities. After thinking, it occurred to him that the elderly man may be unable to live by himself unassisted and perhaps had moved in with a family member, and that may be why the number for Bert Manning was no longer in service. Looking at the list, he took the telephone book and started calling people who shared the last name Manning. On the third call, a woman answered the telephone. As he had done on the other calls, Tucker briefly explained he was a newspaper reporter searching for a man who had the initials B.L.M and had fought in the air war over Europe.

"You are talking about my father-in-law," she said.

"Okay, may I speak to him?" Tucker asked.

"At the moment, he is sleeping, but he should be up this afternoon," she said.

"Would it be possible for me to come by sometime this afternoon and ask him some questions?" Tucker asked.

"My husband will be home at four o'clock. It would be best if you waited until then. Would you be able to come over at that time?" she asked.

"Yes, I can do that," Tucker said.

She supplied their address and directions, and Tucker found himself with a few hours before the meeting. Driving around town, he located the city park.

"Looks like a place to stretch my legs and eat lunch," Tucker said to himself. He found a shelter that overlooked a shallow pond. Once he finished eating, he took a leisurely walk around the park and then back to the shelter where he started writing the beginning of his second article. A little before four o'clock, he returned to his truck and drove to the address she had given him. It only took him ten minutes to arrive at the house.

"Well here goes," Tucker said to himself as he grabbed the journal, a small pad of paper, and exited his truck. He desperately hoped that each step he took toward the house was bringing him closer to the questions that he sought. Stepping up to the door, Tucker gently knocked. A man who looked to be in his thirties opened the door.

"Hello. My name is Tucker McQueen," he said.

"Pleased to meet you. I am David Manning. My wife said you would be stopping by to speak to my father. Please come in."

"Thank you," Tucker took a few minutes to explain to David why he wanted to speak to his father.

"That is an amazing story, but as you know, my father is not well. He is suffering from the later stages of Alzheimer's. What exact piece of information do you need?" David asked.

"Well, I know the author is from Indiana, but I don't know the city," Tucker said.

"I understand. Perhaps Dad will know. Some days are better than others are. We may not get the answers you are after, but we can try."

Tucker followed David down a hallway to the living room. An old man with gray thinning hair was sitting slouched in a high backed padded chair. It was placed in front of a window that allowed the sunshine to warm him and provided a view outside. The man was asleep with his chin resting on his chest. He was wearing a plaid shirt, blue jeans, and white cotton socks with house slippers.

"Please have a seat, Mr. McQueen." David stopped in front of his father and knelt. "Dad, we have a visitor," he said as he gently shook his father's shoulder.

The old man's eyes slowly fluttered open. He looked blankly at his son. "You're my son," he said.

"Remember, Dad, I told you that a man was coming by to ask you a few questions." The old man gazed at Tucker. "This is Tucker McQueen."

Tucker rose from his seat and walked over to shake his hand. The old man looked at his hand, then reached out, and limply shook it. Tucker knelt down beside him. "Mr. Manning, did you serve in the 392 heavy bombardment group?"

He stared at his lips as Tucker spoke, but he didn't appear to completely comprehend what he was being asked.

"I know that much is true," David said.

Tucker reached into his inner jacket pocket and pulled out the journal. Bert's eyes followed his hand and stared at the journal. Tucker placed the journal in his hands.

"Did you know a man named William Pritchet?" Tucker asked. The old man's gaze dropped down to the journal he held in his hands. Slowly he ran his finger across the gold embossed letters. "William," he stated, and a tear started down the old man's weathered face.

"Yes, that's right, William. Did you know him?" Tucker asked. He felt a rush of adrenaline as he waited for the answer.

Without looking up, the old man stated, "Friend. I miss him."

"Dad, do you know where he lived in Indiana?" David asked. "What city did he live in?"

His father stared at him. "You're my son," he said as a smile returned to his face. The old man's wrinkled hands were slowly caressing the journal.

"Do you think my father was friends with the author of the journal?" he asked.

"Yes, the author only calls him Sarge in the journal, but a man with the initials B.L.M. was credited with painting the original artwork."

"I wish that you could have spoken to him prior to his illness as he may have been able to provide valuable information," David said.

"Does your father have any pictures from the war?" Tucker asked.

"Come to think of it, he has a shoe box stored under his bed that holds his war memories. I just saw it when we moved him here with us a few months ago. Excuse me for a minute, and I will go get it," David said. Tucker looked over at Bert who had his chin resting on his chest and had fallen back to sleep.

He returned with a well-worn shoebox that was tied shut with a piece of white string. David loosened the string and then lifted the tattered lid. There were ribbons, patches, and a stack of black and white photographs. David picked them up and placed them in Tucker's hands. A rubber band that was so old it had become sticky and brittle bound them together. Tucker literally caught his breath. The top picture was of William and Elizabeth standing next to another man and woman.

"Well that solves it. I am right about your father being the man William refers to as Sarge. Tucker pointed to William in the picture."

"This is the author of the journal."

"The other man is my father," David stated.

"What is your mother's first name?" Tucker asked wondering why he hadn't thought of it earlier.

"Penelope. She passed away a few years ago," David said.

"She was also spoken of in the journal. William and Elizabeth arranged the first date for your parents," Tucker said.

Working through the stack, Tucker saw for the first time pictures of the airbase, Nissen huts, and William's crew. Near the end of the stack, he stopped on a picture of William, Elizabeth, Sarge, and Penelope at the base dance. Tucker noted the dresses that William had described down to the finest detail in the journal. It was exactly as he had described them so many years ago. The couples were all smiles.

"This was taken at a base dance and was the first date your father had with your mother," Tucker said showing the picture to David. "He had wanted to go out with her for some time. William asked his girlfriend Elizabeth, who was best friends with your mother, if she would be willing to go to the dance with your father. It was a double date. Your father and William were good friends. In fact, he speaks about him often in the journal. They were always cutting up," Tucker said.

Tucker handed the pictures back to David. The box had other personal information in it that they did not disturb out of respect for his father. Some of them looked to be old love letters from Penelope.

"I want to thank you for your kindness and letting me speak to your father," Tucker stated as he stood. David rose, and they made their way to the door.

"Please let me know if you find any more information. Do you know where you are going to turn next?" David asked.

"After I write an article about this new information, I plan on researching military records too as I still need to find out what city he lived in."

"Well, best of luck in your search. Here is my address. Please send me copies of your articles," David said.

"I certainly will." On the way home, Tucker spent his time divided between mentally composing the article he had started writing and thinking about where the next piece of the puzzle lay. The library was on his list again as he had no idea what military records might exist or how to obtain them. It was going on one o'clock in the morning by the time Tucker lay down at his apartment. Physically, he was exhausted but his mind was still working on everything that needed to be done tomorrow, it took a while to unwind, but his bed and feather tick pillow worked their magic, and he finally fell asleep.

Tucker was up early the next morning as he felt anxious about the second article deadline. He set his aluminum coffee pot on the stove to brew as he proceeded to get ready for work. The smell of coffee permeated his apartment when he stepped out of the shower. Once dressed, he filled his thermos and headed to the office. Someone had placed yesterday's paper on his desk. He was pleased to see a very catchy photograph of *The Buckeye* on the front page with his article. The article finished on page five with additional pictures of Tucker exploring *The Buckeye* and one of the journal. On the top of the paper was a note from Mr. Timmons. "See me when you arrive." Tucker picked up the note and headed to his office. The door was open, so Tucker lightly knocked and entered.

"Good news, Tucker. The article caught the attention of several of the larger newspapers. They picked your story up from the AP newswire. Where are you on the next story?" he asked.

"I started on it yesterday and should wrap it up this afternoon," Tucker said. He continued by telling him of his meeting with Sarge. Mr. Timmons sat and listened intently.

"I'll expect a rough draft by one o'clock," he said.

The rest of the morning Tucker was busy finishing the article. Bridget grabbed him a sandwich from the diner, and he worked through lunch. As promised, at a little before one o'clock, he set a draft before Mr. Timmons. He made several editorial comments and then handed it back to Tucker.

"Make the changes and then submit it for print. What's your next move?" Mr. Timmons asked.

"I think I can find his home town or perhaps his address in military records. I need to go back to the library to see if Ms. Simms can help. It took Tucker another hour to edit and retype the story. It was thirty minutes past two when he finished and submitted it for print. Grabbing his cap off his desk, he headed out the door to the library. When he entered, Tucker saw Ms.

Simms re-shelving books. He walked to the reference desk and stood. She heard him approach and turned to speak to him.

"Hello, Tucker, I read your story in the paper yesterday. It was the talk of the town. It stirred the imagination among our patrons as I overheard several of them talking about it. Was your trip yesterday worthwhile?" she said.

"I will let you read about it in the paper," he said winking at her.

"Oh, is that the way I get treated?" she said bantering back. She stepped down off the ladder. "How may I help you today?"

"I am looking for military records that might provide me with answers."

"Hmmm. Well let me start digging," she said. You can wait here or browse books if you like. This may take a minute." Tucker searched for books about bomber bases in England and about the Consolidated B-24 Liberator. He was reading about the B-24 when she returned.

"You ready for another road trip?" she said as she slid a piece of paper before him. "The Army Air Force military records you are searching for are at the national records files located in College Park, Maryland, in military archives. They will have a copy of the Missing Air Crew Report or MACR. That was the document filed when a crew failed to return from a mission and will have next of kin information. If they have one for them, then ask for the…" she hesitated. "For the individual deceased personnel files. They contain reports written by the Army personnel who scoured Germany after the

251

war to exhume the bodies of our men. She then pulled out an atlas and calculated the trip to be about 350 miles. Well you could send for the records in the mail, but I assume that would take way too long," Ms. Simms stated.

"Yep. I don't have the time to wait. May I have the information you have written down?" he said.

"Certainly, and check out the atlas and books if you want."

"Okay," Tucker said carrying the books to the checkout desk.

"Good luck. Be careful on the road and call me if you need any research assistance when you arrive. I will eat my lunch in the library tomorrow so you can reach me at any time," she said.

"Thank you. That is very kind of you."

Tucker checked out the books and dropped by the office just long enough to tell Mr. Timmons of his plans. That evening he called his mother and told her he had met Sarge. She sat in silence amazed that he was able to find him and wanted to hear everything he could remember about the meeting. Once he had finished packing for his trip, he started reading the library books. Knowing he had another long drive the next day, Tucker turned in early. Rising at 5 A.M. to get an early start on the drive, Tucker thought of the times that William and his crew were awakened in the early morning hours. Setting his snacks and coffee beside him on the front seat, Tucker started his truck and headed east. The journey was somewhat of a blur as one small city looked much like the next. A few miles outside the city, he pulled over to take a closer look at his map and the detailed directions Ms. Simms had provided. Following them, he found himself in front of a federal building that was built for function with little thought being given to aesthetics. Walking to the front door, he wondered what additional secrets the documents inside might uncover. Tucker walked straight to the reference desk to ask for assistance. A man in dress slacks and a cardigan sweater looked up.

"How may I help you, sir?" he said.

"Hello, I am looking for information about a man who served in the Army Air Force during World War Two," Tucker said. "I want to know if there is a Missing Aircrew Report for the crew," Tucker stated.

"Do you have his military identification number?"

"No, I am afraid I don't have that information."

"Okay, what information do you have?"

"Well, his name is William Alan Pritchet and he was in the 392nd Heavy Bombardment Group, and I know he lived somewhere in Indiana," Tucker stated. The man took down the information.

"I should be able to find the MACR, but it may take a bit longer for me to locate the file as I will first need to find his military identification number. If you would like to have a seat at that table, I will bring anything I find to you." Tucker walked over and sat down at a long oak table to wait. About fifteen minutes later, his heart sank when he saw the man walking back with a folder. Tucker knew there was only reason that the man would have a file: William's crew had been shot down. How could that be—*The Buckeye* was still flying? Tucker rebounded quickly realizing it was still possible William had parachuted out and survived the war, but something nagging inside him made him feel he was just avoiding the truth. The man set the file on the table in front of Tucker.

"Here is the Missing Aircrew Report that you requested. When you are done with it, please return it to me," he said.

Tucker took a deep breath and then opened the tattered folder. The papers inside were yellowed from age. At the top of the original missing aircrew report was the aircraft identification number. The crew had flown their final mission on *Ole Number 060* and had not returned from the flight. That explained how *The Buckeye* had survived the war with the hidden journal. The mission was a long one back to Brunswick, Germany, and they were targeting . Flak had been heavy as well as fighter opposition. *Ole Number 060* was flying at the back of the formation. The bomber was attacked from the rear by a single engine enemy aircraft and then started it into a spin. Eyewitness accounts stated it had recovered from the spin but still had smoke pouring out of one of the engines. That was the last any crewmember had seen of them as the formation quickly outran the stricken bomber. They were left alone to fend for themselves. Tucker knew the B-24 was never meant to fight one-on-one battles with nimble speedy fighters. They depended upon the enormous firepower of the formation and their little friends to protect them. The report listed the names of crewmembers who were on board. They were all listed Jack, Albert, John, and William Pritchet, as well as many more details including the briefing information, time of departure, temperature, and other information. Turning to the second page he came to the next of kin information. Scanning the list he came to William's name and read "Lyle Pritchet, Rural Route 16, Box 232, Lena, Indiana." "Lena," Tucker said to himself unsure of where that was in Indiana. Tucker took down all of the information and then closed the file. Finished with the file, he returned it to the archivist.

"Did you find what you were looking for?" he asked.

"Yes, I did, but I was hoping his crew had survived the war. This seems to point in the opposite direction," Tucker said.

"A Missing Air Crew Report doesn't necessarily mean all of the crew were lost. It is possible that they parachuted out and became prisoners of war," he said.

"Yes, I suppose that could be," Tucker said with hope reemerging. "Do you know how I could find out what happened to them?" Tucker asked.

"I would suggest we look to see if there is an Individual Deceased Personal File for any of them," the archivist said.

"Yes, a librarian back home suggested that. What information would it contain?" Tucker asked.

"American airman who were killed in action would have been buried by the Germans. When the war was over, the War Graves Commission was charged with quickly removing all American soldiers from German soil. The form was completed when the bodies were exhumed. The families were then contacted and given the choice of having their boys returned to them for burial or moved to a national cemetery in Europe," he said. "It would contain all information related to exhuming the bodies from Germany and how they were identified. Shall I go review the records to see if I can find a file for any of the crew?" he said.

"Yes, would you please?" Tucker said.

"This may take a bit."

While waiting at the table, Tucker started working on his next story for the newspaper. He had a good start on it when the man came back to his table. Tucker was happy to see his hands were empty. "There were no such files," he said.

"That is a bit of good news. Thank you," Tucker said. With the information collected, he started his long journey home. He passed the time by mentally constructing the remaining portions of his next story. There was still hope that William had bailed out or perhaps Pappy had successfully crashed landed in a neutral country where they were interred for the remainder of the war. All hope was not lost. When he arrived back in Mitchum, Tucker stopped by his apartment, grabbed a change of clothes, and then drove to his mother's house. Pulling down the driveway, he could smell leaves burning, a familiar sign of the fall time. A soft inviting glow could be seen in the windows. So that he wouldn't startle her, Tucker lightly tapped on the horn when he was close to the house. He watched the front door to see his mother look out. After such a long drive, he was happy to be home. He walked to the front door and on into the house as his mother held it open for him.

"Well, this is a pleasant surprise, and your timing is perfect as supper is just about finished," she said.

"That sounds good. I am starving," Tucker said. Entering the house, he could smell a wonderful aroma wafting from the kitchen. "That smells delicious. What are you fixing?"

"Fried chicken with mashed potatoes, corn, and I am making some chicken gravy. I was tired of frozen dinners," she said.

"Sounds like I came on the right evening," Tucker replied.

"It should be ready in about ten minutes," she said.

"That should give me time to get cleaned up," Tucker said. Once he had washed up, he entered the kitchen and started setting plates and silverware on the table. Sitting down, he told his mother about his long drive and the new information he had uncovered.

"So you are still uncertain what happened to them?" she said.

"Yes, I still hope that they made it through the war," Tucker said as he filled his plate. "The most important piece of information that I obtained was his next of kin information. I now know that he lived in Lena, Indiana," he said.

"So what do you have planned for the next few days?" she asked.

"Tomorrow, I will finish the article about this trip. In the afternoon, I will visit the library to gather information needed to plan my trip to Lena."

After supper, Tucker turned in early as he knew another early morning awaited him.

The next morning, Tucker was eager to start writing the article as he felt the familiar anxiety building within him that only receded when he put his thoughts on paper. Arriving at work, yesterday's paper had again been set on his desk. His article was again on the front page. A note from Mr. Timmons was lying on it. Tucker grabbed the note and headed to Mr. Timmons's office.

"Mr. Timmons, do you have time to talk? I would like to provide you with an update," Tucker said as he stood just outside his office.

"Yes, come in, Tucker," he said. He appeared in a better mood than usual. "Before you start, I am pleased to tell you that your stories are appearing in many renowned newspapers across the country. You have piqued the curiosity of many people and have a large following."

Tucker felt a sense of deep satisfaction in knowing that so many people were on this journey with him. It was more than just personal pride. He had a growing sense that he was honoring the crew by telling their story and bringing attention to the sacrifices they had made for the country they loved. He took a few minutes and retold the details of his journey to Maryland and the new information he had obtained.

"Where are you on the third article?" Mr. Timmons asked.

"I have a good start and should be able to get it typed and submitted to you late this afternoon," he replied.

"Well, I won't keep you from your work," Mr. Timmons said.

Tucker had mentally worked out the remaining portions of the story in his mind on the drive home, which resulted in it quickly pouring out onto the paper. At eleven o'clock, hunger kicked in, and he took a break and headed to the diner for a bite to eat. He was starting to become somewhat of a local celebrity with people at the diner, who questioned him about the fate of the crew. At two o'clock, he had a rough draft ready for review and approached Mr. Timmons. He looked it over and scribbled a few editorial comments on it. Once corrected, Tucker delivered it to Mr. Timmons who proofed it and directed him to submit it for publication. Tucker dropped it off and then headed for the library. Ms. Simms spotted him coming up the steps and met him at the door.

"Hello Tucker, what bit of information are you after today?" she said.

"I need to find out where Lena, Indiana, is located," he said as they made their way to the reference desk.

Ms. Simms flipped through several maps until she pulled out one of Indiana. Once she located Lena on the map, she dug deeper and came up with the location of the home. "Here is where William Pritchet lived in 1944," she said pleased that her talents were contributing to the story. She would get a real surprise with the next story to hit the newspaper as Tucker planned to give her credit for all of the assistance she had provided to him.

"This is likely to be my last trip," he said.

Tucker wrote down some driving directions and then drew a simple map showing the location of the house in Lena. It was a difficult night's sleep as Tucker struggled to turn off his thoughts. He woke up at 4:00 AM and couldn't go back to sleep, so he decided to get up an hour early. Compared to his other trips, this would be his shortest one, at only five hours one way, but he had a feeling it would seem much longer as he was anxious to arrive. Once dressed, he brewed a cup of hot coffee, prepared a bowl of oatmeal with brown sugar, coarsely ground peanuts and added milk. With breakfast finished, he grabbed his briefcase, the journal, and headed to his truck. It was hard to imagine that in a few hours he might meet William. Each hour seemed to pass as slowly as two on a normal day. Tucker finally passed by Indianapolis and knew that he was a little more than an hour away. He thought about how many years had passed since the journal was given to William by his mother and father and of the amazing journey it had taken only to have him taking it back to Lena so many years later. Turning off the paved highway onto a dusty gravel road, he drove deep into the rural countryside. Tucker wondered how many times William had looked at these same sites. The road snaked through wooded areas and then opened up with farm fields on both sides. Rounding a corner, he saw an old one-lane bridge ahead. The high arched bridge prevented him from seeing if anyone was starting up the other side. He honked to alert anyone coming over from the other side that he was crossing. Looking off to his left, he could see he was passing over a railroad track that stretched for miles in both directions. He stopped at the top of the bridge and looked out over the small Midwestern town that lay before him. "Lena," he said to himself. To his right, he could see a small country store with a few cars pulled up in front and a round Texaco sign above a single gas pump. Beyond the store, he saw the white steeple of a church. Directly across the road from the store was a two-story house with a modest front porch. Behind the house was a detached garage. Tucker could feel adrenaline rush into his system. He tried to push down the nervous excitement that he felt. So this was it. The farm that he had read about and imagined so many times in his mind. Driving down off the bridge, he made an immediate left hand turn and in a few hundred feet pulled into the driveway. He took a moment to take a closer look at the house. An old wooden swing was hanging on the front porch. He reached over and grabbed his pad of paper, the journal, and exited his truck. Walking up the steps to the porch, he gently knocked on the front door. Footsteps drew near the door, and he saw the curtain pushed aside before an elderly woman opened the door.

"Hello, my name is Tucker McQueen, and I am looking for a William Pritchet." The elderly woman stared in silence and then took hold of the door to steady herself.

"Lyle," she said in the loudest voice she could muster.

Tucker wanted to reach out to steady her but hesitated as he didn't want to frighten her. "Ma'am, are you okay?" he asked genuinely concerned.

Her husband came as quickly as an old man could. "What is it, dear?" he said gently.

"I need to sit down," she said softly.

Tucker watched as he helped her to the couch. Once he had taken care of her, he returned to the door.

"Is there something I can do for you, son?"

"I am looking for William Pritchet," Tucker said.

"He is my son," the old man stated.

"I am trying to find him so that I can give this to him," Tucker said holding out the journal.

"Oh my, where did you get that?" the old man asked reaching for the journal. "He was our eldest son and never returned from World War Two. This was a present I gave him when he left for the war," the old man said. "My name is Lyle Pritchet. Would you like to come in?" he said.

"Thank you," Tucker said as he removed his hat and entered the front door. The woman he had spoken to was no longer sitting on the couch. Tucker followed the old man as he moved slowly to the kitchen.

"Have a seat at the table, and I will get us some coffee," he said.

Tucker watched him disappear into the kitchen and could hear the clinking of coffee mugs. Looking around, he saw simple decorations and pictures of family sitting on top of an antique dark brown buffet. The decor had not been updated in years. Gazing out the window, he could see the old country store. There were hushed voices in the kitchen, and then both Lyle and his wife came back in the room with coffee mugs and an old aluminum coffee pot.

"Tucker this is my wife, Mary," the old man said politely.

"I am pleased to meet you, ma'am, and I am so sorry that I upset you," Tucker said hoping she would accept his sincere apology. She looked at him and smiled.

"William was never found and returned to us," Lyle said. "We would like you to tell us the entire story of how you came into possession of his journal. He was listed as missing in action and the War Department was never able to find him. A year later, they declared him killed in action." As Lyle spoke, Mary was daubing her eyes with an old, white, delicate handkerchief. The emotional wound had never healed.

Clearing her throat, Mary spoke. "Perhaps we could gain some measure of closure if he were brought home," she had to stop, as her emotions took control, and she struggled to speak. Lyle reached out and took her hand.

"I am so sorry. Perhaps I should go," Tucker said.

"No. Please stay and tell us about our William," Mary said.

Starting from the beginning, Tucker explained his accident on the bomber that led to the discovery of the journal, how he and his mother started reading the journal to try to discover information about the owner, and then how he set out to return it. He finished by explaining that he was in the middle of writing a series of articles about his attempts to return it to

William. The two sat in silence and listened. He told them some of the contents in the journal, but spared many details as he wished to avoid the pain he knew was just below the surface and could emerge with any careless comment.

"Although I never met him, my mother and I came to admire and respect him," Tucker said.

Lyle spoke up. "Thank you for bringing it to us." They sat and talked for another hour, and Tucker learned far more about William than he had read in the journal. Mary retrieved pictures, and he sat for over an hour and listened to funny stories and how blessed they felt to have him as a son.

"He was such a cheerful lad always willing to lend a hand to lighten another's load," Mary said. At times they were all laughing at something silly William had said while just a small boy, and then just as suddenly their emotions would swing the opposite direction with a story of deep loss. Tucker felt a bond with them, and he in return believed they felt the same. At the end of the conversation, Mary reached out and patted his hand.

"We are so grateful for what you have done," she said smiling through the teary eyes.

"Would you like to see the farm and hear more stories?" Lyle said.

"Yes, I would," Tucker stated.

Lyle led him on the barn path. Walking along, Tucker noticed the walnut trees that William had planted and spoke of in his journal. They entered the barn, and Lyle continued with the stories. The entire farm had the fingerprints of William on it. Looking across a mowed lawn, Tucker again saw the small country store that William described in the journal. Noticing that it was open, he asked Lyle if they could walk over to it. The two started across the side yard, and then crossed the main street and entered the store. Tucker saw a group of old men sitting on foldable wooden chairs. Close by them was an old style Coke-Cola machine and a coffee table that sat in the center with several open soda bottles sitting on it. Lyle spoke to them as Tucker stood off to the side until he was introduced. After visiting, the two walked back over to Tucker's parked truck where Mary met them.

"I would like to bring you copies of the articles I have written," Tucker said.

"Thank you," Mary said

Tucker said goodbye and then started his drive home. Reflecting on the conversation, he found himself at times smiling and at others tearing up as he realized there was a sad ending to the story he would need to write. When Tucker arrived at the office the next day, he received much praise from writers and photographers alike. Setting his lunch and briefcase on his desk, he spoke to himself. "Just one more to write and probably the toughest one," he murmured. He wasn't sure he could convey the emotions he felt in words. Seeing that Tucker was in, Mr. Timmons made his way across the office to him.

"Tucker, were you able to find William?" he asked.

Tucker informed him of the meeting with Lyle and Mary. "I suppose no one will ever know what actually happened on his last mission. I had hoped for a happy ending," Tucker added.

"When do you expect it will be done?" Mr. Timmons asked.

It was the first time he had ever asked and not stated a deadline, a clear sign of the respect Tucker had gained.

"I should be able to submit the story to you this afternoon," Tucker replied.

With great anticipation, readers snapped up the final story and sent *The Daily*'s sales to some of the highest they had ever experienced. A few days after the story ran, he was invited to appear on a local television station. This notoriety had never been given to another one of the staff writers.

Chapter 13

Two weeks after the big story ran, Tucker found a note on his desk to call a man in Durant, Oklahoma. Dialing the number, he allowed it to ring several times before he hung up and decided he would try later. High profile assignments that he never would have been given before were now making their way to his desk. Later that morning, he called again. After the third ring, a man answered.

"This is Tucker McQueen with *The Daily Reporter*, and I had a note to call this number. I am sorry, but the secretary forgot to put a name on the note." There was a pause.

"I did not provide one as I was afraid you may not call me. My name is John Eagle Feathers Thompson."

Tucker sat in stunned silence. "John," Tucker said wondering if this was a cruel hoax.

"I realize it is hard to believe, but I was the bombardier on *The Buckeye* many years ago," the man said.

Not wanting to be duped by some mentally deranged reader who had concocted some wild story, Tucker asked him if he could prove his claim. The man told about his experience and added details that only a crewmember would have known. As crazy as he knew it was, after ten minutes of listening to him, Tucker became convinced that he was speaking to John.

"How did you survive?" Tucker asked.

John started telling the story of their last raid. "The mission started out with a bad omen. When we arrived at our hardstand *Ole Number 060* was sitting where *The Buckeye* should have been. She had been pulled from the line for some upgrades. *Ole Number 060* felt like someone else's shoes, which may look like yours but are worn in all the wrong places. We were never comfortable in another aircraft. Our crew had been clobbered last time we flew a mission in *Ole Number 060*, and we feared this would be a repeat. It was a foggy morning, which happened more often than not in England. We finally pulled out of our revetment behind another bomber and slowly lumbered out toward the main east/west runway for departure. The briefing revealed our target as Brunswick, a deep mission into Germany, which required the aircraft to be loaded to gross weight. Our long hauls came with an added stress at the beginning of the mission. If one of the engines quit or even coughed shortly after takeoff, we would not be able to maintain our altitude and would become a statistic off the end of the runway, which is what we witnessed when we were in line for takeoff. A huge fireball and then dark sooty black smoke was the evidence that some poor fellas had bought the farm. No one spoke a word, but all of us knew dreams lay shattered off the end of the runway, and several families would never be the same when word reached them. Death was our constant companion, but we rarely spoke about it; such pressure will show you what is at the heart of a man. After watching several aircraft depart into the murky mist, it was finally our turn. Pappy taxied *Ole Number 060* out onto the runway and lined the bomber up on the centerline. With brakes applied, he smoothly advanced all of the throttles and brought all four of the huge engines up to full power. When he finally released the brakes, *Ole Number 060* strained forward, groaning and creaking under the heavy load. With each second, valuable speed was gained. The scenery outside sped by until it became a blur. I could feel the aircraft start transitioning its weight from the wheels to the wings as we started to break free from the bonds of gravity. Airborne and gaining altitude, everyone breathed a sigh of relief. We all frantically searched for our wildly colored battle weary formation airplane. Lew called her out. 'There she is at two o'clock high.' Pappy swung *Ole Number 060* over to put us in our respective position in the rear of the formation, which receives a lot of attention from the enemy fighters. Our formation then tacked onto the larger formation, and we headed out across the English Channel enroute to our target. After we were across the channel, the cloud cover started to break, and I moved to the nose of the aircraft to take up my battle station. 'Looks like whitecaps down on the channel,' Albert said from the waist window. I stood up and leaned forward to look out. The wind was whipping up waves, and I knew anyone who came back and ditched in the sea today had better get out in a hurry because they certainly wouldn't last long. Stretched out as far as I could see, out in front of us was a continuous stream of bombers.

'Not long, now fellas. Better do your test firing,' Lew said. I heard the guns rattling off around the ship.

'Well time to show'em who is boss, boys,' Pappy said breaking an unusually long period of silence. 'Let's work this as a team and remember, smooth handoffs.'

His pep talks had become part of the superstitious repertoire. In some form it was repeated every mission. There was an expectation by members of the crew that even the trivial aspects would be repeated in the same manner before and during each mission. His talks were expected.

'Okay everybody check in,' Lew said.

When we entered German airspace, the fighters started in on us. They were using new tactics in an attempt to exploit our weaknesses. Lining up as many as thirty abreast, like a cavalry charge, the heavily armed Focke Wulf 190 fighters started working us over. To protect them, the Germans had the lighter highly maneuverable Messerschmitt Bf 109 flying high cover. They would deal with any of our escort fighters that entered into the fray.

'Got some friendlies at two o'clock high. Looks like Mustangs,' Archie, our nose turret gunner said.

I saw them scatter the enemy before they attacked us.

We were about half way to our target area when Little Frankie called a warning. 'Looks like we have company at three o'clock.'

'I see more of them forming up to come and pay us a visit,' Ben said perched in the tail.

'Wow, look at all of them. I'd say there must be over fifty,' William said.

'Everyone ready? It won't be long now,' Lew said.

The 190's were agile planes that were deadly in the hands of an experienced pilot. They were capable of taking out bombers with their twenty millimeter cannons and were equally dangerous in a dogfight. I watched as Archie rotated in the nose turret to get a bead on them as they swung out in front of us. 'Their coach is running parallel to us just out of gun range,' Jack said from the waist window. It was a nickname we used for their leader, who tried to coordinate the attack and would position the squadron for the attack. I hated them, but had respect for them too. They were brave fighters knowing that our gunners were capable of turning their aircraft into a flaming coffin. When they were well out ahead of us, first one rolled and then another on down the line until all had turned back into us and started a head-on pass. Their military precision and discipline was impressive. There was about a dozen of them forming up. As they were above our altitude, Jim, our top turret gunner, and Archie in the nose turret were initially the only ones who could get them in their sights. They spoke calmly throughout the entire attack. It amazes me how calm we were during the battles. The fear was usually felt after a battle when we reflected on the danger we had gone through. One of our gunners or perhaps one from another bomber made a direct hit, and I saw a flash as one of the enemy fighters exploded. At close range, the fighters would break right before colliding with

the formation and then dive below us. The closure rate, when
they attacked head on, was about 600 miles per hour, which
made for a tough target. Everything was moving. It's a wonder
we ever hit any of them. We had several more passes much like
the first, and some of them made hits on us. I watched through
the windows in amazement as battles were going on all around
us. There were so many targets it was hard for our gunners to
pick just one to focus on. This was by intent. They were
attempting to overwhelm us and cause complete chaos. Perhaps
even scatter our formation.

'B-24 going down at 5 o'clock,' Albert said.

The aircraft started into a long dive with smoke pouring
out of two engines. It finally exceeded its structural limits, and a
wing folded back. It plunged straight down to the earth, five
miles below. I can't imagine the hell those fellas must have been
going through to try to escape. I only saw one parachute from
that aircraft. I watched as Jim, firing from the top turret, found
the correct range on one and let him have a good burst from his
twin fifties. Striking the aircraft, it sent out a huge glycol spray
as it sped past us. Just as soon as the first group were finished,
another wave started in on us in the same manner. A ferocious
fight between the fighters and the gunners in the bombers was
taking a toll on both groups. One Bf-109 passed so close that I
could plainly see the German pilot seated inside it, the huge iron
crosses painted on its wings, and hear his engine whining as he
must have been pulling every possible ounce of power out of it.
He barrel rolled through our formation. It grew hotter in our
hell as they then attacked simultaneously from multiple
directions. They were determined to stop us. We did our best
in *Ole Number 060*, but I had a feeling it wouldn't be enough.

The crew was becoming overwhelmed. I have no idea how much time passed during the battle. It could have been five minutes or fifty. We were concentrating on surviving each individual attack. It felt like the entire Luftwaffe had singled us for destruction. Bullets were ripping through the aircraft as we continued on to the target. I looked over to see three single enemy aircraft that had snuck in while attention was diverted to the other large formation attacks. What has always stuck in my memory is that we again were being singled out by the aircraft with the yellow painted spinners. I am sure they were some crack outfit. After their attack, our right inboard engine, known as the number three, was hit. I looked over and saw oil streaming back across the engine nacelle and then smoke followed. I called it in to Pappy. Lew was already working the problem, and shortly after the instructions, he confirmed the steady drop in oil pressure. At 35 pounds, he shut down the engine and feathered the propeller. Lew informed Pappy that he was bringing the power up on the other three engines to try to stay in formation. The fighters knew we were hit and were relentless in their attempts to knock out another engine, and thereby, cripple us so much that we would have to drop out of formation. I noticed again that the yellow-nosed Bf-109's were concentrating their attacks on us. There was constant chatter among the crew.

'Hit him from the waist window, Albert,' Jim said while tracking a fighter from the top turret.

'Swing the ball around and throw some lead over this way, Frankie,' Jack said as he let out a short burst to a fighter that had broken from the pack and was inbound for a strike.

They were very skilled. I recall hearing some of the other crewmembers talking about those yellow nose Messerschmitt's. The German 109's pressed their battle with increased ferocity as we neared the target area. I looked over to our left side and saw *Battle Wagon*, a bomber we had seen many times at our side. One minute they were fine, and then a minute later I watched them come under attack by some FW-190's. They knocked out the tail gunner and then sat behind them and poured cannon fire into the bomber. I could see bits and pieces of metal hurtling out the front of the bomber from the bullets passing clean through it. The tremendous damage of the rain of bullets rushing through the fuselage must have made it hell inside. I don't see how any of them survived such an intense barrage. First one engine caught on fire, and then another burst into flames. The fires grew in intensity streaking back along the sides of the fuselage. They were doomed. As I watched, another German fighter made a head on pass scoring strikes on the cockpit. He must have hit the pilot because the bomber pitched up vertical and momentarily stood straight up. It was surreal to watch it struggle to stay in the air. The aircraft shuddered with its engines running wildly and propellers screaming. It was like a huge beast entering its death throes. The crew inside had seconds to make their exit. Flames were everywhere as it fell over on its back, and I watched crewmembers jumping. One man exited on fire. The bomber broke hard to the left and started into a death spiral. I watched it drop a thousand feet below us and then explode. I noticed another one of the solid yellow-nosed Bf 109's at distance start strafing the bomber crew that had just parachuted. There was nothing we could do but watch in horror as he murderously flew from one to the next and shredded them with his deadly machine gun fire.

'Somebody needs to get that SOB,' Ben said as he watched the same scene that my eyes were fixed on. The only three men who had exited the aircraft were now hanging lifeless in their parachutes. The Germans had broken a basic unwritten rule of aerial warfare to not shoot a man in a parachute as they were completely helpless. As quickly as they had appeared, the enemy fighters seemed to evaporate. We all knew what that meant: flak, thick, black, and ominous. The run through the flak was worse than the fighters as we had to fly through it with no way to fight back. The gunners below were rapidly cycling their 88mm anti-aircraft guns. The sky was dark and dangerous like an angry thunderstorm.

'Okay fellas, we are on the bomb run. The ship is all yours John,' Pappy said while being jostled about by the exploding flak.

We entered flak alley, which was what we called 'the bombing run' that was between the initial point and where we dropped our bombs. It was only about 5 minutes, but it seemed like an eternity. They burst all around us, and I will never forget the sound of that flak peppering the aircraft. It sounded like hail on a tin roof. Each burst of flak sent thousands of pieces of shrapnel in all directions. The aircraft shook and bucked from the explosions and the turbulence created by the bombers ahead of us. When we were ready to drop our bombs, I heard a loud explosion. I knew it was closer than ever before and looked behind me to see that Albert was clutching his leg. Jack immediately turned to him to provide first aid. One of the crew called the cockpit and informed Pappy. He sent William back. His secondary duty was to serve as our inflight medic. I saw Albert on his knees still firing his gun. Lew reported to Pappy that the flak burst had punched through the side of the aircraft leaving a several jagged holes. At bombs away, Pappy immediately took evasive action. With the pounding we had taken, we were ready to get the hell out of there. On the return trip, the yellow nose Bf-109's reappeared and seemed intent on finishing the job they had begun. Ben warned us that several enemy aircraft had lined up astern and were starting their attack run. I could hear Jim operating the top turret, Frankie in the ball turret, and Ben in the tail turret coordinating their efforts to try to bust them up. The fighters finished the attack and zoomed over us only to rally out in front with others to make a frontal assault. I heard a cry out in my headset, and shortly after William informed Pappy that Archie had been hit. At that time, William was busy tracking our position, so I made my way to the turret to check on Archie. He had been hit in the chest and was lifeless at the controls. There was blood splattered all over the plexiglass. I told Pappy that we had a gaping hole in the front turret and Archie was in bad shape. He asked me to take over the turret. I pulled Archie from the turret. William came over and started applying first aid, but I think he was already dead. I climbed in the turret, but it would not turn as the hydraulics had been damaged. We continued on, but with the added drag and running on only three engines, we quickly started falling behind the group. It wasn't long before the formation was no longer in sight. Pappy gave us a pep talk about making it home and that we had a lot of fight in us, but I am not sure it helped as the crew and *Ole Number 060* were shot up pretty bad. A sense of despair was starting to set in. The 109's with the yellow spinners reappeared. They came line abreast on a coordinated strafing run. On one of the passes, they hit the top turret, and Jim crumbled. I looked back and saw William guiding him to sit down by Archie. His face was all bloody with shards of plexiglass in it. One of the crew called out that we had fuel leaking from the left wing. We all knew that the B-24 had a nasty habit of exploding when the wing tanks were hit. A minute later, I heard a call that the number four engine was on fire. We were still at about 15,000 feet. I knew the bomber could blow up at any moment. William was busy wiping the blood from Jim's face and making him as comfortable as possible. I yelled at him. "We have to jump.' He looked up at me. 'I can't leave them', he said. A second later he rushed me shoving me onto the bomb bay doors. My weight tripped them, and I fell from the bomber. Free falling, I looked back up. The bomber heeled over on a wing and started into a spin. Pulling my ripcord, I watched as the *Ole Number 060* continued down. I didn't see any parachutes. Once a bomber lost control and started spinning, the centrifugal force would pin the crew against the sides making it impossible to escape. I came down in a forested area. I was in shock but had no time to think of anything as the Germans would immediately come looking for me. Slipping out of my parachute harness, I cut off as much of the cord as I could and then buried the parachute. I traveled perhaps ten miles and then built a simple lean to for the night. Using the leaves, I made a bed and also covered myself with them to hold in my body heat as it was the end of October. When darkness came, the temperature plummeted.

For a month, I slowly worked my way across Germany. I survived on edible plants and snared wild game with the parachute cord. Several times German patrols passed within fifty feet of me. Eventually, I crossed into France where I made contact with the resistance. They wanted to help me get back to

England, but I had vengeance in my heart. Over the remainder of the war, I worked with them to cut communication lines, attack troops, and relentlessly harass them. I killed at least ten German soldiers for every one of my friends. It wasn't enough to satiate the hatred I felt toward them. The Germans learned of me and put a bounty on my head. They must have known personal information about me as I was told they had nicknamed me Geronimo.

At the end of the war, I worked my way home on a cargo ship and slipped back into the country. As far as the army knew, I had been killed in action. Once I was back in the states, I melted into the Choctaw nation. Years after the war, I found out that we were right about the Bf-109's that had the yellow spinners. Another crewmember told me that on an earlier mission, one of the gunners on board *Ole Number 060* had taken a long shot and killed a German pilot as he was parachuting. From then on, they marked that aircraft for destruction at any cost. They wouldn't have known that we were a different crew and not the ones who had killed their friend. William was always writing in the journal that you found. He must have hid it under his navigator table as it was illegal to keep a record of our missions.

I fell into a severe depression when I tried to settle back into the reservation. For some time I struggled with alcohol abuse. Eventually, I married and had a daughter, but the pain remained. Nothing could quench my anger. On a bleak winter day, I was thinking about William and what made him stand out among so many men. It occurred to me that he always placed the well-being of others above himself, even when it cost him his life. He spoke to me many times about his faith in God, and

I remembered he had given me a small New Testament. When the Army Air Force listed me as missing in action, they shipped all of my possessions home to my parents. I dug through them and found the small pocket testament that he had given me. I had never read it. Some of the pages were folded over to draw my attention to specific Bible promises. The first was John 3:16, which provided hope to me. Once I started reading it, I was pulled in and found a peace that I had never known. Slowly life started turning around for me. After a few months of reading it, I was baptized, gave up alcohol, and started to be the father and husband I should have been all along. I attend church every Sunday now with my wife and children. William played a key role in my salvation."

So many questions entered Tucker's mind at one time that he had trouble sorting out which to ask first. "Do you know what happened to Elizabeth?"

"A few years ago, I felt drawn to go back to England. I am not certain why but think I was looking for closure. It was deserted, so quiet—such a lonely experience. I visited the mess hall and saw the large eagle mural on the wall. I slowly walked through the large aircraft hangar where Glen Miller had played and the hut where William and I had bunked. With all of the men long gone, it felt like a dead body devoid of a soul. Vandals and weather had taken their toll. The next day, I visited the old pubs and spoke to the locals. In speaking to them, I asked about Elizabeth. I was told that she had complications during childbirth and died a few hours after giving birth but had lived long enough to name her baby."

"So, she was pregnant?" Tucker asked.

"Yes, but William didn't know it. I visited her grave, and back dating, I figured out that the baby had to have been William's child. They said the baby girl was placed in an orphanage as Elizabeth's mother was unable to take care of her." Tucker paused and thought of the multiple layers of sadness in the story he had just been told. His thoughts then turned to the crew.

"How about the crew. Were they ever found?"

"No, they are still somewhere in Germany, and that is why I had to call you. It has always haunted me that they never returned home to their native land. With the declassified documents that you uncovered, I think you may be able to find them. You have a starting point as the missing aircrew report has the last known latitude and longitude of the aircraft. We flew for about an hour past that point in a westerly direction. That should be enough to create a search area," he said. "Your investigative abilities and the financial backing of the newspaper put you in a unique position to go after them."

Tucker realized that even with that information, the search area would cover many hundreds of square miles, but he also knew he must try. "I am willing to go, but will need the resources of *The Daily Reporter.* Ultimately, the decision is one for my boss," Tucker said.

"I understand," John said.

"Let me speak to him, and I will call you back."

Tucker sat at his desk for a while just looking down at the two pages of scribbled notes he had taken during the telephone conversation. Picking up the pad, he headed to Mr. Timmons's office. When he approached the office, Mr. Timmons looked up.

"Come in Tucker. You look like you have seen a ghost," he said.

"I didn't see one, but I did just speak to one," Tucker said.

For the next ten minutes, Tucker retold the conversation he had with John. Mr. Timmons was amazed. He leaned forward in his chair.

"I thought we had plumbed the bottom on this story, but clearly I was wrong. Are you interested in pursuing the story across the ocean?" he said with a slight grin.

"Yes, for multiple reasons," Tucker replied.

"Bridget, hold all my calls for the next hour. Let's plan out the next few weeks. The first order of business is for you to reopen the story by writing about the conversation you just had with John. I would like to have it this afternoon as we need to strike while the iron is still hot, and right now your story remains fresh in the readers' minds. We need to determine what international airport is closest to the last known position of the bomber. You are going to need help getting around in a foreign country, and you will need to get an expedited passport. Let me reach out to some of my contacts and see what I can put together. I think we both know that the odds of you locating the bomber after this much time and such a large search area is extremely slim. However, the readers will enjoy the adventure and human aspects of your journey even if you don't find it. Most importantly, it will sell newspapers," he said.

Tucker left his office and started writing the story. The words came quickly, and he had cleared Mr. Timmons's critical review and submitted it for publication by the afternoon deadline.

The following week Tucker was given light assignments so that he had ample time to prepare for the trip. He placed a call to John to let him know that he had been cleared to go look for the crew.

"I will pray for your success," John said.

He stopped by the library to learn more about the area of Germany he would visit. When he entered the library, Ms. Simms was tending to another patron. Tucker waited patiently at the reference desk until she had finished.

"Hello Tucker, what story are you working on now?" she said.

"Believe it or not, I am back on the same story," he said. He explained the telephone call and his plans to go to Germany to hunt for the downed bomber. She sat in rapt silence as he told of John and his escape and his experience harassing the German army with the French partisans.

"This is too much to believe. You must have come close to falling off your chair when speaking to him," she said.

"I had and still have a hard time believing it," Tucker said.

"Well, how can I assist you?" she said eager to help.

"John said that he spent considerable time in a forest when he parachuted. I wonder if we could pinpoint the latitude and longitude that is given in the missing aircrew report and then look for a large forested area that they would have passed over fighting their way back to England."

"Let me get a map of Germany, and we can spread it out on one of the large tables," Ms. Simms said.

Tucker made his way to the closest table, and she returned with a German map with lines of latitude and longitude marked on it. "We need to create a search area, but I am not sure how to proceed." She sat silent for a moment. "Tucker, do you know any pilots that could assist us?"

"I do. May I borrow your telephone?" Tucker placed a call to the airport and spoke to Bob. Half an hour later, he arrived at the library. Providing him with the latitude and longitude that was recorded in the missing aircrew report.

"This x is the last known location of the bomber according to the aircrews from the other bombers," he said. Next he drew a line from the last known location of the bomber to Wendling airbase. He then pulled an aeronautical sectional plotter from his bag and placed it where his line ran across a line of longitude. The magnetic heading from that point to their airbase was 310 degrees. "Do you know their airspeed?"

"John said he heard Pappy tell William they had slowed to about 160 knots," Tucker replied. "How long did John say they flew past the last known position?" Bob asked.

"About an hour."

"I think we should estimate they flew no less than 30 minutes past that point and no more than 90 minutes. If we are correct on the heading, right here would be 60 minutes past their last known position and where John bailed out and shouldn't be far from where the bomber came down." Bob pulled an E6-b flight computer from his flight bag. "This is a mathematical slide rule created for aviators." Spinning a metal dial on the front of the instrument, he determined two more points along the line. "It may be on this line, but we have to take into account that their heading was not 310 degrees. We know that there is some error in all of this, so let's expand the search area. In the end he had drawn a trapezoidal search area.

"The bomber should be located somewhere in this area," he said pointing to the area he had marked on the map.

Tucker sighed when he realized how large the search area was. "It makes sense that it could be in that area as it falls within the black forest which explains what he told you about making his way out of a large forest. It could also account for why the bomber was never found. You definitely have a lot of ground to cover. It will have to be an aerial search."

Tucker felt overwhelmed as he looked at the sheer size of the search area. He had envisioned hiking to the last coordinates and working from that point, but he now saw how impossible that would be.

"There may be a cleared area from where it came down and the wreckage burnt, or you may be able to see some portion of the bomber," Bob said optimistically. "Aluminum is highly reflective on a sunny day. You may see a reflection. Let's lay out the search lines so a pilot can use this aeronautical sectional." Bob meticulously calculated the latitude and longitude of various points and laid out a search grid that would assure the entire search area would be covered. "I would do more, but the wind has to be taken into account, and thus, the pilot will have to work out some time, speed, and distance calculations," Bob said. "If he uses this sectional chart, he should be able to keep on track and assure that you fly the entire area."

"I owe you one," Tucker said as Bob placed his equipment back in his flight bag.

"Just bring the men home, and that will be payment enough," Bob said as he shook Tucker's hand.

Once Bob had departed, Ms. Simms pulled out books on traveling in Germany and a few on hiking. She helped compile a list of essential wilderness hiking gear and explained the weather patterns typically experienced in early October. Germany could be rainy and cold.

"One last request: Would you look up the telephone number of William's father, Lyle Pritchett?" Tucker asked.

Ms. Simms found the correct directory and produced the number. That afternoon, while at the office, he called and explained the new information that had surfaced and that he was going to Germany to look for the missing crew. There was a long pause until Mr. Pritchett finally spoke

"We will be praying for your safety and success," Lyle said.

Over the following few days, Tucker packed his gear including his heavy warm outdoor clothing.

On Friday, he was called to Mr. Timmons's office.

"Everything is set. Your tickets have been purchased, and I have a contact for you. A German man named Hans Fischer. He lived in the U.S. for several years and worked as an engineer. Dr. Fischer retired a few years ago and owns a home in the Stuttgart area. He has agreed to hire some college students to aid in the search. Here is his telephone number. Call him once you are settled in at your hotel. We booked you a room in a small city that is 20 minutes south of Stuttgart. That will put you close to the search area that you showed us. Do you have all of your gear ready to go?" he asked.

"Yes, I am packed," Tucker replied.

Mr. Timmons stood. "Call in every few days and keep plenty of notes as I will expect several articles to be generated from this trip. Best of luck. We're all pulling for you."

Tucker stood and shook his hand and started out of his office. The night before his departure, Tucker called his mother to tell her goodbye. They spoke about the amazing journey and reminisced about when they first opened the journal and read it in her living room.

"Be careful and call me when you safely arrive," she said.

At five o'clock the next morning, Tucker loaded his gear in his old Ford truck and headed toward an unknown outcome much like William had many years ago. The journey to the Cincinnati airport was made in the dark. Although it was still early, the terminal was bustling with people arriving and departing. There was a constant stream of traffic, and it was a bit overwhelming. His flight was from Cincinnati to Chicago O'Hare to Washington Dulles Airport and then on to Stuttgart, Germany. Tucker checked his luggage and boarded with a small carry on that contained essentials. He slept on the first leg of the journey and made a successful transfer at a complex terminal in Chicago. The flight to the East Coast was a bit uncomfortable as a large man sat beside him and spilled over into his space. A two-hour layover at Washington Dulles Airport allowed him to stretch his legs, grab a sandwich, and review a translation book. Tucker memorized common words that he thought would be beneficial to know. Boarding the Boeing 707 for the transatlantic flight, he was pleased to see larger seats and more space. He was also pleased to sit in a window seat. The thrust of the four engines accelerated the aircraft quickly. Tucker dug in his bag and retrieved a novel he had packed for the long flight. Between it and making conversation with a woman who sat beside him, he found the flight to go by more quickly than he had anticipated. A few hours from Stuttgart, he fell asleep and was awakened when the pilot briefed the passengers about the local weather, time of arrival, and of course, thanks for flying on Pan Am. Looking out the window, he thought about how only a few decades ago, he would have been an enemy of the people whose help he now sought in finding the crew. Tucker departed the aircraft and headed to the luggage carousel. Several bags passed by and still he did not see his suitcase. He began to worry as it contained the maps of the search area. About the time he was going to report it missing, he saw it and breathed a sigh of relief. After exchanging his currency, he was off to the rental car company.

Verifying his driver's license, the clerk then handed him the keys. Proceeding out to the parking lot, he found his car and sat in it while he studied his map. Once he had a general idea of where he was heading, he put the car in drive and began following the signs to exit the parking lot and find his way to Highway 81. Following the map that Ms. Simms had given him, he started south. Carefully watching the signs, he came to an exit with the city name on it, and after some wandering around, located the inn. Walking to the entrance, Tucker passed a couple who spoke to him in German. He said "hallo" in return, but was uncertain that his reply made sense as he had no idea what they had said. They politely smiled in return. Tucker entered the hotel, walked up to the counter in the restaurant, and spoke to a man.

"Hello, would you be able to tell me where there is a pay telephone?"

The man stared at him and disappeared behind a door. It was becoming clear that everyone wasn't bilingual like he had been told. Tucker looked around at couples eating and felt hunger pains as he smelled all kinds of enchanting aromas coming from the kitchen. He had turned his back to the counter and was somewhat startled when a man behind him said, "May I assist you?" He was instantly relieved to hear someone speak English and felt a friendship with this stranger.

"I need to place a telephone call. Do you have a pay telephone?" Tucker asked.

"There is no pay telephone here, but you can place a call on this telephone," he replied as he set it up on the counter top.

"Thank you," Tucker said. Pulling the telephone number out, he started to dial. He counted the rings up to six and then set it back on the receiver.

"No answer," Tucker said.

"My name is Gunther. I am the inn manager."

"Pleased to meet you. My name is Tucker," he said.

"Do you have a room reserved here at the inn?" Gunther said.

"Yes, there should be a room under the name Tucker McQueen," he replied.

Gunther checked the registrar. "Here it is. You are in room ten," he said. He pulled the correct skeleton key off a hook on the wall and handed it to Tucker. "Perhaps you would like to freshen up a bit and then come down for something to eat," Gunther said.

"It has been a long journey," Tucker replied.

"Wolfgang, zeigen ihn in sein zimmer," Gunther said to one of his staff members. Turning to Tucker he said, "Wolfgang will show you to your room."

They walked up a flight of steps to the second floor and passed several doors until Wolfgang stopped, drew a key from his pocket, and let Tucker in. Entering the small room, Tucker saw a regular size bed with a white bedspread, a dresser for his clothes, and a private bathroom. Wolfgang looked at Tucker "Das ist Gut?" he said smiling at him.

"Yes, this is good," Tucker said.

He unpacked his clothes into a simple wooden dresser, splashed water on his face, and then headed back downstairs to the restaurant. Siting at one of the booths, he picked up a menu and hoped to find pictures to assist him in understanding what he was ordering. While looking at it, a young attractive woman came to his table.

"Darf ich Ihre Bestellung," she said looking expectantly at him.

Tucker, wondering how to get out of this predicament, remembered Gunther who had helped him earlier. He clumsily strung together words that he hoped she would understand "Gunther bitte, nein Deutsch." She disappeared into the kitchen. While Tucker studied the menu, Gunther approached his table.

"What would you like?" he said.

"Well, what would you suggest?" Tucker said.

"The wiener schnitzel with pommes frites will not disappoint you," Gunther said. "It is thin sliced breaded veal served with what you call 'French Fries.'"

"That sounds good and a glass of tea or coffee too, please. Oh, and thank you for all of your help."

"You are welcome," Gunther said. He then handed the order to the waitress so that she could place it. About fifteen minutes later, the young waitress brought his plate with a large glass of cold tea. Setting it before him, she smiled but did not speak. Tucker was pleased to see it was a large portion as he was hungry and not sure what he would find at breakfast time. Once finished, Gunther came back to his table.

"Did you enjoy the meal?"

"Yes, it was delicious."

"Perhaps some dessert?" Gunther asked.

"Oh, no thank you." Tucker replied.

"If you don't mind me asking, why have you come to Germany?" Gunther asked.

Tucker tried to give him an abbreviated explanation, but it still took him several minutes to explain.

"I wish you the best of success in your search and let me know if I can help in any way while you stay here at the Heeseburg."

"May I borrow the telephone one more time?" Tucker asked.

"Of course," Gunther replied.

Tucker dialed the number and was relieved when he heard.

"Hallo?"

"Dr. Fischer, this is Tucker McQueen."

"Yes, I have been expecting your call. Are you at the airport?" he asked.

"No, I am at the Heeseburg," Tucker replied.

"Okay, very well. Shall we meet in the restaurant tomorrow morning at seven o'clock?" he asked.

"Yes, that would be nice," Tucker said.

"We shall eat breakfast, and then we can start the search," Dr. Fischer said.

Tucker returned to his room and set his alarm for six o'clock. Lying in bed, he read until he fell asleep. The next morning he awoke ten minutes before his alarm clock was set to go off. Reaching over to turn it off, he rolled out of bed, showered, and dressed. Grabbing his jacket, he headed downstairs to the restaurant. Entering, he looked around for an older man. Seeing no one, he sat in a booth that gave him a good view of the door. At exactly seven o'clock, the door opened, and a slender man walked in. He wore tan slacks, a buttoned short-sleeved shirt, and a well-worn dark green felt Tyrolean hat. It was accented with a delicate braided rope around its base and a small dark red feather. Removing the hat he exposed his thinning white hair. He slowly scanned the restaurant. Tucker stood and made eye contact with him.

"Dr. Fischer?" Tucker said.

"Tucker, it is nice to meet you," he said with a German accent.

They sat and spoke, becoming acquainted. After finishing breakfast, they spoke of the mission details.

"I have hired some college students to assist us. We will direct them to search any targets that we identify from the aerial search. Do you have a general search area?" Dr. Fischer asked.

"Yes, I have an aeronautical chart of the area and a search grid marked on it," Tucker said.

"How many days do we have to search?" Dr. Fischer asked.

"Five days," Tucker said.

"Very well. I have contacted the airport and hired a pilot who will fly us in a four-seat airplane. I have it booked for today and will book it for four additional days."

"Shall we head to the airport?" Dr. Fischer asked.

"I am ready if you are," Tucker said.

Arriving at the airport, they found the small charter outfit where Dr. Fischer spoke to a manager who introduced him to their pilot. Once Dr. Fischer had explained to the pilot their mission, he asked Tucker for the aeronautical charts. Tucker pulled them from his bag and handed them to him. Laying them out on the table, Dr. Fischer asked Tucker for clarification and then translated the information to the pilot. Just as Bob predicted, the pilot obtained the wind speed and direction to determine his ground speed and then used the information to calculate how long he had to fly on a given heading to arrive at various spots in the search grid. They were finally in the aircraft at 9:00 o'clock and ready for departure. The pilot motioned for them to put on their headsets. Tucker found himself extremely excited to finally be getting underway. He sat behind the pilot so that he could search out of the left side of the aircraft while Dr. Fischer sat in front and searched on the right side. Tucker heard the pilot speak to several individuals, but had no idea what was being said. They finally lined up on a runway and started accelerating. After about fifteen minutes into the flight, the pilot spoke to Dr. Fischer and told him when they were entering the search area. He, in turn, conveyed the information to Tucker. Both of them scanned the ground for any signs of plane wreckage. When something caught their attention, they would use binoculars to take a closer look. They searched for two hours before they flew back to the airport for a much-needed break. It was mentally draining. Since it was close to lunch, they ate at the airport restaurant and were back in the air at around 12:30.

"I see something shiny at about our three o'clock position, Tucker," Dr. Fischer said.

He then spoke in German directing the pilot to orbit the target. Tucker could see debris on the ground and did see the sun shine off a reflective surface. He felt a rush of excitement. Dr. Fischer instructed the pilot to mark it on the map. They finished the day at around four o'clock. When they reached the airport, Dr. Fischer wrote down the latitude and longitude from the map so that the students he had hired could investigate the site. Tucker knew the odds were against it being the bomber, so he tried to not become excited as he knew the backside of excitement was disappointment, something he desperately wanted to avoid. Regardless of how hard he tried, a little optimistic voice inside him whispered that it was possible that this was it. On the way back to the hotel, they planned the next day's activities beginning again with breakfast. Tucker ate dinner alone at the hotel and spoke with Gunther about the day's events.

"So no success, but some hope," Gunther said.

"Yes, there is hope that it will be wreckage from the bomber, but it's unlikely. If the wreckage were obvious, it would have been found years ago, and by now the ground cover may have covered any exposed pieces," Tucker said.

"I suppose you are correct, but even if you do not find it, you have done a noble deed," Gunther said.

Worn out from the day's search, Tucker retired to his room to read a little and then fell asleep.

The next morning over breakfast, Dr. Fischer and Tucker spoke about the search and the hope that the wreckage they had seen the day before would be the bomber. "The students should find the site late this morning, but we should keep up the search as the clock is ticking," Dr. Fischer said. They arrived at the airport and were recharged and ready to begin again. For a change, Tucker took the front seat, and Dr. Fischer sat in the back. The pilot flew them to the search area and started where he had left off in the search pattern. The drone of the airplane made Tucker sleepy, and he found himself fighting sleep. He engaged Dr. Fischer in conversation to stimulate his mind and shake off the boredom induced head nods. They broke off the search after three unproductive hours and flew back to the airport. Tucker wondered if he had three and a half days of searching left in him. It was around noon when the students called the airport. Tucker desperately hoped to hear good news. Dr. Fischer walked back to the lunch table and sat down.

"It was an old cabin sight. The metal we saw was from debris on the ground." Devoid of emotions, Dr. Fischer spoke. "Well, shall we resume the search?"

They climbed back aboard the aircraft and were soon over the search area. An hour into the flight, Tucker saw a glint.

"I see something shiny in a cleared area at about three o'clock," Tucker said. His heart started racing as they drew nearer to the area. Looking down, he could see a stream running into a small pool of water. Orbiting the area, none of them could see anything other than the water in the clearing. "It must have been the sun shining off of the pool of water," Tucker said. Dr. Fischer instructed the pilot to resume the search. After three more hours, Tucker began to feel the futility of the search working on his optimism. He tried to remain reasonable without diminishing all hope, but it was a challenge as he knew the odds weren't in their favor. On one hand it was unlikely that they would find it, but it was not impossible. He was relieved when the pilot landed. Back at the hotel, Tucker spoke to Gunther about the search.

"Well, it sounds like you are doing everything you can, and that has to be good enough," Gunther stated.

"Perhaps, but I want to find them. So many good people want a happy ending, and going back without the crew will leave the wounds unmended," Tucker stated. Before he climbed the stairs to his room, he called his mother and spoke about the difficulties of the day.

Tucker awoke the next morning to the sound of rain. Dr. Fischer was waiting for him at their usual spot in the restaurant.

"Looks like we're washed out today," he said as Tucker approached the table.

"I suppose so," Tucker said much in need of a cup of coffee to lift his spirits.

"You seem a little down this morning," Dr. Fischer stated.

The gloomy day brought out his honest feelings. "I fear I may fail at this," Tucker said.

"You just need a day off to pick up your spirits," Dr. Fischer stated. "Here you are in Germany, and yet you have seen so little of our wonderful country. Let's go see some of the sights," he said patting Tucker's hand that was lying on the table. "But first, some breakfast," he said while waving for assistance from a waitress.

Tucker finished a cup of steaming hot black coffee and then started into sausage, eggs, and sliced cheese and finished with fresh fruit. Leaving the Heeseburg, Dr. Fischer took him to a local city where they walked into small shops, and Tucker purchased a gift for his mother. It was a Hummel figurine of a little girl wearing a bonnet and holding a basket of flowers.

At lunch, they ate bratwurst and enjoyed the locally brewed beer. The rain was trailing off when they arrived back at the inn. As Dr. Fischer had predicted, the day was therapeutic, and Tucker felt more optimistic about the next two days.

The next morning, the sky had cleared but the high-pressure center had also ushered in a biting wind and lower temperatures. The morning search did not turn up any signs to be investigated nor did three more hours in the afternoon.

Arriving back at the airport, Dr. Fischer spoke to the pilot who was unloading his gear from the aircraft. Once he was done, he briefed Tucker.

"He said we are on schedule to finish the search area tomorrow."

Mentally fatigued, Tucker was happy when they arrived back at the inn. They ordered a couple of mugs of beer, and Tucker munched on pretzels as Dr. Fischer conversed in German with a few friends. "One more day and then back home to break the bad news. Perhaps I was a fool to even hope. What shall I tell John and William's parents?" Tucker said to himself. He knew they would understand, but it stung when he thought about delivering a sad chapter to an already painful past. It was as if the crew had just vanished, and if he wasn't successful in finding them then, what had been the point of all of this? With nowhere else to turn, he whispered a simple prayer, "Help me do this for them."

"Well, one more day," Dr. Fischer said seemingly undaunted by their lack of success. He pulled on his coat. "We will begin again tomorrow. There is still hope," Dr. Fischer said as he departed.

Tucker envied him as tomorrow he would walk away; whereas, Tucker would have to carry home the sad news. The thought occupied his mind and stole his appetite. Sitting alone, he ate a meager supper, returned to his room, and read. It was hard to concentrate on the book as he found himself thinking that he only had one more day. He closed his eyes to escape the thoughts and drifted off. The stress made for a restless night's sleep. He dreamt that he was driving out to William's parents' house to break the bad news to them, and then later while telling John on the telephone, he could hear nothing but breathing. He woke in the night and tried to clear his mind by thinking of anything but the next day's search. It didn't work. His last dream was of John parachuting down and the bomber exploding in the background.

The morning sunshine poured into Tucker's room. It was as if someone was shining a bright light in his face.

"Tucker!" he heard his name hollered out and sat up right in bed. It startled him as no one was around. There was no reason to push back the curtain to see if the sky was clear as the early morning sunshine poured into the room. He had been so caught up in his thoughts before bed that he had failed to set the alarm, and looking at his clock, he realized he was due downstairs in five minutes. Frustrated by his oversight, he hurriedly readied himself and rushed downstairs. Dr. Fischer's breakfast was just arriving on the table when he walked in. Tucker ordered coffee and some bagels with cheese as he knew it would be fast and simple.

"Well, the last day is here," Dr. Fischer said.

"Yes, this is it," Tucker replied still groggy.

Arriving at the airport, they loaded their gear and assumed their positions. Airborne again, Tucker began his scanning and periodically used his binoculars if anything looked abnormal. After an hour of searching, he saw a quick flash that caught his attention. Looking back, he could not find the object. Not willing to lose the possible target, Tucker spoke. "I just saw something flash on the ground but lost it. Will you ask the pilot to turn ninety degrees to the left?"

Dr. Fischer conveyed the information to the pilot who made the turn. Scanning with their binoculars they frantically searched for whatever he had seen.

"I see some type of metal panel that is partially hidden," Dr. Fischer said.

Tucker looked over at him to see where he was looking, brought his binoculars up, and found the object. He saw weathered markings on the metal sheet, but a major portion of the object was hidden under some of the evergreen trees. The target was in an opening that had only small trees. There were other suspicious pieces lying around that were covered with pine needles and moss and had the look of something manmade.

"Should we go back and ask the students to investigate the site?' Dr. Fischer asked.

Tucker was afraid of making a quick decision as precious time would be lost if they returned to the airport. "What do you think?" he asked.

"Well, it looks better than anything we have seen. The clearing could be a result of the post-crash fire. If we don't send the students now, they may not have time to reach the site before it gets dark," Dr. Fischer said.

"Let's go call them," Tucker said with excitement.

301

Arriving back at the airport, Dr. Fischer called the students and relayed the coordinates to them. "They think they can take a look and be back in around two hours," Dr. Fischer said.

"It is 10:30. If we wait for the call and this is not the bomber, we will have lost more time, but it is close to lunch; perhaps we could eat a little early," Dr. Fischer said. Tucker felt the gentle nudge to wait and decided to take the gamble. They sat in the lounge talking until they felt the pangs of hunger and stepped into the restaurant to eat. After lunch, they returned to the lounge for more waiting. It took longer than expected to receive the call. When the pay telephone finally rang, Dr. Fischer walked over and answered it. Tucker followed him and was encouraged when he saw him start to smile. He also could hear an excited voice on the other end. Hope crept into his mind that this could actually be the remnants of *Ole Number 060*. They had seen reflective material on the ground. He could hear the student talking excitedly, and Tucker felt the rush of excitement wash over him. Dr. Fischer tried to calm the students so that he could get a clear understanding of what they had found. Since Tucker could not understand the language, he focused on Dr. Fischer's facial expressions to determine if he was being given good news or bad. He looked away too fearful of being let down and returned to the table. Dr. Fischer hung up the telephone and walked over to him. His smile was gone.

"They found a piece of an aircraft, but after they described it to me, it became clear that it was only the crash of some small twin engine aircraft."

"Are you absolutely sure?" Tucker asked with despair sweeping over him.

"Yes, I am afraid so."

The two sat in silence for a moment.

"Well shall we get back to it? We still have a few hours left?" Dr. Fischer said smiling.

Tucker was uplifted by his dedication and suddenly felt ashamed at his feeling of despair. As Gunther had said, regardless of whether or not they found the crew, they had done a noble deed. They had given it their best. Perhaps it was not meant to be.

"If you like, I could ask the pilot if we could stay out a little later to make up for some of the time we lost. Perhaps we can complete the search area."

"Yes, please do," Tucker said.

Dr. Fischer turned and spoke to the pilot. "He said we could fly until six o'clock."

"Let's give the crew our best," Tucker said as they headed out to the aircraft.

The methodical search began again with their straining to see anything out of the ordinary. Three hours of endless searching resulted in no targets, and they were down to the last leg of the search pattern. Tucker had resigned himself to the fact that they would not find them, but felt at peace.

"That's it," Dr. Fischer said. The pilot turned the aircraft back toward the airport cutting across the middle of the forest. Dr. Fischer was chatting with the pilot, and from the general chuckling, Tucker could tell it was unrelated to the search. Leaning his head against the door, his mind drifted from the search to the fact that if he could only turn back the clock, he could witness what happened. It was hard to believe that he was flying over the same ground that years before had been a battlefield, the final resting place of a crew lost forever. He relaxed his vision and just stared at the ground as it sped by in a sea of green treetops. It was the contrast that caught his attention and shook him out of his trance like state. As a matter of curiosity, he mentioned it to Dr. Fischer. "Look at that red tree in the clearing." Dr. Fischer swiveled towards him to see what he was talking about but could not see it as he was on the opposite side of the aircraft. He spoke to the pilot to reverse his course and circle around. In order to direct the pilot to the correct spot, Tucker pulled up his binoculars and started searching for the tree. He slid his lens along a sea of green and brown until he caught a glimpse of bright red crimson. The sunlight was highlighting the tree's magnificence. Before Tucker directed them to it, Dr. Fischer spoke. "I see it. It looks so out of place; how did we miss it?" Tucker searched the ground around it with his binoculars and thought he saw a dull dirty rim and tire.

"Look just south of the tree. Is that a tire and a rim?" Tucker asked.

"I believe it is, and there appears to be a large metal beam sticking up just west of that piece," he added.

Dr. Fischer asked the pilot to make several orbits so they could make a thorough search. Tucker memorized some prominent landmarks to aid in finding the site from the ground.

The pilot marked where they were on the aeronautical sectional in case they needed to fly back over it. Flying back to the airport with one last lead, Tucker and Dr. Fischer discussed the target and again wondered how they had missed it.

"Wait a minute," Dr. Fischer said. "We would have passed over that area on our second day out probably sometime in the afternoon. There was a dull overcast on that day. Without the sunlight, there was most likely much less contrast between the colors. That would explain why it didn't catch our attention."

"Do you think we could investigate this one ourselves?" Tucker asked.

"I think we will have to as the students have most likely gone home. I told them we would be done at 4:00 today, and it is a little past 6:00," he said.

Arriving back at the airport, they grabbed the aeronautical map and transferred the location onto a topographical map. It took them over an hour of driving on an old logging road before they were as near as a road would take them. Pulling out his compass, Tucker determined a course line, and they started into the forest. After working through some difficult terrain, they came upon a large open area that had a few sparse trees. Looking across the area, Tucker saw the crimson colored tree highlighted by the fading sunlight. The tall dark green spruce trees stood as proud sentries around the outer edges holding back the forest. He made it a mere ten yards into the cleared area when he started finding debris. First a scrap of metal, then some electrical wires sticking out of the back of some type of radio. Heading toward the tree, they found part of a bucket style metal seat. When they reached the tree, Tucker reached up to pull some leaves off to identify it. After studying the leaves, his eyes started to tear up.

"It's an Ohio buckeye tree," he said as he handed Dr. Fischer the leaves so that he might inspect them.

Dr. Fischer looked at the leaves.

"How could it be? This is not a native tree," Dr. Fischer asked.

Tucker spoke in a hushed voice out of respect and reverence for the men that he knew were near. "This is the crash site," he said. William carried a buckeye in his pocket on every mission. His younger brother Charlie gave it to him as a good luck charm when he left for war." Tucker stared at the tree, watching its branches swaying in the light breeze. They both stood in silence as the cool wind rustled the leaves. He reached down and picked up some of the buckeyes that had fallen to the ground and put them in his pocket.

"It stands as a natural monument to the men," Dr. Fischer said quietly.

The realization that he had found the bomber was still so new in Tucker's mind he struggled to believe it. With the light fading fast, Tucker knew they needed to make their way back to the car.

"We need to get some army experts in here to recover the remains," Dr. Fischer said. Walking back to the car, Tucker tried to memorize as many landmarks as possible as he was fearful that they might struggle to find the site the next day.

Once back at the hotel, Tucker telephoned his mom and told her of their discovery. Throughout the story, she periodically interrupted him saying she just couldn't believe it.

"Tucker, I think there is a higher power at work in this," she said.

"Mom, I thought the same thing the moment that we found them. By all accounts, we shouldn't have."

"The story is so amazing. I can understand how people would be inclined to think you made it all up or at a minimum embellished it," she said.

Mr. Timmons was beside himself with excitement and admitted he had never really believed Tucker would find them. Before Tucker even asked, Mr. Timmons promised to have Bridgett change Tucker's date of departure by two days. The last telephone call that he made was to the nearest U.S. Army base to inform them of the discovery and to request assistance. They agreed to send out personnel to investigate the site the next morning. Tucker provided them the registration number of *Ole Number 060*, the names of the crew, and the number on the missing aircrew report. For the rest of the evening, Dr. Fischer and Tucker sat around and relived the week's events in light of the day's success.

"There are so many reasons I am happy about our success, but none more than being able to bring this news back to the families," Tucker said.

"Wonderful, that says volumes about who you are," Dr. Fischer added.

Dr. Fischer stayed until nine o'clock. The two made plans to meet at first light the next morning. Tucker walked to his room, cleaned up, and then returned downstairs for a beer. He was still in a talkative mood and was happy when he found Gunther was tending the bar. Tucker retold the story and found it difficult to believe. He felt as if he would wake from a dream at any time.

"So you have done the impossible. I am so pleased for you and happy for the families. This is just one more piece of healing that helps mend some of the pain that was endured by so many," Gunther said.

The next morning, Tucker was met with clear skies and another beautiful sunrise. He was up early, but still found Dr. Fischer was waiting in the restaurant.

"Hallo, Tucker, and good morning."

Shortly after seven o'clock, six army personnel walked into the dining area. Since Tucker had his back to them, Dr. Fischer motioned to Tucker to alert him to their arrival. They rose, and walked over to meet them. The officer in charge identified himself as from the Army Graves Registration Service in charge of recovering the remains of U.S. soldiers. After individual introductions, the group walked outside and headed to the site. Leading the way, Dr. Fischer drove ahead of them. Tucker checked the landmarks he had memorized as they followed him deep into the forest. Thirty minutes later, the tall spruce ended, and they entered the clearing. Looking across the open area, Tucker turned his attention to the tree. Dew had collected on it and made it glisten in the early morning sunlight. The team immediately set out to positively identify the aircraft. After combing the debris field for 15 minutes, they located a piece of the vertical stabilizer. On it could be seen the sun faded serial number 42-95060. A sergeant showed it to Tucker.

"The bomber that they had been assigned was *Old Number 060*. Obviously they had abbreviated the tail number when referring to it," Tucker said to the group of men. The lieutenant in charge flipped through a clipboard of documents and confirmed what Tucker had stated.

Upon positively identifying the bomber, Dr. Fischer unfurled an American flag that he had concealed in a backpack and hung it from the limb of the Buckeye tree. A soft breeze brought the flag alive. Upon placing it in the tree, the Army personnel came to attention and saluted. Tucker reflected over the loss of the men and the suffering that had occurred among friends and family. His thoughts turned to the enormity of the sacrifice that this one crew had made for freedom. It was a fight worth fighting, a victory worth the price; they hadn't perished for nothing.

They expanded the search area and came across a large piece of the fuselage. The horizontal and vertical stabilizers had been sheared off it as the aircraft tore through the trees at high speed. One hundred yards from the tree, another large portion of wreckage was found. Partial remains of five of the crew were found within or strewn around it. Another two hundred yards away they located the tail turret with the skeletal remains of another man wedged in by the twisted metal. Considering the state of the finds, Tucker realized that it would have been nearly impossible to see it from the air as the aluminum had oxidized and everything was covered by moss or littered with leaves. In addition, most of it was being shielded from the air by a canopy of large pine trees. Whenever a crewmember was found, the Army personnel stopped their activities and gathered near to salute, as an American flag was used to shroud the remains. They stood at attention until the remains passed by them and were placed in the transport area. Once the above ground remains were found, they split into teams of two. One member carried a shovel while the other worked a metal detector. One of the teams received a positive tone for metal about 50 yards from the Buckeye tree. They gently started removing dirt to find the remains of another member of the crew. It was in the afternoon that they worked close to the Buckeye tree, and Tucker heard the audible whine of a metal detector. He knew they had found the remains of William. A plain gold ring had set off the detector. Exhuming him required the cutting of some of the roots that had interwoven around him cradling his remains. Tucker stood and watched as the anguish of so many shattered dreams and broken hearts descended upon him. As he personalized the loss and thought about what his death would mean to his mother, his eyes filled with tears. His chin quivered as the tears rolled down his face. Dr. Fischer seeing his sadness came beside him and placed his hand on his shoulder. They stood until the last of what was left of William's shattered body was respectfully laid on the army litter. Everything done at the sight was conducted in a dignified and respectful way down to the last details. The soldiers understood the tremendous responsibility that they had undertaken when they joined the recovery team. By the end of the day, they had recovered all but two of the crewmembers. The team searched until the last light. They would leave no man behind. Dr.

Fischer and Tucker spoke to the Army officer in charge and requested permission to accompany them the next day to locate the remaining men. Permission was granted, and the following day they witnessed as they found the remaining men who had been thrown wide of the main body of wreckage. When the team had departed, Dr. Fischer walked over to the tree and took down the flag. Carefully folding it, he walked over to Tucker and placed a hand on his shoulder. His eyes were watery.

"I want you to have this as a reminder of a job well done." he said. Tucker felt the tightness in his throat as emotions welled up inside him.

"Thank you for your help. This would not have been possible without you," he said in reply. When they reached the edge of the clearing, they stopped and looked back at the buckeye tree standing as a living memorial to the sacrifice made by the crew. Its brilliance was a testament to the best that was given during the worst of times.

When they reached the hotel, they sat down for one final meal together.

"What are your plans now?" Dr. Fischer asked.

"On the way back to the states, I will start writing a series of articles for *The Daily*. I imagine it will take several days to complete them. Then I am going to request a few weeks off work to take care of some personal business."

"Would that personal business involve finding a certain young lady?" Dr. Fischer asked smiling at Tucker.

"I hope to tell her about her parents," Tucker said.

"Yes, she deserves to hear about them," he replied. At the end of the dinner, Tucker walked Dr. Fischer to his car to say goodbye.

"You will keep in touch and send me copies of your articles?" Dr. Fischer asked.

"Of course, and you will visit me when you're back in the states?" Tucker said.

"Yes, my American friend, I will."

"Good bye," Tucker said.

"How about, until next time?" Dr. Fischer said.

Tucker smiled. "I like that better."

That evening Tucker telephoned his mother, who as usual, sat silently listening to every detail.

"You know your father would be so proud of you," she said. Tucker, already very emotional from the last two days, broke down. He was silent as he tried to clear the thought from his mind so that he might regain control and continue.

"It is going to take a while for me to sort all of this out," he finally replied.

"When will you contact John," she asked.

"I didn't bring his number so as soon as I get home I will call him."

Later that night, Tucker walked around his weeklong home and said his goodbyes to his new friends and realized he would never see any of them again. He was mentally and physically spent, so when he lay down, sleep quickly found him. His journey home was productive as he had individual outlines for each story he would write, and the first article was ready for Mr. Timmons review. It was closing in on nine o'clock when Tucker arrived at his apartment.

Chapter 14

When Tucker walked into *The Daily* the next day, the word had already spread of his success. To his surprise and amazement, the staff and reporters stood and clapped when he came through the front door. With the draft in hand, he walked straight to Mr. Timmons. He was standing looking down at an article on his desk. His head rose when he heard him enter. "Tucker, the world traveler. Welcome back."

"Thank you," Tucker said.

"I see you have the first article ready for review."

"I completed it on the airplane."

Mr. Timmons set it aside and sat down. "Well, tell me more about your trip." They sat for an hour in discussion.

The second story was ready before noon, and so Tucker requested and received permission to take a trip to Lena,

Indiana. Before he left, he sat down at his desk, took a deep breath, and dialed the phone.

"Hello"

"John, it's me Tucker. I am calling to tell you that I found them…they are coming home. There was silence.

"Are you still there?" Tucker asked.

"Yes, I am sorry. It's just that I have wanted to hear that for so long."

For the next fifteen minutes Tucker told of the eye straining days, hopes dashed by false targets and finally the forest clearing created by the violent crash which made an opening for the buckeye tree to grow. One by one, he respectfully explained in detail how each crew member was found and the wreckage they were found in or near. John listened and softly said the crewmembers names with each description.

"You have brought peace where turmoil has lived for many years. I would like to attend William's funeral," John said.

"I am driving to deliver the news to his parents this afternoon. I will give them your telephone number and tell them you wish to be informed," Tucker said.

"Thank you. You have brought honor to your family name. I will see you at the funeral," John said.

Taking the long drive to Lena afforded Tucker time to gather his thoughts and determine how he would tell them details without offending them. Arriving, he walked up to the front door and knocked.

"Hello, Tucker. Won't you come in?" Lyle said.

"Hello, Mr. Pritchet. Thank you." They sat down at the kitchen table.

"Do you have any news for us?" Lyle asked as he and Mary sat looking at Tucker. Tucker collected his thoughts and took a deep breath.

"We found them," Tucker said. Lyle looked out the picture window across the front lawn, and Tucker noticed a tear start down his face. Mary stood and came behind Lyle's chair and placed her arms over his shoulders. He took out his white handkerchief and dried the tear.

Still looking out the window, Lyle spoke. "Very good. We wish to hear everything."

Tucker recalled each day of the search and the moment he spotted the buckeye tree. He pulled out pictures he had taken of the buckeye tree and others of the crash site. Lyle took the pictures and stared at them as Tucker spoke.

"The pictures are for you and so is this," Tucker said as he handed Lyle a buckeye from the tree.

"Thank you. This means so much to us. Our other children wished for us to express their gratitude," he said as he took his other hand and patted the top of Tucker's arm.

The next few minutes were spent in discussion about Julia and Charlie. When the conversation trailed off, Tucker became noticeably quiet. Lyle sensed something and asked, "Is there something more?"

"Yes," Tucker said pausing uncertain as to how to proceed. He knew that as Christians the news of a baby born out of wedlock would be a major blow to their beliefs about their son. "I am not certain how to say this."

"It's okay, son. Just tell us," Lyle said.

"You know he met a girl?" Tucker said

"Elizabeth?" Mary said.

"Yes," he replied timidly.

"In his letters home he spoke about meeting her, and after reading the journal, we now know just how dearly he cared for her," Mary said.

"I didn't tell you previously as I didn't want to upset you...," Tucker said stopping short. They both were staring at him correctly reading the hesitancy shown on his face.

"There was a child," Tucker said

Mary let out an audible gasp. She looked to Lyle. As usual he remained steady.

"What additional information do you have concerning this?" Lyle said.

"I know that Elizabeth died shortly after the birth and that the baby was a girl," Tucker said.

Lyle was quiet and then looked back at Tucker. "Am I correct in assuming you will be making a trip to England?"

"That is my plan." "I am going to ask the newspaper to send me so that I can try to locate her. I think she should know about her mother and father." Tucker said.

"Do you know when you will make the trip?" Lyle asked.

"I hope to leave in the next few weeks," Tucker replied and continued to explain how he planned to find her.

"You will tell her about us and that we would hope to meet her?" Mary said.

"Yes, if I find her, I will certainly tell her. I should tell you also that the Army will be contacting you about your wishes regarding William's final resting place," Tucker said as he stood to make his way to the door.

Mary stepped over to him. "God bless you for bringing our boy home and for the news of our granddaughter."

"You all sacrificed so much for our country. I am glad to have brought you some closure," Tucker said as he fought to maintain his composure. They walked him to his truck.

"We look forward to hearing from you when you return," Mary said.

"I will contact you as soon as I arrive home."

Over the next week, he turned out two more articles. Some of the largest newspapers in the country and a few overseas picked up the articles. Two weeks after he returned, he received his first job offer from a major newspaper. He turned it down and focused his attention on the one remaining piece of the puzzle, one that had been on his mind for many months. As with all of the others, his first task was to visit the library.

"Hello, Ms. Simms," he said upon entering.

"Hey there Mr. Celebrity, back for more research?" she asked.

"I need to find someone who lives in England.

"I hope we can narrow that down a bit," she said.

"Yes, of course, but I really don't have much information. I mean, I don't know her name or anything, just some fragments." He handed her a slip of paper that had her mother's name, the city where she would most likely have been born, and a range of her possible birth dates. "Her mother died after she was born, so she may have been adopted or grew up in an orphanage."

"Well, let's see what we can find out," Ms. Simms said. "Let's look into how to find birth records in England. Have a seat and give me a minute to locate some resources," she said. For the next half an hour, Ms. Simms jotted down notes as she moved about the library. After fifteen minutes she came over to his table. "Let me make a few long distance calls."

Tucker sat down and thumbed through a few magazines as he loosely listened to her conversing with a variety of people.

"Well, that is about as far as we are going to get sitting on this side of the ocean," she said. "I found two ways to find birth records. One would be through the government registration office and another source may be the public library in Beeston. You know her last name, gender, the area that she would have been born, and have a range of six weeks that you think contain her birth date. You could determine an exact date by visiting her mother's grave. You have quite a bit of information when you put it all together. If you can recover birth records, you may be able to then check orphanage records. I think you are going to have to go there and start knocking on doors and overcome obstacles as they present themselves," she said.

"That's the plan," Tucker said. "As always, I appreciate all of your help."

She smiled. "I am pleased to use my talents to assist you in all of this. As always, best of luck in your search."

Tucker returned home and started planning his trip. He hadn't cleared it with Mr. Timmons, but he felt confident that *The Daily* would cover the expense as there was the possibility of more stories. A few days later he asked the question, and without hesitation, Mr. Timmons approved the request with the mandate that he produce one or more stories.

A week later, Tucker was back aboard an aircraft crossing the Atlantic Ocean enroute to Heathrow Airport. To pass the time, he read and worked out the details of his search. A few hours from England, he fell asleep. An hour from his destination, a crying baby woke him. During the descent into

Heathrow, he peered out the side window and saw the Thames River. As they drew closer to the ground, he could make out the blur of city activities. A jolt and faint screech of the tires announced their touch down. The terminal was a sea of people intent on their own purposes. Tucker gained his bearings and headed to the ground floor to retrieve his luggage. Once collected, he found a small bank in the terminal and exchanged his U.S. currency for British pounds. Working his way out to the main doors of the terminal, he flagged down a small black hackney carriage. The driver hopped out and opened the front door for Tucker. He then quickly picked up the luggage and set it in the rear seat. Sliding into the driver's seat he asked, "Where to, Mister?"

"I need to go to the train station," Tucker said.

Making their way out of London, the drive took him past many scenic sights all of which the knowledgeable driver pointed out and added interesting facts. Tucker tried to take in as much of it as possible as the taxi wove its way through the crowded busy streets. He hoped to return someday on vacation and take his time exploring the city; that would have to wait as he had one mission in mind. Arriving at the train depot, he thanked the cab driver and grabbed his luggage. Entering the depot, he approached a man at the ticket window.

"How may I be of service?" he said.

"I need a ticket to the Wendling Depot," Tucker said.

Fifteen minutes into the train trip, he accepted a hot cup of tea. With no other options for lunch, Tucker pulled out a peanut butter and jelly sandwich that he had packed. He sat back and slowly enjoyed the sandwich and tea. It was peaceful to just relax and gaze out the window as the train wound through the beautiful English countryside out into the rural area. An hour and half later, he arrived at the Wendling station. He disembarked from the train and started his short walk to Beeston. Entering the small city, he walked down Main Street and made his way to the Ploughshare Inn where he had reservations. Tucker walked up to the small check in counter and waited. While he waited, he looked around. The floors were well worn oak, and heavy roughhewn wood beams ran the length of the ceiling. A large stone fireplace was at the opposite end of the room with a small fire lit in it.

"Good morning, sir. How may I help you?" said a woman who had entered through a door that was directly behind the counter.

"My name is Tucker McQueen, and I have reservations at the inn."

"Pleased to make your acquaintance. I am Ms. Fortner."

Taking the ledger, she scanned the names. "Oh yes here it is. Follow me, Mr. McQueen, and I will show you to your room upstairs," she said.

Tucker picked up his suitcase and started up a narrow staircase. There were only four doors upstairs. "Here it is, room number 2," she said as she inserted a key and opened it. There is a community bathroom at the end of the hallway with a sign-up sheet for bathing," Mrs. Fortner said.

"Thank you," Tucker said.

"If you need anything, please let me know," she said as she handed him the key.

Tucker sat his suitcase on the bed and looked out the window down onto the cobble stone street below. He unpacked his clothes and placed them in the dresser. After he had washed up, he grabbed his research information and headed down stairs to find some dinner. Ms. Fortner suggested an old pub that was within walking distance named The Dog and Pony. Entering the pub, he felt the warmth of the British decorum. Darkened hand hewn wood beams and paneling created a cozy atmosphere that invited quiet conversations and reflection. There were several locals sitting at the bar. Tucker walked over and sat in one of the booths that ran along a wall. After several minutes, he noticed that everyone was ordering at the bar. Leaving his research on the table, he placed his order. A woman with dark hair in her fifties came over to him.

"What will you have?" she asked.

"Fish, chips, and a beer," Tucker said.

She grabbed a pint, filled it, and set it back on the bar. "Here you go, Yank. What brings you to our island?"

"That's a long story of which I will try to shorten." For the next five minutes he stood and told her the story. As the story unfolded, she stopped cleaning on the bar and intently listened.

"Well, that is an amazing story," she said. Tucker, sensing disbelief, walked to his seat and picked up his satchel. Returning to the bar, he reached in and pulled out some of the newspaper articles. She looked through them. "I must say I had my doubts. Well, I wish you the best in your search," she said.

"Thank you," Tucker said in reply.

He picked up the mug of beer and returned to his booth. Ten minutes later, she set his supper before him. "My name is Molly," she said.

Tucker stood. "Pleased to meet you. My name is Tucker." After he finished with dinner, he explored the town.

The next few days were filled with visits to governmental offices, orphanages, and hospitals; but as anticipated, he struggled to collect any meaningful information. The standard reply was, "We wish we could assist you, but the information you are requesting is confidential." Every evening he retired to The Dog and Pony where he poured over any new information he obtained from the day and carefully sifted through it for any clue.

"How is your search going, Tucker?" Molly asked.

"After four days of searching, I haven't made any real progress outside of marking leads off my list."

"Well keep at it—luck will break your way"

"I am not going home until I find her or what happened to her"

Tucker finished dinner, gathered up his documents, and walked back to the inn. Passing by the check in area, he started to head upstairs when Mrs. Fortner entered the room.

"Mr. McQueen, I have a message for you. A woman stopped by to see you. I did not know when you would return, so she left her telephone number for you."

Tucker stepped off the bottom step and walked back over to her. She fumbled through some loose notes and found the one with his name on it.

"Oh, here it is," she said. Tucker set his satchel down to open the note and read it.

"May I use the telephone?" Tucker asked.

"Certainly," Mrs. Fortner said and lifted it up and set it on the bar. Tucker dialed the number.

"Hello," a woman said.

"This is Tucker McQueen. I received a note to give you a call."

"Hello Mr. McQueen, I was at the orphanage when you visited. I know the girl you were inquiring about. Her name is Penelope Pritchet." Tucker sat down on a stool and took a deep breath. "I wanted to help you when you visited us, but legally I couldn't say anything. Actually I am risking my job, but she deserves to hear what you have to say. Please do not let it out that I supplied this information as it could easily be traced to me. After the war, when I had just started working at the orphanage, she was placed in our care. We were told that her mother had secretly married a U.S. airman who was killed in action prior to Penelope's birth. There were complications during birth, and her mother only lived a short time after she was delivered, just long enough to whisper her name. I was assigned as her primary care giver at the orphanage. Such a sweet little girl. Had it not been for the strain that the war placed on society, I am sure she would have been adopted, but there were so many war orphans. It was only a few years ago that she moved out. She lives a few miles from where you are staying over in Swaftham. I have her address for you." Tucker opened his satchel and grabbed a pencil. He quickly scratched down the number and profusely thanked the woman for her kindness and assured her he would not name his source. When he lay down that evening, his mind was racing. Somewhere in considering what he would say to her, sleep overtook him. He awoke early and knew he would never quiet his racing thoughts. Looking at his clock, he realized it would be at least 3 hours before most people would be out of bed. Turning on the bedside light, he read for an hour. Unable to sit still any longer, he moved downstairs where he read the morning paper while he ate a breakfast of sausages, eggs, biscuits, and tea. After dragging out breakfast, he couldn't wait any longer and started walking to Swaftham. The journey only took about 15 minutes, but Tucker's eagerness to meet her made it difficult for him to walk. He kept telling himself that walking quickly would just amount to more standing around when he arrived. Turning down her street, he counted down the address. He walked toward a metal bench that had a street lamp over it. Drawing closer, Tucker could see it was a bus pickup, and looking across the street, he noticed it was across the street from her address. There were no lights on, so he sat down and started what he knew would be a long wait. When the sun just started to crest the horizon, a solitary light appeared from a window on the second floor. Tucker watched as shadows were momentarily cast on the blind of her window. A half hour later, the sun was up, and the light above his bench shut off. He knew that there was a real possibility that he would frighten her, so with the remaining time, he tried to settle on the best way to approach her. It occurred to him that she would instantly know he was a stranger when he spoke. That alone might alarm her. He decided there was no best way, and so he prayed. A few minutes later, the outer door opened, and a young woman appeared. She stepped off the sidewalk and walked directly across the street towards him. She was coming to the bus stop, thus, eliminating the need to approach her. When she drew near, he knew more about Elizabeth's beauty than William could have ever conveyed in writing. She had inherited her mother's high cheekbones and large expressive brown eyes. Simply stated, she was beautiful.

"Good morning," he said as she approached him.

"Hello," Penelope replied.

"Heading to work?" Tucker asked.

"Not today. I am heading into town to pick up some miscellaneous items. You are not from here. Are you on holiday?" she said.

"Well, that's a long story."

Penelope looked at him but said nothing. "My name is Tucker McQueen, and I am a journalist. I work for a newspaper called *The Daily Reporter* located in the state of Ohio," he said. "How long do we have before the bus comes?"

She glanced at her watch. "Perhaps 10 minutes, but it's not always on time," she said.

Reaching into the satchel, he pulled out the newspapers and told her the story that eventually led him to England. After several minutes, he finished by saying, "I am here to try to locate William Pritchett's daughter to tell her the story of her parents," Tucker said.

She sat quietly. "You are looking for me," she said softly.

"Yes, I have no doubt. You resemble your mother," Tucker said handing her the newspaper that had the picture of her parents. She stared at it. When she looked up, he noticed her tears.

"Please tell me everything you know about them," she said as she held the newspaper in her lap. Tucker told her details of William and Elizabeth and about his interactions with her grandparents.

"Thank you for finding me. I have missed so much in not knowing them," she said.

"It was the least I could do. I have great respect for your father and mother. After the journey I have been on, I feel as if I know them," Tucker said. Penelope handed the newspapers back to him. "No, I brought them for you." She smiled at him and held them tightly.

"The only keepsake I have of hers is this cross necklace," she said. Reaching behind her neck, she grasped a gold chain and worked a necklace out from under her sweater. She unclasped it and handed it to Tucker. Your father spoke about this necklace in the journal. His sister gave it to him when he left for the war. After speaking for well over an hour, they made plans to meet again.

Penelope took the next few days off from work. They spent considerable time talking and sharing their life stories while at other times their conversation drifted to the subject that bound them together. A few days before he was set to leave, they traveled to Beeston to visit the abandoned airfield. Vandals had rocked the windows, and vines were climbing and invading the buildings. The runways, taxiways, and ramp areas were still clear, but there was noticeable vegetation growing through the cracks. Penelope had read the articles that Tucker had given her but still asked him many questions about the function of the numerous dilapidated buildings. Walking the airfield, they located the old mess hall. Tucker was only able to open the door a couple of inches as a concrete step in front of it had cracked and the door was caught on it. Locating a metal pipe, he put one end in the opening and pushed hard on the other end, to force the door open far enough that they could squeeze through. There were a few tables strewn about and wooden foldable chairs. Dappled sunlight worked in through the windows and lit the interior. The stainless steel sinks and appliances were all gone, and pipes jutted out from the walls where they had once sat. At the end of the hall on the wall was a large mural of an eagle. It was soaring with B-24's flying out in multiple directions. After the mess hall, they walked to the main hangar where the dance had been held. Tucker slowly explored the hangar and envisioned the base dance. Exiting the hangar, they made the long walk around the perimeter track to the huts where the 578th squadron had bunked. They all looked alike with rusted roofs and overgrown vines and vegetation.

Some doors were open while others hadn't been opened since the men left the airbase. Birds and other wild animals had taken up residence in some of them. Walking along, they occasionally opened a door and stepped in. Some had a bed frame or the potbellied stove. A few had faded pinups on the walls while others sat completely empty. Tucker looked down a row of Nissen huts.

"I think I see your father's hut," Tucker said.

"Which one?" she asked.

"Just up ahead. The fourth one on the left," Tucker said. "See the one with an extra chimney pipe sticking out of the roof?"

Yes, I do," she said. Arriving at the hut, Tucker reached down, twisted the handle, and opened the door.

As he looked around for something to stand on, he spoke. "Your father wrote in his journal about a secret hiding place in his hut. There was little privacy from other crewmembers in such tight quarters, and there was always the possibility of an inspection. One of the unique characteristics about his hut was they had bored the stovepipe hole for the chimney in the wrong place. Instead of patching the hole, they just left the original chimney on the roof, bored a new hole, and set a second chimney pipe in the correct location. Your father spoke about it in his journal. I think he may have hidden something in it," Tucker said and pointed to a round piece of thin metal that covered the hole. "I need something to stand on and something that can serve as a screw driver to remove the screws."

"Let's search some of the other huts for something to stand on and perhaps we could just pry it off," Penelope said. They searched until they found a wooden box, a foldable wooden chair, and a broken piece of a metal strap hinge. Placing the chair under the patch, they then set the box upon it. "Would you like to try it or shall I?" Tucker asked. Penelope took the tool and started up on the chair while Tucker steadied it. It was a shaky perch. She stretched and tried to get the metal underneath the patch. The box she was standing on moved, and she dropped the piece of metal. Tucker reached down and picked it up for her. Reaching again, she found a gap and forced the metal underneath it. Pulling down on it, she pulled loose one of the screws. Stretching, she worked to get the piece of metal under the other side. "I wish the chair were a little taller," she said.

"Be careful," Tucker said. No sooner had he said it than she pulled down on the metal strap. The patch broke free, and the box rocked throwing her off balance. Tucker let go of the chair and caught her. Off balance, he was unable to stop their fall. Everything came crashing down. They both sat up. Tucker looked over at her. "You okay?" he asked.

"I think so. How about you?" she said reaching over and brushing some debris off his jeans.

"Yeah, I am fine," he said. The patch sat on the floor beside them. Tucker looked up but was unable to see into the dark hole that the patch had covered. "Let's set it back up. Nothing fell out, but something could be wedged in."

"I will let you reach inside and find anything that might be lurking in there," she said.

"Lucky me," Tucker said.

They reassembled the chair, reset the crate on it, and positioned them below the opening. "Your turn," she said and smiled. Tucker carefully climbed on top and slowly stood up. Reaching up into the opening, he felt the bottom of a container. "I feel something, but I am not certain what it is." He was able to get his fingers on each side of it and started working it down until he freed it. "Here, can you take it?" he asked handing it to Penelope. She set the container on the floor so that she could help him. Once down, Tucker took the wooden crate off the chair, turned it on end, and placed it across from the chair. "Have a seat," he said offering her the chair. Tucker picked up the small wooden box and handed to her. He could barely make out the faded name of "Velveeta" on the side of it. Turning it over in her hands, they could faintly hear the sound of something shifting inside. Grasping the container, she used her thumbs and slid the top back to reveal the contents. Laying aside the top, she reached inside and gently pulled out a collection of folded papers. When she removed them from the box, Tucker knew by their color and size that they were the missing journal pages.

Opening them, she softly started to read. Tucker interrupted her.

"Penelope, I wouldn't be offended if you read it to yourself. I don't want you to feel like you have to share this with me."

She lowered the papers to her lap. Tucker felt the power of her unwavering gaze and could see the emotions in her face. "I know how you feel about them and want to share this with you," she said.

"Two days ago was the best day of my life. Elizabeth and I were married. It seems too wonderful to be true. It all occurred so quickly, but we both were so certain about our feelings for each other. Pastor Wimbley knows the depth of my feelings for her. I did not seek the required approval of my commanding officer, nor did we file any paperwork with the local government. According to their manmade contracts, we are not married, but I do not consider that to be what creates a true marriage. Our marriage was created by the vows we swore to each other and before God. We dressed in casual attire so that we wouldn't attract any attention. I wore my every day army uniform while she dressed in blue jeans, a pink shirt that had small white dots, and white low-heeled slippers. She used an extra piece of fabric that matched her shirt to pull up her hair. It was late in the afternoon when we set out for the lake. We walked a few steps ahead of the rest in route to the lake.

"Sorry, I don't look much like a bride."

"I wouldn't change a thing." She smiled and reached down and took my hand. The tall mature trees, shimmering lake, and water lapping against the pebble shore created a picturesque setting. Pastor Wimbley stood with his back to the lake and invited us to join him. We stepped forward, hand in hand. He opened with a prayer of blessing for us. When finished, he spoke of God's plan that a man and a woman should become one. He held an open Bible before him and asked that we place our hands on it for the recitation of our vows. She laid hers upon it first, and then I put mine over them. When we finished, he looked at us and said, "William, you may kiss your bride!" I gently took her in my arms, and we kissed.

"Does this mean William will be around for good?" Timmy asked.

"Yes Timmy, he will be around for good," Elizabeth replied laughing. Her mother came over and hugged me. Timmy was beside her, and then she moved to hug Elizabeth. Timmy stood before me and held out his hand. I shook it.

Pastor Wimbley hugged me and whispered in my ear. "You are a blessed man." At the house, we said our goodbyes and walked to Beeston where we rented a room and spent our first night together. Over the next two days, we traveled via rail and visited nearby villages and shops. We shared our hopes and dreams of having children, making a home, and building our lives together.

Clutching the papers in her hands, she lowered them to her lap. Penelope stared out the dusty window. "They were thinking of me," she said and then began to softly sob. Tucker reached out his hand and placed it on hers. She brushed away her tears. "Well, there is nothing that can be done about it now. She picked up the box and pulled out a small white booklet that had a pair of gold rings embossed on the front of it. She opened it and then handed it to Tucker. It was a marriage certificate that was signed by Pastor Wimbley.

Leaving the hut, they walked to the perimeter gate of the base and on to Elizabeth's house. Little had changed along the old country road. The scenery was a blend of pastures, fields, and farmhouses. Arriving at the house, Tucker noted the barn was falling in and a garage had been added in the side yard.

"Shall I knock?" Tucker asked.

Penelope looked at him. "I would like to see inside," she said.

Tucker walked up to the door and knocked, but no one answered. There was one more area left to explore. Leaving the residence they walked down the road to the small stone bridge, removed their shoes, and proceeded down to the lake.

"This must be the spot we just read about," Tucker said. Standing at the edge of the lake, they stood silently and let their minds carry them back to those many years ago. It was a quiet walk back to her flat as they both were caught up in their own reflections of the days.

At the end of Tucker's stay, Penelope rode the train to London to see him off.

"You will write," she said.

"Often, and you will come visit?"

"I should have enough saved in a couple of months."

Tucker began missing her the moment he boarded the aircraft. They kept their promise, and over the next few months, communicated through letters and an occasional telephone call. She came to the United States and stayed at the old home place with his mother. They made the drive to Lena and ate dinner at her father's house. At dusk, they laid flowers at his grave. The original spark that Tucker had felt fanned into a flame, and they were married exactly one year from the day they met. With Penelope's grandparents in the states and since she had no known family in England, they chose to build their life in Ohio. They bought the old home place from his mother and a few years later were blessed with two children: Willy and Beth.

Chapter 15

Tucker continued his rhythmic motion in his rocking chair. He lifted the white ceramic mug and savored the last of his coffee. The last rays of the waning sunlight pushed through the trees and laid long black crooked shadows across the tranquil backyard. With a reduction in light, the brilliant crimson colored leaves on the buckeye tree were now subdued. Tuckers thoughts drifted to all of the life lessons he had learned through the experience. His life contained so many visible reminders that some portion of the story regularly emerged in his mind. Considering the tragic loss contained within the story, it might be expected that a melancholy pall would be cast over his life with each remembrance, like a portentous dark storm cloud always overhead searching for happiness to rain down on. However, the experience had the opposite effect. With each warm hug of his children, each laugh shared with Penelope, and each family gathering at her grandparents' home, he was reminded how precious life is and the price paid in blood that allowed him to enjoy it.

He believed that it was not as important how much time a person is given but how much living they do in that time. William and Elizabeth had lived a lot. They found in a short period what many people fail to find in an entire lifetime. The one.

He learned other lessons from the other men of *The Buckeye*. Pappy, Lew, Jim, Ben, Little Frankie, John, Archie, Albert, and Jack. Real men. The kind that when a war has to be fought, they run toward it. When called on to protect what was theirs, they flew into the face of the worst the enemy could throw at them. They may not have considered themselves heroes or that they were doing a noble deed, but the citizens of their nation would disagree with them. Tucker knew his career, wife, and children were the harvest from the seeds of freedom these good men had sown many years before. As Tucker lived life and tragedy splashed across the news on a daily basis, he remembered that along with the very bad in society are the very good. He worked hard to be counted among them. After years of reflection, he understood how the journey had taught him lessons that his father would have. In the end, the most enduring lesson he learned was that sad endings are but the beginnings of happier ones.

Philippians 4:8 Finally, brethren, whatsoever things are true, whatsoever things are honest, whatsoever things are just, whatsoever things are pure, whatsoever things are lovely, whatsoever things are of good report; if there be any virtue, and if there be any praise, think on these things.

About the Author

The author has undergraduate and graduate degrees in aviation and over twenty-five years of professional experience. He has a passion for WWII aviation history. Over a two-year period, he completed investigative work regarding the downing of his great uncle's WWII B-24 bomber. His investigation led him to the crash site in Germany and inspired him to write this novel.